FAITH IN THE STABLES

By the same author:

THE TEACHING OF FAITH

FAITH IN THE STABLES

Elizabeth Bruce

This book is a work of fiction.
In real life, make sure you practise safe sex.

First published in 1996 by
Nexus
332 Ladbroke Grove
London W10 5AH

Typeset by TW Typesetting, Plymouth, Devon
Printed and bound by
BPC Paperbacks Ltd, Aylesbury, Bucks

ISBN 0 352 33062 7

Chapter One

Alex had been quietly busy on the telephone for most of the morning; snatches of business conversations about shares, client accounts, *arbitrage* and investors reached an uninterested Faith. Stockbroking was something Alex did very well, but the subject bored her. Now as the darkness of the late evening grew around them, the powerful BMW drew steadily away from the Garland estate and, with each passing mile, Faith felt her inner tension easing. She felt that perhaps a few days (or even a week) in the country might do her good.

It was odd to think that over the weekend she had lived through so many diverse and pleasurable experiences. First, the rejection by the members of the Chosen had caught her unexpectedly at her most vulnerable. She had been certain that their acceptance of her was a mere formality; instead of which she found herself chained naked to the cold bars of a cage, her only source of warmth being the hot flesh of her behind where Marigold had warmed it with a strap.

This had been followed by them giving her too much wine – getting her drunk, in fact – before they aroused her sexually, only to chain her on the cold tiles at the bottom of Marigold's empty swimming pool and then jeer at her while she sought relief by working herself against the bar to which she had been fastened. The abrupt changes had confused her,

1

making her more vulnerable while she swung between the conflicting emotions of elation and despair.

Faith thought she had given up all hope of becoming Chosen. She felt she had told someone; was it Lillian Brampton? Or Julia? Someone, anyway. She thought that at some point the cold and the rejection had been too much for her to take and had voiced her intention of quitting. No one had listened to her. Releasing her from the bottom of the empty swimming pool they had soaked her in warm water then welcomed her with their previous affection. It had been a means of making her appreciate what she was obtaining; entry to their closed circle of friendship. What was it Lillian had said? 'You don't value anything unless you pay a high price for it.' Something like that. She had paid the price in discomfort, humiliation, cold and shame.

Then they had sat around watching while she had ridden the 'three-horned god'; kneeling on the floor in the centre of the circle with the erections of three men penetrating her at once. Simon in her vagina and Max in her mouth, while Alex, the man who occupied the driving seat behind her, had taken 'the master's right' – her backside. They were right. She knew that the middle-class young woman she had once been was now a complete stranger. Now she was able to enjoy sex to a far greater degree than she had thought possible.

Yet since her initiation into the Chosen, Faith found Alex much more solemn than he had been. There was a reserve about him (as there had been about the others, prior to their departure) with everyone seeming to avoid answering her questions about the Stables. Why? Several times when she broke their silence to put questions to him, he had answered in a quiet, curt manner, as though concentrating on his driving, though her instincts told Faith he was avoiding the issue.

'Where are we?' she asked, looking at the darkening landscape.

'We're on the M23. You'll see Gatwick soon.'

'And where is it we're going, exactly?'

'Exactly? I couldn't tell you the name of it, though I've been there before. I just don't know the names of the little places. Roughly; between Horsham and Crawley, though not in a direct line.'

'I see.' Faith nodded. She recognised the names of Gatwick, Crawley and Horsham, though she had been to none of them. They were convenient reference points. 'Who are these people who run the Stables?'

Alex smiled to himself in the darkness, falling silent until the overloaded family car in front weaved back into the centre lane to allow him to smoothly power past. Faith thought he looked particularly handsome in the reflected light from the vehicle ahead of them, his Gieves and Hawkes suit a perfect fit. When the road was clear, he answered.

'It's old riding stables with some land around it; nothing much. A couple of fields of grazing; that sort of thing. Woods too, that come right down to the buildings. The horses are gone, though you'll ride every day. Clive Jackson's a bluff character; doesn't say much, but he's got his head screwed on. I was at school with his younger brother. Then there's his housekeeper. Mrs Marryat; Martha. Like Clive, her manner conceals a lot.'

'It's only for a couple of weeks.' Faith shrugged, feeling that perhaps these were people with whom she had little in common. 'I expect I can survive!'

In the darkness, Alex wondered whether he should explain about what she was letting herself in for. Yet how was he to do that when it would probably put her off attending the Stables altogether? Surely she was intelligent enough to take a hint?

For several seconds there was silence between the broad-shouldered, fair-haired man who topped six feet and the dark-haired young woman who sat beside him. Alex Pellew's ice-blue eyes swept the dark road ahead, his hands automatically steering while his mind turned over again the events of the previous fortnight.

At a party in Belgravia, one look at Faith had convinced him she was someone he had to see again. Though she had been stupefied at the time, he had taken her back to his Chelsea flat for some of the most satisfying sex he had experienced. A second look had convinced him she should become his companion, a member of the Chosen. A pleasure slave. So far he had no regrets, although it was now time to further her education; possibly the most difficult part.

Faith Small was just 23 years old. An Oxford graduate who had worked in a lowly position at an advertising agency when they met, she had been living with her boss while trying to learn the business from him. She had abandoned all that security to move in with Alex, allowing herself to be introduced to the advanced sexual techniques practised by him and his friends, all fellow members of the Chosen. This select group of wealthy individuals was dedicated to the enjoyment of sex and pleasure in all its many forms.

At five feet ten, Faith had become accustomed to smaller men, until she met Alex. There was no one like him. They contrasted and complemented each other in so many ways besides the purely physical. He was wealthy while she was comparatively poor; he was a sophisticate while Faith, despite her expensive education, was only just beginning to discover what life was about.

4

For two weeks Alex had taught her about sex, improved her wardrobe as well as her appearance, and introduced her to other wealthy and important people. He had also spanked her, fastened her to his bed while he made exquisite love to her and taught her to appreciate outrageous sexual stimulation. At his hands she had scaled the heights of ecstasy, making love while being restrained, as well as plumbing the depths of fear and doubt. She had found that bondage could be wildly exciting, and the effects of a spanking were not all painful. Especially bondage. It was a subject which thrilled her to her very core.

Under Alex's tuition she had learned to walk in tight, thigh-length, black, high-heeled leather boots, pacing his flat naked with her wrists cuffed behind her.

Now he was sending her to these people to learn discipline. Why? All the members of the Chosen present at her initiation had claimed she needed it, but no one would tell her what it entailed.

'Remember, Faith.' He sounded anxious. 'Their job is to teach you discipline. It's not easy, and don't think you'll find it so either.'

'You're joking!' Faith answered at once. 'I'm sorry. I didn't mean to sound superior. It's just that ... well, I think I can handle it.'

'You'll survive, I know, but you'll find this beyond anything you might have imagined.' He nodded and from his faint smile Faith understood that he found her predicament amusing. 'The pleasure of discipline, and the discipline of pleasure. They're not subjects to be undertaken lightly, but without them you'll suffer greatly, believe me.'

Just when Faith was about to ask for an explanation of this cryptic utterance, the BMW swung into an open space between long, high, straight hedges, thick enough to conceal everything on the other side behind their long, dark, glossy leaves, stirring in the faint breeze. Large, high, wrought iron gates barred their progress but there was an intercom on a pedestal. Without leaving the driving seat, Alex was able to announce himself and when the machine had given the final squeal, he looked at Faith.

'I'd like to see anyone get in here; or out. There's a ten-foot mesh fence in the middle of that.'

'Why all the security?' Faith asked, relieved when the gates ahead of them began to slowly open.

'It dates back to when Clive's father ran the place. He had several very valuable animals here; racehorses and the like. Before the sophisticated facilities for transporting them we have now. Horses would be brought here for a few days before a meeting at, say, Epsom or Sandown, Kempton or Brighton. That sort of thing. Ideal place to "nobble" a horse, so a high level of security.'

'Yes.' Faith relaxed against the firm leather upholstery again. 'I'm impressed. Does it go right round the property?'

'Of course. It wouldn't be much good if it didn't. There's quite extensive woods here; lovely in autumn. Peaceful too. No ringing telephones or people demanding answers.'

'That must be heavenly.'

Faith smiled, feeling herself liking the place as the car eased forward, and in second gear Alex drove slowly along the tarmac ribbon which wound sinuously between wood covered slopes. The headlights picked out the stark scene in front of them – the budding plants with an occasional fresh green leaf or shoot providing contrast to the brown of the earth, the russet of the dead leaves and the dark green and black of the tree trunks.

The house was part of a complex of buildings built into a hollow square, as though to withstand a siege. As the BMW approached the corner, Faith saw one end of a long, low, stone building reaching away into the darkness, with a series of dormer windows evenly spaced across the neat, new slates of the roof. There were lights on in only some of the windows which faced out on to the black tarmac into which some white chippings had been set, giving the end of the drive a curiously freckled appearance.

Off to the right of the house and attached to it was another low, stone building though the wall facing them was blank and the roof above was less well tiled, being devoid of windows in the sloping surface. At the far end was a wide and high gateway, filled with a wide and high gate, the wood painted a dull brown, but neat and looking as if new. There were marks on this wall as though vehicles had stood there with the engines running; small, black, circular patches at various heights.

As the car arrived in front of the house, three bright lights spaced across the front of the building came on, flooding the space with harsh illumination. While Alex turned to bring the boot of the BMW level with the single glass door which gave access to the porch, he said, 'Damned thing catches me every time. It's a security light, though why he needs one, God alone knows. It makes parking easier when the eyes get used to it, but it's so sensitive that foxes set the thing off.'

Faith stepped out of the car, feeling the sharpness in the chill air and shuddering against it. After the warmth of the car (or perhaps a memory of her incarceration in the cage by Marigold Garland) it was inevitable.

'Hello Alex!' a gruff, well-modulated voice called

7

from behind them as Alex tried to lift out the case. Faith, who had been trying to help without interfering, turned.

Clive Jackson was of middle height, with sandy hair which already glinted here and there with grey. His round face had the flush of the country about it, but his eyes were concealed (as was most of his face) in shadow. He wore a light tweed jacket and a pair of old, green, corduroy trousers with boots projecting from beneath them. Squinting against the light, Faith could make out the shape of a knotted tie at his throat, but that was all.

'Here! Let me give you a hand with that.' Jackson stepped forward, passing between Faith and Alex and reaching into the abyss of the boot.

Between them they managed to lift the case out and Jackson then carried it, one handed, and led the way through the door into the house. Faith hovered between following Jackson and waiting for Alex, but the latter shut the boot then gestured for her to walk ahead of him towards the house.

Both the high, thick, light-coloured doors had been opened to allow Jackson through with the case. When Faith stepped through into the hallway, their host was already bent double securing the bottom bolt which held one of them in place. A woman stood at the entrance to the corridor which led down to the left, attracting Faith's immediate attention.

She was taller than Jackson, about Faith's height of five feet ten, but slimmer and younger, too; Faith put her age at about 35. Her pale complexion contrasted with Jackson, yet there seemed to be a serene severity about her. She reminded Faith of the actress Jean Marsh. She wore a plain, light oatmeal-coloured dress with a green brooch pinned on her left lapel, and plain brown shoes.

8

'Alex! Good to see you,' Jackson rumbled cheerfully again, his ruddy cheeks becoming more prominent as they clasped hands.

'This is Faith.' Alex extended his hand towards the tall young woman, half-turning to include her. Faith watched the friendly and yet almost professional greeting, as though they were still unused to each other.

Yet Faith was surprised to notice that it was Alex, usually the most urbane of men, who was slightly distant, as though unhappy about meeting this man. It was as though this man was someone for whom he had no real liking. Why?

Jackson, having greeted Alex, advanced on Faith, asking, 'Just Faith is it?' He took her soft hand in his hard, firm grasp. 'Is that all?'

'Just Faith,' Faith answered, looking into Jackson's light grey eyes. 'My middle name's Michaela, which is a bit of a mouthful.'

'Faith.' Jackson nodded his understanding, still holding her hand as he half-turned.

The woman had advanced, apparently without moving a muscle, for she was in the same position; hands clasped in front of her at her waist, right over left, her neutral expression not a whit different. Close to, Faith could see that her skin was flawless. She had pale blue eyes under heavy lids, almost as pallid as Alex's, which seemed to shoot straight through her, the intensity of her expression reminding Faith of Marigold Garland. For no reason Faith shuddered.

'This is Mrs Marryat. Faith is to stay with us for a while, Mrs Marryat.'

'How pleasant.' Her voice was low and well modulated and her smile genuine as she took Faith's hand in her own slim, soft hand. There was a coldness about her grasp which surprised Faith at first, for she thought that her own hands were cold enough, yet Mrs Marryat made no comment, her eyes remaining fixed on those of the guest.

'I can't stay; got to get back.' Alex checked his watch. 'How are things with you?'

'Mouldering on. Got several pupils at the moment. Might make something of them yet, though it's too early to say. You know how they are. Not to worry.' Jackson smiled at Faith, yet the light in Mrs Marryat's eyes made her uneasy.

'I'm awfully sorry, but I really must get back.' Alex sighed, turning to Faith and looking at her in silence for a few moments. He put his hands on her shoulders. 'Faith, this is where I leave you. Remember, you do what they say, right?'

'Yes,' Faith answered, surprised that he was spelling it out. 'Of course.'

He released her and began walking towards the door Mrs Marryat held open for them. 'You're to learn discipline.' Alex turned to her again, his expression anxious. 'Without it, you'll get nowhere. You've made a good start and it would be a pity if you were to be let down by a lack of it. Clive and Martha are good at what they do, they'll keep us informed about your progress.' He paused then added, 'It's not just *you* now; it's *us*.'

'Yes,' Faith assured him, 'I'll try.'

'We'll teach her,' Mrs Marryat said quietly. 'Won't we, Mr Clive? Faith will be perfectly disciplined when she leaves.'

'Of course,' Jackson agreed.

'Do what you're told and you'll have no trouble. Right? The more you knuckle down, the sooner we'll meet.' Alex reached up behind her and, with a metallic sound, operated the lock on the gold choker about her neck, removing it. Faith felt the weight being removed and the sense of cold air on her skin again.

'Alex!' Faith could feel the tears welling up but refusing to release. She wanted to reach out to him, but already he was disengaging himself from her.

'I've given them all your things, though you won't need much while you're here.'

He was torn between telling her what she would have to do at the Stables and allowing her to discover that for herself. He felt he should warn her, but Clive and Martha were strict about there being little or no preparation. Surprise played a large part in their work. If they could surprise their pupils, it was sometimes the only way to maintain control.

The alternative, they had found, was that pupils became frightened; sometimes violent. Which usually meant they had to use the restraints more; something neither wanted. This was a training establishment, not a punishment one.

'No.' Faith swallowed, fighting back her tears and trying to remain calm. She knew he could see her distress, but refused to give in.

'And wear your boots,' he urged. 'This is an ideal place for that. Wear them as much as you can.'

'Yes.' She gave a little laugh that trembled on the verge of overspilling tears before she recovered herself again.

'God bless.' He kissed her forehead, gripping her shoulders, and was gone with a nod to Mrs Marryat, who followed him. Faith went to the doorway but found her progress barred by the woman, who stood on the step until the car started and in a smooth, almost silent movement, vanished into the darkness.

Long before the headlights vanished behind the first slope, Jackson turned, closed the door of the porch, then went indoors. Faith had retreated into the hallway with Mrs Marryat. Jackson sighed and closed the door behind him, locking it. Then he looked at Faith.

'We'd best start by showing you your room, Miss Faith. This way.'

Leaving her case in the hallway, he mounted the broad stairway which curled round the hallway to the left, in three right-angled turns. Above the hallway was a corridor, narrower than the one below. He led the way until he reached a door at the end. Unlocking it, he went in.

The room was of modest size, though the sloping roof cut down on the available space. It was dominated by a large brass-framed bed just inside the room on the left of the door, while a fireplace was set into the far wall. This was bricked up, though an electric fire had been built into it.

'This will be your room.' Jackson looked round at her, as though checking to make certain she was with him. Mrs Marryat closed the door and stood before it, her face still calm, as though awaiting Jackson's instructions.

'It's very nice, thank you,' Faith said. There were two windows, one on either side of the room, giving a view of the courtyard and the outer greenery, though now they were both black, the reflection of the room showing in them.

Mrs Marryat moved to the bed, turning down the covers to expose the pillows. Something brightly metallic gleamed amid the white pillows, but Faith thought nothing of it, her attention being taken by Jackson, who was saying, 'We expect you to keep it tidy. Do you like riding?'

'Yes.' Faith was surprised at the sudden switch of subject. 'I love it. Though I haven't ridden in years, and I haven't any kit.'

'That won't be a problem.' Mrs Marryat spoke from where she had now finished attending to the bed. She moved towards the other side, behind Faith, who smiled.

12

'Right.' Jackson gave a relieved sigh, nodding, then looked her in the eye before he quite distinctly said, 'Take all your clothes off, Miss Faith. Lay them on the bed.'

'Sorry?' Faith's jaw dropped as she looked at the man in stark surprise, unable to believe what she thought she had just heard.

'I said strip!' He paused to let the message sink in. 'Put your clothes on the bed,' he said again, his tone firm and with a slight edge in it. This was the beginning of the process – the stripping of the pupil to remove an association between their old ways outside the Stables and the new regime within.

'I will *not*!' Faith answered, too surprised to be angry.

There was a sudden pain in her left arm as it was twisted up her back, the shock taking her breath away. Faith yelped in surprise as her torso was bent forward. Mrs Marryat, who was holding and twisting her left wrist, had raised her knee to support her. Jackson took charge of her right hand while Mrs Marryat brought her own right hand down on Faith's unprotected rear three times, sharply. Each slap was mitigated by her skirt, but the speed of the assault, added to the surprise, had an effect Faith would never have imagined. She burst into tears, her body shaking with sobs.

'Stop snivelling, Miss Faith!' Mrs Marryat's voice snapped, hardly any different in timbre from normal. 'You were told to obey us by Mr Pellew before he left, which I distinctly remember you agreed to do. Now remove your clothing, or shall I strip you? Which will mean you will get a spanking into the bargain.'

'I . . . I . . . I will *not*!' Faith struggled vainly against the tight grip which pinned her. She knew that Mrs

Marryat stood on only one leg and it should have been easy to topple her over, but Jackson's grip on her other arm restrained her. She thought of kicking, but Mrs Marryat was too quick.

Quickly she scooped up Faith's skirt at the back, hauling it to her waist, where Jackson held it. The thin black knickers were her only protection, enhancing her pink, rounded bottom. Mrs Marryat hardly hesitated a second before slipping them down to mid-thigh, grunting every so often as Faith tried by force to shift her weight. It was impossible, for she was held between two people who had a good deal of experience in restraining recalcitrant young women. All Faith did was confirm that she was reacting, not thinking. With a little less panic and a bit more thought, Faith could have freed herself, but they took advantage of her natural reactions.

Once her knickers were down, Mrs Marryat began to slap. Her soft hands were surprisingly strong and she knew how to slap too; beginning at the top of Faith's buttocks and slapping the cheeks alternately, making the flesh wobble. Each slap left an imprint of a hand. When the first landed, Faith jerked, shrieking as Mrs Marryat called, 'One!' then proceeded with another, evoking a similar shriek, and a third, by which time Faith's vain struggles redoubled. When twelve had been delivered (each accompanied by Mrs Marryat calling out the number) Faith had stopped struggling and was crying the tears she had refused to shed on Alex's departure. They fell profusely as the half-remembered occasional pain of her youth and the memory of Alex's bittersweet ministrations swept through her.

Yet she knew something was happening deep within herself, something over which she had no control. She could feel the reverberations sweeping through

14

her body, setting up a familiar surge of pleasure. Faith knew she was beginning to enjoy the sensations, even though they were being produced by the love balls which Alex had carefully inserted prior to her departure. Faith thought the vibration in the BMW had begun to affect her, but now she was sure. This woman was spanking her quite hard, yet despite the stinging flesh she could feel herself lubricating. Would these two people realise they were leading her to a climax? She hoped not; the shame would be too much to bear. And in any case, why were they doing this to her? They were supposed to be educating her, not spanking her like this. She had long forgotten Alex's comment about pain sometimes making an educational point.

Mrs Marryat reached 25 before she stopped assaulting Faith's behind, still holding the sobbing young woman as firmly as ever, though she had given up struggling long before.

'Mr Clive, it seems that our new pupil quite enjoys a spanking, don't you think? She's quite wet, you know.'

'Sounds like it,' the man answered, nodding as Faith blushed and closed her saturated eyes in horror. 'Since you reached double figures, Mrs Marryat, she hasn't closed her legs at all. I think she enjoyed that.'

Faith's features burned.

'You are going to remove your clothing now, at once,' the woman said to Faith's bent head, the fringe of hair concealing her scarlet face.

'Yes, yes,' Faith sobbed, eager to be released and anxious to have the terrible spanking stopped. Her behind felt on fire – she had never known anything like it – while the shame she felt at having been spanked like that (with her knickers round her thighs) in front of Jackson, made her hot cheeks even more

15

incandescent. The worst part was to have the woman tell Jackson that she was lubricating. Faith had forgotten that her musk, like that of most women, was quite distinctive. Even when Alex had spanked her for no other reason than the fact that he loved her, she had not been so upset. Yet there was a sexual thrill running through her, a sensation which mitigated everything else. The pleasure she felt far outweighed the discomfort.

When Jackson nodded they released her, yet stood on either side while her skirt slipped down her legs. For a few seconds Faith stood, gasping and swallowing, trying to control herself but half-expecting one of them to seize her again. She needed a few moments to recover her poise, but was denied them.

'Are you going to undress?' Mrs Marryat broke the silence. Faith's answer was to look doubtfully at Jackson's impassive expression, at which Mrs Marryat said, 'Mr Clive has seen many young ladies without clothing. You'll find, Miss Faith, that young women are all made pretty much the same. Undress as you promised, or I shall take a leather strap to your behind.'

Faith was unfastening her blouse before the woman finished, her fingers trembling as she fumbled with the buttons at her wrists, her wavering lips making her exhalations sound like shuddering sobs. Neither interfered or tried to hurry her. It was the beginning of a preparatory psychological process in which Faith (as others had before her) removed their clothing and, by threat of worse punishment, gave themselves up to the strictures of Jackson and his housekeeper.

Had Faith's clothing been torn off by Jackson and his housekeeper, she could have preserved her independence, but now she had promised to obey. By

16

complying, Faith started the process where she would eventually acquiesce to further instructions, so becoming a party to what was happening. Becoming obedient and disciplined.

Once Faith had removed her outer garments she began on the underwear, removing first the brassière, not seeing the look of relief passing between Jackson and Mrs Marryat. Surprise and co-ordination had won out. When she was naked Faith stood waiting, tensed and ready for flight or fight, yet if anything they stood further away, examining her like farmers with the livestock at the cattle market.

Surprised, Faith sneaked a look at them sideways, not daring to turn her head in case they took exception to it.

It was Mrs Marryat who spoke first. 'Her skin's not as good as it could be; not too bad, of course.' She lifted some of Faith's hair, an expression of dislike on her face. 'Her hair needs attention, but both of those could be diet; we shall have to see. Well cut. Bad posture, of course. Can't you stand up straight, Miss Faith?'

'I *am* standing up straight!' Faith answered in a sullen tone. They weren't exactly Mr and Mrs Universe.

'You slouch.' The woman spoke as though Faith had remained silent. 'You are round-shouldered.'

'Yes.' Faith shrugged a little then stopped in case they took exception to that. 'My friends at school were all short.'

'A good many young women have the same problem.' Mrs Marryat nodded with a tone and expression which suggested understanding. 'We can cure it, though.'

Faith sneaked another look at Jackson. His right forearm was held across his body, the hand supporting

17

his left elbow, while his left hand cradled his chin in a thoughtful pose. He moved around so that he could see Faith better as Mrs Marryat began testing her muscle tone by gripping her arms and thighs between her fingers. Then she took hold of Faith's buttocks in both hands, squeezing tightly and making the young woman wince and hiss at the discomfort to her rosy flesh.

'Good tension.'

The woman nodded, then instructed, 'Spread your legs, Miss Faith.'

'Do ... do I have to?' Faith asked, her sobs threatening to overwhelm her again. Her breathing, which had returned to almost normal, became shallow again at the thought of spreading her legs so that Jackson, who stood in front of her, would have an unrivalled view of her sex. Alarmed, Faith realised that her breathing was changing because she actually relished the thought of displaying herself to this man.

'Yes you do,' Mrs Marryat answered quietly. Slowly Faith began to slide her legs across the carpet while Mrs Marryat kept flicking a finger outwards until she nodded for Faith to stop when her legs were sufficiently widely spread to allow both of them to see her sex.

Mrs Marryat knelt in front of her and with her cold fingers, gently teased the hot sex lips apart while Faith's breath came in even more short, hesitant gasps. She was being sexually aroused by this examination; she was afraid and yet found being touched and examined as though she was an animal quite exciting. The woman nodded her understanding a few times, but whether at Faith's lack of protest or something she was thinking about, Faith never knew.

'Sexually experienced, of course, but we knew that,' she said, then felt the lower abdomen just above

Faith's pubis. 'You have the balls inserted at the moment, don't you?' she asked, looking up at Faith.

'What?' Faith's frightened features peered down at the older woman's upturned face.

'You have two balls inserted, don't you? Mr Clive, would you fetch some others, please? They're almost identical and will work equally well.'

While Mrs Marryat expelled the love balls from Faith's cervix by pressing against the top surface indicated by the slight distension of her lower abdomen to make them descend to her vaginal entrance, Jackson took a small box from the dresser, opening it as he returned and handing the contents to the kneeling woman.

'They're cold, I'm afraid,' Mrs Marryat said softly, then pressed them, to Faith's gasps, into the open pink flesh of her aromatic vagina, inserting her long middle finger to push them higher. Finally she felt up Faith's pubic mound with her fingers, adding the final, external push which settled the balls within Faith's cervix. 'There! That's better, isn't it?' She rose again but remained in front of Faith, her eyes on Faith's breasts. 'Yes. Nipple rings each night, I think.' She looked round to Jackson, who moved closer. 'She's had them before and we'll continue with them until they're permanently enlarged. Her teats will look lovely.'

'Yes.' Jackson nodded, then from the box produced two familiar rings.

As he handed them to her, Mrs Marryat said, 'Stand still, Miss Faith, this won't take a moment as you know, but it must be done.'

Before Faith could protest, or even move, she fastened her lips around Faith's left nipple. While Faith gulped her surprise down her throat, Mrs Marryat extended a hand towards Jackson, who placed a ring

19

in her fingers which she then transferred to her mouth.

Within seconds, Faith felt the familiar suction and sudden pressure as the ring slipped over her nipple, which felt chilled when Mrs Marryat moved to the right breast where the process was repeated. Her frightened gulp matched her expression; the only comment she made on the process. Yet she knew the flush of arousal had not left her face. She knew too that both of them knew it and expected a comment, which never came.

'There!' Mrs Marryat smiled at the young woman, frightening her even more. 'That didn't take long.'

'I was thinking.' Jackson frowned. 'Alex was right. The boots, too. She can be taken for walks.'

Mrs Marryat smiled at Faith. 'We'll have a lovely time. There are some very beautiful walks in the woods here, though in certain places one has to be careful. Turn around, Miss Faith.'

Faith paused but there was no change in either of her tormentors; they merely waited, ready to seize her should she refuse. This was when Faith would think about how much she should co-operate, so they were both close enough to act.

When Faith turned, Mrs Marryat commented, 'Good round behind, I'm glad to see. So many young women have flat buttocks due to too much sitting about. Though I think it could do with a corset. What do you think?' She looked at Jackson, then back at Faith to give another instruction. 'Bend forward over the bed, Miss Faith.'

Faith objected. 'Why? Why do I have to?'

For her answer they grabbed her and, holding her legs straight, bent her forward over the bottom of the bed, each pressing her shoulders into the covers. Then they moved her legs further apart, securing them with their own and, once again calling out the numbers, Mrs Marryat spanked Faith. Thirty deliberate, regular slaps. Once over her initial shock Faith tested her muscles in an attempt to struggle free. To her surprise, she found herself absolutely unable to move, yet the reverberations of the spanking were setting up a climax despite the stinging in her behind. She could feel the swelling, pounding climax surging up from her abdomen while her sex soaked the covers of the bed.

Chapter Two

Faith tensed her limbs, trying to fight against them, but they knew exactly how to hold her. The parts of Faith's buttocks which had been relatively untouched by the previous spanking were now as red as those originally treated, but nothing made any difference. Her orgasm was severing all but the most basic connections to her brain. In the intellectual part of her brain she was aware of the pain, but that was all. The messages the nerves were sending had been blocked by the pleasure overwhelming them.

It was not just the fact that she was lubricating over the bed which made her feel ashamed, it was the knowledge that the process had begun even earlier, during the previous spanking, making her wonder whether her control was slipping. Yet some spark of defiance made her try to grit her teeth against this loss of control. She would refuse to allow them to dictate when she had a climax. She was a modern young woman who claimed that right for herself.

Faith could feel herself begin to tremble with the understanding that there was nothing she could do to mitigate or even change her situation. She had to lie across the bed, held firmly in place, while Mrs Marryat brought her to a climax by spanking her. As the delicious feeling surged through her, lending strength still unequal to the task of moving her captors' grip, Faith's cries were muffled by the bedcovers.

The familiar hardness in her abdomen as her muscles tensed alerted her to the imminence of release. Then the overwhelming sensation swept over her, drowning out all other stimuli in a surfeit of pleasure, centred just behind her pubis but spreading like a brush fire through her system. She bit the covers to conceal her delight.

When her crying and shaking were done, she was released from their grasp to lie inert in the same position, feeling the glow on her behind beginning to warm again the sensations of arousal. Shocked at herself, yet knowing that even after the orgasm she had just experienced she had another seeded and ready to sprout, Faith caught her breath while her mind turned over the information. She felt an awe within her at the discovery.

To Faith, bondage had always meant being held fast, as Jackson and Mrs Marryat had held her fast, while unspeakable tortures were inflicted on her. Alex had fastened her securely to the bed at his friend's house, rendering her incapable of resisting him, yet that had never seemed proper bondage in her mind. It had been the stuff of nightmares ... or was it dreams? The pain of the spanking was diminishing by the second, being replaced by warmth. That in itself was fuelling the early stages of arousal. Would these two people who seemed to know her so well provoke another climax?

'There!' Mrs Marryat said in a voice which expressed as much sorrow as annoyance. 'Now we can proceed. Do *not* draw your legs together, Miss Faith!' This was said in a sharper tone.

Mrs Marryat knelt again and, with her delicate fingers, pressed and tested Faith's buttocks before she took the hot, rounded globes, pulling them gently apart to open up the vista of Faith's anus. Mrs

Marryat looked up at Jackson, who immediately took over the task of holding Faith's buttocks apart while Mrs Marryat's questing finger moved on again to more sensitive flesh.

Faith could feel herself blush again as she realised what was happening and twitched as that cold finger, surprisingly unwarmed by the spanking, pressed and prodded her perineum, then tested the pulse in her anus with first a delicate push, then some steady pressure. Each of these intimate touches made Faith gasp in a mixture of apprehension and fear, not passion. Mrs Marryat smiled to herself at the almost unharmed sphincter before her. Yet though the discomfort of having the finger pressed lightly on to her anus was unusual, Faith found herself being further aroused. It seemed as though every part of this examination, including the spankings she had received for her disobedience, were part of a grand design to bring out all the facets of her most lubricious nature. Once again she blushed as she realised just how much this woman knew about her; more than she knew herself.

'Apart from your initiation, Miss Faith, I take it no one has ever entered your bottom?'

'No.' Faith gulped an answer, then a longer more drawn out gasp as, quite deliberately, Mrs Marryat pressed the centre of the ring of muscles, her finger finding entry relatively easy, freezing Faith into immobility at the sensations which surged through her body. While the warmth of her buttocks had started another cycle of arousal, now the questing finger provided a measure of discomfort to counterbalance it, the difference bringing other sensations into play. Despite herself, Faith lay inert, her eyes partly glazing over as she gave herself up to Mrs Marryat. If, after this, Jackson wanted her, then she would make not the slightest objection. She was ready to be satisfied.

'You're very fortunate, Miss Faith,' the woman said evenly. 'Your bottom seems willing to accommodate my finger, right to the top.'

Faith groaned. Mrs Marryat's knuckles rested against her labia, the pressure parting them to admit them to the scarlet flesh of the vulva within. One knuckle pressed against her vaginal opening from which the musk still oozed. The mixture of the two emotions – the excitement of the knuckles and the pressure of the finger – set up another set of familiar waves of pleasure within Faith.

'Stay there.' The woman withdrew her finger, rising to her feet. Wiping her finger, she crossed the room to the box from which Jackson had taken the love balls, where she selected a long thin rod. About six inches long and half an inch across for the majority of its length, the tip was rounded. At the other end it was necked down to less than half that, before a round, flat plate, about an inch across, completed the end. When Faith's head half-turned in that direction, she saw the woman turn with it in her hands. She took a deep breath when she recognised the dildo.

Mrs Marryat brought this and two bottles of colourless liquid with her when she returned to the bed, kneeling again. She poured some of the liquid from one bottle on to her fingers before beginning to massage it into Faith's anus, applying it gently yet persistently, listening to the cooing sounds the young woman made. Unseen by Faith she smiled confidently up at Jackson.

Faith gasped at first, from the surprise of the touch and the cooler temperature of the liquid but, after a few seconds, subsided. Submitting and waiting for the massage to end, Faith realised that Mrs Marryat knew more about young women than even Alex did. The tension within her and the sudden contraction of her muscles at her spanking, her penetration and now this massage, had sent the balls moving around. The old sensations were being aroused again even as the liquid was soothing her inflamed tissue, adding to the familiar tingling in her breasts from the nipple rings.

When Mrs Marryat was satisfied with the preparations, amid the familiar sounds of appreciation from Faith, she tested the pulse of the oiled anus again, nodding. She then applied some of the thicker liquid from the second bottle to the end of the rod as she said, 'Just one more, Miss Faith, and it'll be all over and you can get into bed. There!' She applied the rounded end of the rod to Faith's bottom. The young woman gasped as the pressure overcame the natural resistance of the muscles, but it was too late. Even had she wanted to resist, she would have found it difficult as the rod was slipped and twisted clockwise into Faith's rectum. Faith gulped and gasped her faint protests into the covers.

The familiar sensations of sexual arousal being produced within her made her gasp, for there was no real pain. In fact, there was pleasure; but the shame of having this foreign object pushed into her bottom by strangers made Faith blush yet again. This shame was compounded by the knowledge that Mrs Marryat obviously knew she would enjoy it, and Jackson had witnessed everything. These two people had taught her a lot about herself in the short time since Alex had left her with them. They seemed to instinctively understand her liking for bondage; but did she have other desires? Did they know of them and, if they did, would they see to it that she indulged them, too? The problems were mounting thick and fast.

When it was securely lodged, the round flange flush against her, Mrs Marryat rose to her feet as Jackson released Faith's buttocks.

'That has to stay in all night, Miss Faith, so I hope you don't want to evacuate your bowels. I should have asked, I'm sorry. Do you want to use the lavatory before you go to bed? There won't be another chance.'

'No,' Faith answered while Mrs Marryat wiped her hands again before instructing her.

'Stay on your front, but move up the bed, Miss Faith.'

Thinking she had best comply instantly before she was spanked again, Faith moved up the bed by hauling with her arms until her head was on the pillow on the right of the bed, her legs still held apart. She was unable to see the smile on Mrs Marryat's face, or the look she exchanged with Jackson at this show of submission. Not many learned that lesson so early.

But Mrs Marryat also moved quickly. From between the two pairs of pillows she took a bright metal collar which was padded internally and, before Faith could even react, placed it around her neck. There was a key-operated lock which she turned, then she withdrew the key, telling her, 'You can get into bed now, Miss Faith.' She stepped back quickly in case she struggled. Faith lay there for some seconds while the realisation sank in.

Faith took several deep breaths as her circumstances were brought home to her. Around her throat was a metal collar. Not a beautiful, decorative gold collar like the one Alex had given her, but a simple stainless steel one, for all the padding. Designed for use rather than decoration. It was bondage, but of a kind she had not previously experienced. This was serious. Not part of sexual arousal or a prelude to a bout of lovemaking. This was not pleasure slavery, but the simple, old-fashioned kind. The concept took her breath away for a moment.

Faith knelt on the bed. The chain connected to the collar (a light, shiny, stainless steel chain with forged links offering no hope of being prised apart) rose from the top of the bed with her. She stood by the side of the bed looking at them, a fearful, almost pitiful expression marring her face.

'Why are you doing this to me?' she asked, trying to keep her tears in check.

'You are here to be disciplined, Miss Faith,' Mrs Marryat answered. 'We're disciplining you, that's all.'

'But why are you *doing* this to me?' Faith wailed.

'You heard Mr Pellew, Miss Faith, you are to be taught discipline; which we are to do. It may take a few weeks; it may take longer. We have never had a young lady who left as ill-disciplined as she arrived. Some had a pleasant time; some were whipped daily. We had one whom we locked in a cage for six weeks, chained to the bars. Yes!' she said quickly as Faith's eyes widened at the mere mention of a cage. 'We have cages here, too. How you are treated depends on how you behave; how you respond to the training. Do you understand?' When there was no response apart from an expression of blank incomprehension, Mrs Marryat nodded. 'Goodnight, Miss Faith. Have a good night's sleep. You've had a difficult day, but things will seem better in the morning. I will turn out the light now and the chain isn't long enough for you to reach the door, far less the light switch. Goodnight.'

Faith moved towards them but she was suddenly brought up short when the chain refused to stretch any further. Wordlessly they turned, opened the door, the light went out and the door closed, leaving her in darkness.

For a moment Faith despaired. She turned and moved back to the bed, misjudging the distance and falling forward on to it, where she suddenly burst out into sobs of frustrated anger. They had worked well together and taken her by surprise. They had made her do their bidding, but she would be ready for them next time.

Here she was, chained to a bed in a miserable old house deep in the country, and who knew? Alex. That was it! Alex would find out about how she was doing; he said he'd get reports, perhaps even telephone. Yet they could put him off with excuses. There was always the possibility of escape, of course. Jackson had said that she could go for walks and unless they kept her in those boots, she felt confident of out-running either of them and a chain-link fence shouldn't be too difficult to climb.

As she lay in the darkness, her tears drying on her hot cheeks, Faith began to think of how she could distract them for long enough to get a head start. Yet there was something rather thrilling about being there. Her throat was held fast in a collar fastened to the bed, her buttocks felt on fire but the sensation was translating into sexual pleasure, and she thought she recognised the liquid which Mrs Marryat had used on the dildo. An aphrodisiac. Would tomorrow mean that she was sexually used? Or did they intend to keep her until she begged them to mount her?

Downstairs on the telephone, Mrs Marryat heard Alex ask, 'How did she take it?'

'There was some initial difficulty, but there always is, of course. She was spanked twice before we got her into bed, but she's no worse for that. Enjoyed it, even.'

'Yes. I found that. What about tomorrow?'

'I expect we'll be spanking her again; possibly even the strap. And it wouldn't surprise me if she didn't spend some time in the cages. I might even demonstrate them, just to prepare her. Is there anything special you want her to learn while she's here?'

29

'Just discipline and deportment, as we agreed,' Alex answered. 'And of course, the usual polish.'

Faith did not have a good night. The rod lodged in her behind was slightly larger than the others she had known. Alex had always made sure that when Lillian Brampton inserted one during the day, it was removed on going to bed. Usually it preceded Alex mounting her. She felt her anus beyond the warm, smooth tissue of her backside, her fingers finding the flat flange tight against her skin and, when she gently tried to use her muscles to expel the rod a little, they refused to move.

She would have to use them in greater strength if she hoped to shift it at all. Faith reasoned that in trying it, she could produce unfortunate consequences. If they spanked her so much for refusing to strip and bend over, what would they do if she made a mess? Though perhaps it would mean another climax. Somehow she thought it was better not to try it.

For the first time in many months, Faith was sleeping alone. She was lying in a large double bed; she was warm, she was weary, but sleep refused to come because of the very necessary presence she required of her partner. Albert had wanted sex every day when she lived with him. His idea of sex was so insignificant that catering to it presented no problems. Though there had been times when Alex and Faith had not made love, they had been perfectly happy together. Sex was not all that she wanted from him though it had been wonderful. She needed the companionship of the bed; the ability to put out a hand to touch someone else, to hear him breathe softly in the darkness. Lacking it, she was miserable.

So she sought solace in the way she so often had with Albert but never with Alex. Her fingers first caressed her almost hairless mound, then stole down the smooth sides of her labial lips, lightly pressing and caressing. Faith knew that the longer she delayed touching her clitoris, the more intense would be the arousal when it finally came; and the more satisfying. She may not have Alex with her, but she had imagination and a greedy little pip at the top of her labia with an insatiable appetite for sensation.

Faith was not going to escape that morning. Her first vision on waking was of Mrs Marryat leaning over her, pulling back the covers. Faith's hands were still down between her legs, gently massaging her sex, comforting herself with the unconscious action.

'Good morning, Miss Faith.'

Mrs Marryat's voice was the same, even tone as it had been the night before after having administered the spanking. Startled, Faith lay wide-eyed looking at this woman, the 'Wicked Witch of the West' in her nightmares. Mrs Marryat's skin was flawless, but the only colour was provided by her light blue eyes and the pale lipstick. She wore another plain dress, over which she had a plastic coverall like a long macintosh.

Behind and to one side, a short, slim, dark-blonde girl waited, her head inclined at 45 degrees to the floor, a wooden box held in her hands. She wore only a pair of white knickers, her small breasts with hard nipples looking out of place.

'Did you sleep well?' the woman asked. Faith allowed her breathing to return to normal, looking defiantly at the woman until the latter asked, 'Not speaking to me this morning? Oh dear, I wonder what I should do about that?'

'Good morning,' Faith ground out. Her mouth felt dry and there was an itching between her thighs – a feeling of desperate longing as though she had been too long without sexual release.

'And where are our manners this morning, Miss Faith?'

'Good morning, Mrs Marryat.' Faith tried to keep her voice neutral, but her expression made that difficult.

The woman nodded, still smiling, asking, 'Masturbating, were we? That's not allowed; I shall have to do something about that.'

'I wasn't ... masturbating!' Faith protested, then flushed. 'I had an itch; I was scratching it.' She knew it was the weakest excuse ever. Even though she did have an itch, it was just where Mrs Marryat guessed it was. Perhaps she had put something more than oil on the dildo in her bottom. Lillian had, and it usually produced the same results.

'And a liar too,' Mrs Marryat said sadly, nodding. 'Well, we *have* taken on a problem child, haven't we? Never mind, we've had worse. We can discipline you too. Move down the bed and stand facing it, Miss Faith.'

With a sullen reluctance, Faith did as she was bid, turning to face the bed on which she had passed the night. Mrs Marryat was quick. Before Faith had hardly finished moving she was beside her, her sharp voice insistent.

'Hold out your wrists, Miss Faith!' she snapped. The young woman had come with her and as Faith stood, shocked into compliance, the woman opened the box her companion carried. Quickly Mrs Marryat delved inside, displaying a series of thin metal rings in her hands which were hinged at one side.

They were D-shaped in section, with a thick padding on the flat, inner side. On one side, the open end had a notched tongue which fitted into a hole on the face of the other side. As on the collar around her neck, four steel rings were spaced equidistantly around the rounded outer curve lying flat against it. Faith looked at them reluctantly, then back to the calm woman who, despite being slightly shorter, seemed to tower over her.

'Why are you doing this to me?' she asked, her mouth trembling. Mrs Marryat looked steadily at her then shook her head, her expressive features showing her disappointment at the question.

'Have you forgotten what I said to you last night, child, when you asked that same question? You're here to be disciplined.'

'But I haven't done anything wrong!' Faith protested.

'No one has said you have. Now, silence. Don't make so much fuss. Hold out your wrists, and then your ankles and, in a little while, you'll be taken to the lavatory. I'm sure you must be eager to get there.'

Furious but unable to resist, Faith held her wrists out in front of her, watching as the woman sorted through the four rings, juggling them to find the right one. Eventually she had the first metal tongue through the hole and it was secured to her wrist. The padding helped to take away the cold feeling which came over her and she wondered why she was going along with this as Mrs Marryat worked on her left wrist.

Faith was still secured to the bed by the metal collar around her throat. Should Mrs Marryat encounter any difficulties with Faith, the latter would be at a distinct disadvantage. Mrs Marryat could always get her assistant, who retreated through the doorway, to help. Struggling was useless, at this stage, anyway. Later, perhaps.

'Lie on your front with your hands behind your back, resting on your behind, Miss Faith.'

'Why do you call me "Miss Faith" when everyone else calls me Faith?' Faith spoke in a sullen snarl, though complying with the instruction.

'Faith is your given name, isn't it? Faith Michaela, Miss Faith?' the woman asked, fastening her wrists together with a snap similar to that used on dog leads.

'Everyone calls me Faith.' Faith was sullenly aware that her position was immeasurably worse now that her wrists were fastened together.

Mrs Marryat was quicker with her ankles, snapping the rings on to the narrowest parts just above the protruding bone, then moving her ankles sideways. Almost before Faith was aware of what was happening, her ankles were secured to the foot of the legs of the bed.

Faith lay bent, face down, her arms fastened behind her, her ankles secured, her neck secured, her body taut. As Mrs Marryat moved back towards her, Faith realised her vulnerability; she was unable either to defend herself or to prevent this woman touching her intimately, though she discovered that the woman's mind was far from that subject.

'Apart from many other transgressions, we do not allow lying, Miss Faith.' Mrs Marryat spoke severely. 'If nothing else, it shows your total want of discipline. Each and every lie will be punished, like this!' She brought her hand down sharply against Faith's exposed buttocks.

Long before the tears began to flow, even before the howls of pained surprise had died away, the stinging sensation in her behind was renewed. The familiar feelings of sexual desire came far more quickly than on the previous evening, yet so did her apprehension, for the smacking also increased her very real need to urinate. The pressure within her abdomen was acute.

Part of the reason for her bad night was her waking every so often with the feelings of wanting to urinate, which she had managed to successfully suppress. This shifted her focus from the pain of being spanked to the real need to concentrate her muscles on not disgracing herself. Yet alongside these needs was the pleasure which was again building up within her. Was it to be a race between climaxing and peeing?

If she was being spanked like this for a 'white lie', what would happen if she urinated all over the carpet? And would that punishment, whatever it was, arouse her further? With thoughts like these she distracted herself from the steady rise and fall of Mrs Marryat's hand on her backside.

Eventually, when 40 slaps had been administered, leaving her with a glowing behind, the spanking stopped and, in a voice hardly different from that normally used, Mrs Marryat asked, 'There. Perhaps that may deter you telling more lies, Miss Faith. Do you wish to use the lavatory and wash?'

'Yes,' Faith answered. The woman merely looked directly into Faith's eyes, her expression unchanging, until Faith, controlling her sobbing, looked up. 'Yes please, Mrs Marryat.'

'That's better,' the woman said, smiling. 'Social, as opposed to sexual, intercourse is eased by the petty politeness of convention. "Please" and "thank you" makes the most sordid transactions acceptable. And before you leave us, you will beg me fervently, I know, to whip you.'

The woman unfastened Faith's ankles before moving to the head of the bed where, reaching between the pillows to pull up some chain and operate the lock which held them together, Faith was released.

'It's like being back at school,' Faith glowered in a partly cowed, surly fashion. Three spankings within

24 hours, not to mention the orgasms, had been a shock to her system.

There was no answer, though the woman said, 'The facilities are next door.'

At first Faith thought Mrs Marryat held one end of the chain, but closer examination showed that the end was actually fastened to a similar ring attached to the woman's left wrist. It meant that there was no chance of her suddenly breaking free and making a run for it. Mentally Faith sagged for a moment, then decided that if she was unable to escape, she should at least find out more about the regime she had to endure.

'Why must I be dragged on a chain like a wild animal?' she asked, as the woman opened the door.

'Because, until you're disciplined, Miss Faith, you *are* a wild animal – a dangerous one.'

Pondering, Faith followed her through the door into the bathroom. It was a pleasant enough bathroom without being luxurious. Had Faith not experienced Alex's opulent facilities she would have been content with it, for everything she could have wanted was there. Before she stepped into the shower, Mrs Marryat removed both the nipple rings and dildo, but not the chain connecting her wrist to Faith's throat. Faith thought the splashing water would deter her, but realised that the woman had already thought of that. Her dress was protected in the plastic coverall.

After her ablutions they returned to the bedroom where the bed now sported a tray with a bowl of muesli and mug of hot tea on it. The chain of Faith's collar was refastened to the bed and she ate the Spartan breakfast, supervised by the fair, silent young woman who looked a year or so younger than herself. Despite Faith trying to make conversation, there was

36

no reply and eventually she gave up. If they refused to speak to her, there was nothing she could do about it. Mrs Marryat entered the room as she was finishing, nodding to the young woman, who left silently.

'It is time to begin your training,' Mrs Marryat began. 'When you waken each morning, you will kneel on the bed with your back to the door, placing your wrists behind you. You will be conducted to the various training rooms by your guide, who will supervise your education, though I shall be in the background, of course; watching you. You will address her or him as Mistress or Master. You will know the guides by their clothing, and you will obey every word they say.'

'What do I wear?' Faith asked.

'You're wearing it.'

'Nothing?' Faith asked, astonished. 'But she's got –'

'Nothing,' Mrs Marryat interrupted. 'Only guides wear clothes here, no matter how brief. Now, up!' Faith took a deep breath, rose to her feet and stood there, breathing heavily while the woman looked at her critically before stating, 'While you are here, unless otherwise instructed, you will walk upright, with your shoulders back and your head lowered modestly. Like this.' Mrs Marryat pulled Faith's shoulders back into a painful position, smiling at the grunted protest. 'It will improve in time, Miss Faith.' Then she pressed Faith's head forward so that it pointed at 45 degrees to the floor of the bedroom. Faith could imagine just how submissive this made her look and, with a start, realised that this had been the position in which the young woman who had come with Mrs Marryat earlier had stood. 'There!' The woman walked around to the front of her prisoner. 'That's better. You must maintain that posture at all times;

even when walking and when spread out.' Faith could feel her anger seeping back again but Mrs Marryat was already moving. Even as Faith's ire was sending flashing lights before her eyes, the pressure on the chain pulled her forward.

She was led past the stairway to the first door on the right in the opposite corridor, where the same slim young woman waited. The room was about twenty feet square, the walls covered completely in mirrors save for at intervals, where rings set into the walls protruded. The chain being removed from Mrs Marryat's wrist was connected to one of these rings.

Mrs Marryat looked at Faith in silence for a moment, then said, 'Let us see how well you can stand still. Face the mirror.' When Faith did so, she added, 'No movement now!'

For a moment Faith was puzzled, looking at her reflection, then a movement caught her eye, but too late. There was a broad strap in Mrs Marryat's hand, flicking out at her buttocks, landing with a crack which sent a shiver through her frame. Faith cried out in protest as the leather landed, the stinging pain greater than any spanking.

'What did I tell you about how to hold your head, Miss Faith?' Mrs Marryat asked in a quiet, menacing tone. 'Look down, not at yourself. Vanity is not an attribute we admire here.'

With shaking limbs, Faith's head lowered, looking at the bottom of the glass six feet away, her hands pinioned behind her. The woman gave her a few seconds to control herself, then the strap flicked out again, cracking with equal venom on her rump, just below the previous blow. Again Faith yelped and would have protested had not Mrs Marryat been speaking.

'I said stand still!' Her tone was as sharp as a knife,

cutting through the beginning of Faith's protest. Faith looked up at her tormentor's reflection and again the strap slashed against her behind. 'No one told you to look up!'

Mrs Marryat knew that she had to shock Faith into quick conformity and frighten her with harsh treatment, for the training would otherwise take too long. She ignored much of the trembling in the young woman's limbs; the automatic nervous shaking as the system became used to such treatment. In a few days, perhaps a week, this would vanish and Faith would be inured to it, but the only cure was to suffer.

Trembling even more violently than before, Faith stood with bowed head, wondering from what lunatic asylum this woman had escaped. Only a madwoman would slash at her like that yet preserve absolute calm in her voice and features. But Faith had to admit that the position thrilled her despite the stinging in her behind. The sensations in her abdomen felt similar to those just before Alex penetrated her. She tried to control her heavy breathing as her reflexes took over from her senses.

There was something quite sexual about all this; a feeling of helplessness which spread through her. It was as though the stricture to remain still was seeping into her very being, yet her mind rebelled. She had a good mind, an independent mind; a mind which was telling her body that it was outrageous to be so treated. For almost a minute she stood, then the strap was plied again, this time just landing beneath the line of the others.

'Stand still!' came the cold, hard comment, followed by another blow. 'Don't slouch!'

With her backside glowing hot with the strap, tears standing in the corners of her eyes, limbs trembling both from shock and the unaccustomed stationary position, Faith felt that there was no greater hell. The dissonance set up between her mind and her body, each in the opposite camp, was matched by her senses too. Where the flesh of her behind protested that the punishment could be avoided by compliance – by standing still – the pleasure centres were demanding more movement, for there was no doubt that the warmth induced by the strap was working on them.

To add to her conflict, some detached part of her brain posed philosophical questions to distract her from concentrating on either of them. Was she destined to be beaten like this for as long as they chose? Or would they ship her out, once she was cowed (for she knew she could be cowed) to some foreign country, as a whore? Would she like being a whore?

With her mind working furiously, her face almost as red as her behind, Faith tried to control herself. Eventually, Mrs Marryat nodded to her assistant, handing her the strap.

'Alison will keep you company, Miss Faith. You will address her as "Mistress", and if you move from that position, she will strap you, as I have done.'

'But what –' Faith began, only to have Alison lash out at her with the strap, catching her on the top of her thighs, making her yell again.

'You were not given permission to speak, Miss Faith. You will speak when spoken to in future.' The older woman nodded to Alison before she departed, leaving Faith alone with the young woman in the large, bare room.

Standing as still as she could, Faith found that remaining stationary was hardly as simple as she had imagined. Normally, the body is not adjusted to remaining perfectly still and for someone like Faith, unused to it, the discipline was a trial. The first intimation she would get would be when she heard the swish just before the strap exploded on her skin, making her yelp again, followed by 'Posture!' from the young woman behind her, or 'Stand still!'

When Mrs Marryat returned, Faith was glowing from her knees upwards, for Alison struck the undamaged skin on her thighs exclusively. The pleasure was strong within her, fuelled by the warmth and the action of the two love balls as she moved when the strap landed.

'She cannot stand still, Madame,' Alison said in a soft, yet cultured accent; the product of an expensive education and upbringing. Faith's eyes looked up in surprise at this, for there had been no hint of this in the clipped tones she had used.

'She is new, Alison. She will learn. Unfasten and bring her.'

Chapter Three

With Faith on the end of the chain which the silent Alison held, Mrs Marryat led the way out into the yard, a slightly sloping expanse of concrete, bare save for a few poles and uprights set into the concrete and totally surrounded by brick-built buildings. The mildly chilly morning air brought her skin up in gooseflesh. Faith thought it was the lack of warmth, but the sight of these strange features alarmed her. An old Land Rover stood near the large, covered entrance, but there were no people to be seen. It looked bright out there in the open; spring was well advanced.

They passed the poles and uprights without comment, a bleak smile coming to Mrs Marryat's face as Faith asked, 'Can I ask what happens here in winter?'

'You freeze.' The woman paused and turned, obviously considering the question for a moment. 'You come out here when the snow is on the ground, just as you are now. I disciplined one pupil by chaining her to the wall over there.' She gestured towards the gateway.

Faith looked to where four cleats were sunk in the brickwork, each with a short, bright chain trailing from them. Looking back to Mrs Marryat, her throat visibly bobbing, Faith asked, 'In the snow?' Her voice was an awed, hushed whisper.

'For four hours.' The woman nodded. 'We tried

shorter times at first, but it produced no result. She was still wild, so we left her all afternoon one January day. We had to thaw her out when she came indoors, but she stopped urinating on her bed just to annoy us. I'm afraid that, sometimes, there is just no other way. There are some people, no matter how much one tries to be kind, who only recognise brute force.'

'She might have died!' Faith protested.

'She was blindfolded and thought we had gone indoors, leaving her alone. It was the only time I heard her cry. It was the boredom that affected her most; the boredom of standing there in the snow with nothing to do except count the seconds of her life ticking away. In here.'

The room looked like the interior of a clinic, with a single, tubular-framed chair in the centre of the room with a large bowl beneath it. When Faith was told to sit in the chair she found that it comprised a lavatory seat, but was sitting before she asked, 'What are you going to do?' She looked at the brisk woman who stood over her. Alison remained out of sight, behind her.

'I'm going to give you an enema,' Mrs Marryat answered, as though it was the most natural, obvious thing in the world, smiling and stroking her chin.

'You're what?' Faith demanded, but by then it was too late; much too late.

Curved metal clamps attached to the legs of the chair were swung quickly across by Alison, imprisoning Faith's ankles to them and, by wrapping the chain attached to the collar around the bar at the top, Faith was securely held in place, her eyes wide with surprise.

'Your skin could be improved, my dear.' Mrs Marryat bustled about with unfussy competence, ending once and for all any doubts Faith harboured of her being a trained nurse. Regarding her again, Faith realised she even looked the part of an efficient district nurse.

'I can do that with some cream. Savlon would do it in a couple of days.'

'Possibly.' The woman nodded as though in grudging agreement. 'Though it might not affect the underlying cause.' She was arranging plastic tubing, a funnel and a bottle of green liquid in front of Faith. 'There could be a build-up of toxins responsible. If it is, don't you think it would be best to treat that? I've arranged for you to have a balanced diet, of course; plenty of the right foods. We'll take long walks too, so you get some exercise. We have a gymnasium here which you'll also use. I'll let you know when in good time because we don't want you exciting our other pupils. But you'll have enemas alternate days until I'm satisfied.'

'I don't *need* an enema!' Faith protested.

'Is that a qualified medical opinion?' Mrs Marryat asked in a mild tone, her expression enquiring.

There was little point in answering, so Faith looked away in silence, trying to think of another reason for stopping what she conceived to be just another means of humiliating her. After a few moments the woman left, returning with a washing-up bowl of warm water. Some of the green liquid was poured into it while Faith looked on in horror. Seeing her fear, the woman smiled gently.

'It's only liquid soap, Miss Faith. Some enemas have an irritant in them, but I think we'll try this, first. Now, yes, we're ready. I'll just tip you up . . .' It was then that Faith discovered that the two rear legs were fastened to hinges let into the floor, while the front two rested on the tiled floor.

Both Mrs Marryat and her assistant swung the

chair and Faith backwards until the bar at the top of the back rested on an iron rail and Faith was held on her back, her weight on her imprisoned arms, her painfully red thighs and buttocks completely exposed. Mrs Marryat took the half-inch plastic tube then tried to insert it into Faith's anus, finding the young woman grimly clenching her muscles against the hard, smooth probe.

'Oh dear,' Mrs Marryat sighed, shaking her head, looking at Alison. 'What a pity. Very well.' She sighed again as though realising the impossibility of making an entry without Faith's co-operation. 'If you won't, you won't. I think you'll regret it.'

Faith relaxed again only when the chair was tipped upright, feeling that she had won something of a notable victory. Her ankles were unclamped, the chain was unfastened from the bar (though Alison held it) and she was told to rise.

'You'll regret being so silly, Miss Faith.' The woman nodded to Alison, who looped the chain over the iron rail on which the chair had rested. Before Faith realised, she reached beneath and pulled it, dragging Faith's head down until the collar on her throat was secured across the rail with Faith bent over, facing it. The chain was led back to the bar on the back of the chair where it was tied, securing her in position.

Mrs Marryat was in no hurry to proceed, however, for even as Faith called, 'All right! All right! I'll have the enema!' the woman hooked one small foot between her naked legs, pulling Faith's right foot to the support on that side which kept the bar in place. As she did, Alison was using both hands to pull Faith's left foot in the opposite direction. At the bottom of each upright was a circlet of rope and, with very little effort, Faith's feet were forced through them. Faith yelled again, a ragged edge of panic audible in her voice: 'I said I'd have the enema!'

'I know you did,' Mrs Marryat answered while completing her task, looking up at the lovely face, now contorted with anxiety and not a little anger, 'but you will also be spanked. You know the rules, Miss Faith; obedience. Obedience is all I ask.' She rose to her feet and stood to Faith's left.

'Please!' Faith gasped, 'I forgot. Honestly, I forgot.'

'Then this will help you to remember.' Mrs Marryat spoke in the same quiet yet steely tone as she prepared to give the plump pink buttocks yet another dose of the same treatment which had proved so successful the previous night. 'One!' Her hand landed on the taut skin of Faith's behind.

Thirty-five smacks later, when Faith's tears were just a memory on her hot face, the smacking stopped. Faith had tried to release her feet by lifting them, trying to squirm them free of the circlets, but the rope just slipped up the support and she was unable to obtain any purchase on it. When she realised that there was no alternative, Faith had tried to bend her fastened hands down over her buttocks, only to have Alison lift them clear, while Mrs Marryat continued the same application of her hand. She hardly broke the cadence of the count.

Had it been just a punishment then Faith could have borne it with some fortitude, but she had been undone again by her own body. While the hand was turning her backside into a source of some heat, the rhythmic application was also sending jarring shocks through to her cervix where the love balls lurked. Once sent moving about, they generated their own pressures. Long before Mrs Marryat reached twenty, the sounds Faith emitted were less those of protest and pain than of pleasure – the familiar cooing and gasping she knew so well.

Mrs Marryat bent and held her inner wrist near Faith's flame-red buttocks, testing the temperature before she stroked the hot flesh with a single finger, making the young woman shudder with the cold touch on her skin. As she stroked the skin gently, she allowed her fingers to wander into the velvet groove, her pads testing the pliability of Faith's anus.

Faith had surrended completely, and the questing finger opened the ring of muscles between the two glowing hemispheres as the young woman breathed deeply and shuddered, needing the strange sensation to counter the more familiar ones.

Lower down, Mrs Marryat could see the seepage from Faith's sex, nodding to herself as she thought of some of the other lessons this young woman was to learn. Yes, it was good that this new pupil took so much pleasure in the smacking. She would be much easier to teach and achieve a higher standard too. Her master had found a prize indeed. She looked at Alison, but she was looking at Faith's tear-streaked features with that smug expression Mrs Marryat had noticed so often. No; hardly the same material at all, was she? It showed, too.

Withdrawing her finger and wiping it, Mrs Marryat released first Faith's ankles, then the collar, returning her to the chair where she eased her on to the seat, knowing the comparative cold would make her stiffen in position. Fastening her in again and tilting it backwards, she met no resistance while Faith could do little more than dry-sob, but it was the sobbing of the return from paradise. The smacking had not only been a brutal application of force to her person, it had roused her again while underscoring her helpless state.

Her pride had always been that she was witty and intelligent enough to find a way out of any of life's difficulties. Yet here she was, unable to influence this woman in any way at all; while Mrs Marryat could punish her so exquisitely. This woman had said she would give her an enema and was about to insert the tube into her rectum. This woman had said she would be spanked and had done so. This woman had said she would find pleasure in the pain, and to Faith's shame, she had done so.

First there was the shame of finding herself being sexually aroused by the spanking, as well as the shame of finding herself helpless. Both shames – enjoying being made to do something she refused to do willingly and the punishment that went with it – convinced Faith that perhaps Mrs Marryat was right about having the enema. What if the woman was right after all, and that it was needed to cure the slight skin problem?

Still suffering from the shock and with a lot to think about, Faith made no resistance to the insertion of the tube, which Mrs Marryat pushed well in. While Faith lay quiet, recovering as best she could, feeling the filaments of pain shooting through her buttocks from the fourth spanking in just over twelve hours, and countering the desire which had built up such pressure within her, the woman took a portable stand to which she fixed the funnel, and then connected the free end of the tube to it.

Though Faith felt humiliated by her arousal, part of the feeling was that she suspected Mrs Marryat knew all about it. She knew very well the smacking had produced waves of pressure which had sunk through her flesh, disturbing the balls within her and shaking through to the back of her clitoris where they had inflamed that small, desperate little organ. If there was to be no release from this arousal, when would she get some before nightfall found her in the bed again?

Mrs Marryat dipped a cup in the mixture, then poured it into the funnel, where the pale green, lukewarm, bubbly liquid rushed down the tube, making Faith gasp and wince as it poured into her rectum. Another cup followed, and another and another, until the tube was filled up to the bottom of the funnel. Once completed, Mrs Marryat began pressing her fingers gently but persistently on Faith's abdomen, starting at the bottom and working upwards, going round in a circle as though following a trail, turning to check every so often the level of the liquid in the tube.

Faith, despite her other distractions (the pain in her buttocks and legs and the slow seepage of her pleasure fluids) found herself doing the same, and was surprised when the liquid began to descend.

'Good.' Mrs Marryat smiled, topping the level up from the bowl. 'We're working it higher into your large intestine. You'll feel far better for it.'

'I feel I'm going to be sick.' Faith's complaint attracted the woman's attention at once.

'Stuffed up feeling? As though your stomach's about to heave?' Mrs Marryat asked. 'That's normal. You've been having too much rich food. Give it a little while longer, and I'll remove the tube. It won't take long. You'll have to hold it in for as long as you can afterwards; let it scour around. From tomorrow you'll have powdered slippery elm bark every morning. That should flush you out properly, but in case it doesn't, we'll do this on alternate days.'

Faith thought the liquid waste would never stop voiding her body as she sat, eyes closed, feeling disgusted with herself. It was a simple medical operation, yet she felt ashamed. When it was done, and Mrs Marryat pressed her abdomen carefully, avoiding any pressure on the balls within her, the chair was tipped up again and her bottom was carefully washed and wiped dry by Alison, who disposed of the result.

'Good.' Mrs Marryat was once again pleasant. 'Aren't you sorry now that you refused? When I tell you to do something, you do it.'

'Yes. All right.' Faith's head was lowered as much as the free length of chain would allow. Faith had always considered she had a right to determine what was pushed into and drawn out of her own body, and that included plastic hoses. Perhaps especially, plastic hoses containing lukewarm soapy water.

'All right?' the woman questioned dangerously, her irritation gradually rising with her tone.

'Yes, Mrs Marryat,' Faith quickly amended, lowering her eyes.

The last thing she wanted at that moment was another spanking like the last one. The enema had left her feeling weak; her buttocks were sore and the prospect of another 40 slaps filled her with dread.

'We're learning, Miss Faith. It's slow and can be painful at the start, I'm afraid, but we *do* learn eventually. With many tears, unfortunately. It's a pity I didn't have you here five or six years ago; it would have been so much simpler for both of us. But understand this, Miss Faith –' Mrs Marryat's eyes and pale features became serious '– you *are* going to be smacked and strapped, and you will come to like it. You will *love* it.'

'Do people . . . some people . . . like to be hurt? Whipped?' Faith asked. 'I've heard there are some like that.' Faith's eyes widened at the prospect. Mrs Marryat hesitated a moment before answering, then did so with brutal honesty. 'I'll tell you what I tell all the young ladies who pass through here. You will never endure what I did when younger. I was trained to whip people so that no two marks crossed, and you only learn that after being whipped yourself. It's mostly when lines cross that marks are formed. I was trained to avoid that. Once the skin had healed (usually the abrasions take about a week) you could be whipped again. I know one young woman who endured that, each week, for two months.'

'What happened to her?' Faith asked, her wide-eyed expression turning to anxiety, making the woman smile fondly.

'You're the first young woman to ask about her. She married a young man called Marryat, who was killed two years later. Which is why I'm here.'

'You . . .?'

'Have you been beaten, Miss Faith? I mean, spanked sexually? There are times (and you will experience them here) when that will happen. You will have a strap taken to your bottom, expertly. I will use a strap on your buttocks or vulva or anus. If I have you in the right position; both. In case you don't already know, it hurts at first, then it becomes warm and terribly arousing. After the first pains have subsided and the flesh becomes numb, the pressure affects you internally. If I apply the correct strength, you will plead with me both for more, and to be mounted in your injured orifice. I know. I've been in that position, begging for sexual release.

'I've pleaded for penetration and cried bitterly when it was refused. But I want to teach you. Hurt you a little, yes; but not harm you. Any and all violations of normal good behaviour will be punished, I promise you, though perhaps not quite the way you expect. I *will* enforce discipline, and there are worse punishments than pain.'

'Who ... who ...?' Faith stopped, trying to frame the question. If Mrs Marryat was in the mood to let her ask them, she would like some answers.

'Who wants you disciplined?' The woman shook her head. 'Don't you know?'

'No.' Her anxiety showed as Faith felt sweaty again.

'Someone who loves you, otherwise you wouldn't be here. Mr Pellew made the arrangements for you; you realise that, surely?'

'I live with Alex.'

'Mr Pellew has sent other young ladies here. Each had lived with him. I don't know who your sponsor is, except they must be fairly wealthy; we don't provide this service free and the training costs quite a bit. They must be well connected too, to know about our facilities.'

'Why would –'

'Because they want you to achieve your potential.'

'Or they want an abject slave,' Faith responded.

'I don't think so. What we do is use modest amounts of pain to teach you about yourself, and then only occasionally. The greatest gift you can give anyone, Miss Faith, is yourself. And in what form? Most women lie back and invite a man to mount them; it's hardly world shattering, is it? So what sacrifice can a woman make to her master? The use of her bottom? That's becoming more and more common; you've experienced it yourself.

'For the true lover, of course, comes the opposite of pleasure; pain in modest amounts. Pain is as transitory as pleasure, and yet, why is it that some individuals recall the happy times of their life, while others recall the sad? But for an attractive young woman such as yourself, obedience is everything. To obediently comply with your master's wish, whatever it is, is unique. The young woman who could have almost any man, offering herself to her master is doing more than accepting his domination of her, she is telling him of the strength of that love. Even though you know by now that the selective application of moderate pain can be very sexually arousing. What we're teaching you is self-control, and the application of moderate pain is but one part of that. Perhaps more important is the ability to receive the instruction to go to a place to be punished, with a whip or strap, whatever.

'Your master expects absolute obedience, even in circumstances such as these, and so you do. You go to the spot, you assume the position he selects, and you are soundly whipped. You may cry out if he wishes (some masters prefer to hear their pleasure slaves cry and weep); you will certainly produce tears. But the emphasis is on "pleasure", Miss Faith; the pleasure you give your master at having such an obedient and loving pleasure slave will more than repay all the love and affection he bestows on you. I am sure you will receive equal, if not more pleasure either from the application, or in the aftermath.

'A simple whip could produce a slave, perhaps even a pleasure slave, in time, but it could not produce what we do. Now. Chatter over; we must proceed with your training. I wonder what has happened to our other pupils? Alison; as Miss Faith has been badly behaved, take her upstairs. Back to the mirror room. She must learn to stand still properly.'

With Alison holding the end of the chain and Faith, her wrists fastened behind her, being obliged to follow, they returned to the yard, where Faith was immediately confronted by a sight which shocked her. Strung between the two tall uprights set into the concrete, a naked young woman was spread out, her wrists and ankles secured in the shape of a large 'X'. Behind her, a young black-haired woman wearing a loose white dress, was wielding a short, multi-stranded whip, each stroke landing on the inflamed bare buttocks of the unfortunate victim, whose soft cries had been unheard in the building.

Her cries soon died to cooing whimpers as, with hanging head, she no longer even struggled against the fastenings which bound her. From the fluid making the inner aspect of her thighs shiny, Faith understood with horror that she was in the throes of ecstasy. Her assailant, red-faced with the effort, was being supervised by Clive Jackson, who stood quietly talking to her as she worked.

Mrs Marryat had moved ahead down the yard to where a bar had been set up between two posts, which two people were bent across. A young man, his ankles held apart with his wrists apparently fastened to them, was writhing and struggling while a short young woman in white knickers plied a strap against his naked buttocks. Sticking out in front of him was a thick fleshy poker of an uncircumcised erection. As Alison moved to pass, Mrs Marryat stopped her, beckoning Faith forward.

'Look, you see? Not only young women are trained here. Roger is coming on famously. Soon he'll accept the strap without complaint. And see? Hilary has put a phallus in his bottom; that's always a good idea with men when they're punished.'

She looked at Faith's wide eyes, then directed her attention to the other backside not four feet away. This was female, with the thighs glowing a deep radiant red from the strap being plied by a powerfully built young man. While the young woman lay inert across the bar, the red-haired young man worked with a steady stroke, standing directly behind her, striking right and left to each side alternately. Starting at the inside of the knees, he worked his way up her thighs and then from the outside, both buttocks.

'Harder, Gerald,' Mrs Marryat said, nodding to Alison. 'She won't break; she isn't made of glass. Put some effort into it.'

'Yes, Madame,' the young man answered without looking at her, and the next crack on her buttocks – which Faith only heard as Alison had continued on their way – was louder than ever. How could she stand it? Would she too feel a sexual thrill from being treated in that way? The question troubled Faith a good deal more than her own immediate fate. How could anyone suffer that kind of punishment without crying? Without screaming in pain?

Faith trembled as she walked into the mirror room behind the impassive Alison, who, without hesitation, fastened the chain to the same ring in the wall.

'Stand facing the wall!' she said sharply, turning away to collect the strap from the table at the far end of the room. When she turned back, Faith stood facing her reflection, her breathing difficult though she was trying to control herself. 'Feet together; head bent at the proper angle. Posture!' she snapped suddenly, just before the strap flicked out painfully.

Though she tried, Faith found that standing as still as she could was useless, for no matter how much she thought she was remaining motionless, Alison's strap was swung at her defenceless rear. At first there were intervals between the blows, periods when she could rest to recover herself, but the longer it went on the more often Alison struck her.

The more often the strap landed across her chubby behind, the more sensitive and inflamed the tissue became, which made it react more to each stroke. From hissing at the pain, Faith's tears began to flow and once that happened, her self-control went with it. She began to howl and twist, which provoked further punishment.

When Mrs Marryat entered the mirror room, Faith lay on her front on the bare polished floor while Alison stood over her with the strap. Her legs had given way – they had been trembling for some time, but Alison was merciless.

'Get up and stand still!' the young woman said as the door opened, then turned as she became aware of the newcomer.

'What's this, Alison?' Mrs Marryat seemed unconcerned about what she found; merely curious.

'This slave refused to stand up, Madame,' the young woman answered at once.

'I *didn't*!' Faith cried out, looking at the cold, stern, pale features through a curtain of dishevelled hair. 'My legs gave way –'

'Silence, slave!' Alison snapped. 'No one gave you permission to speak.'

'I see.' Mrs Marryat nodded, then looked at Faith. 'Up. There is something you should see. Bring her, Alison.' The woman turned towards the door. 'Show her the delights in the rooms opposite and I shall join you in a moment. Room 15 would be suitable, I think.'

Smiling as she removed the end of the chain from the ring in the wall, Alison pulled it and Faith out into the corridor, opening the first door on the opposite side and walking in, trailing the young woman behind her. The room was quite small, but in the centre was a small cage, about three feet high, five feet long and two and a half feet wide. The entire front of the cage was propped open on a piece of metal which, if pulled away as Alison demonstrated, closed the cage door, locking it.

'It's not long enough to lie down in or sit up comfortably. You're usually fastened more severely too so you can't move. No food or water for 24 hours, nor any lavatory.' Alison could have been describing a shade of nail varnish for all the emotion she used. 'Madame usually fills them up with powdered slippery elm bark – it's an efficient purgative. Lots of water, too. For 24 hours they remain there in their own mess. No food; no visitors.' She turned to look at Faith, an expression of smug superiority on her pleasant features. 'It's very effective.'

'Yes.' Faith felt ill at the thought of it.

'This is just one of the cages.' Alison took her into the next room, where a large cage occupied a good proportion of it. There was a long bar spread across the width of the cage from which circlets of rope depended, and outside, another bar with a padded piece in the centre stood at waist height, supported on two uprights. 'In here, they have their ankles passed through those loops.' Alison opened the entrance to it, pulling Faith inside. 'This is Room 15.'

'But I haven't done anything!' Faith began to sweat, the tears already forming in her widening, panic-stricken eyes, her chest heaving.

'Perhaps Madame just wants you to experience what it will be like. She may want you to experience what it's like for no particular reason, or it could be your punishment for disobedience. It's good to be punished for only a very slight reason; or none at all. You realise what will happen if you disobey.' It was clear from her expression and tone that Alison found pleasure in what she was doing. There was a smile of genuine warmth on her face as she began to make the arrangements.

While Faith waited, trembling in her position just inside the door and her eyes fixed on the loops on the ceiling of the cage, Alison placed a small folding table under the bar. Despite her apparent fear, Faith could feel the excitement building up within her. Her breathing was becoming deeper while her abdomen churned, sending the love balls moving about to further tantalise. Faith was made to lie on her back on the table, being pulled roughly on to it when she hesitated momentarily. Still pleading with the young woman not to hurt her, Faith complied, though Alison took not the slightest bit of notice, or of the tears trickling copiously down Faith's hot flushed face.

Alison was happy that she had someone to put in a cage and even more pleased that it was this newcomer. She looked as though she was the daughter of someone important, which always added to the thrill. She would have some fun with this one before she learned too much about how things were done in the Stables. That was the trouble. They quickly learned how to stop her doing just what she wanted. She had to be careful, of course; just as she had at school when self-important girls of famous fathers or mothers had joined. Making their lives miserable had been one way to relieve the utter boredom.

Taking Faith's right foot, she fastened a thick padded leather gaiter securely to her ankle before she pushed it through the loop at one end of the bar, then put the other through the loop at the opposite end, so that Faith's heels were slightly over five feet apart. Remembering how Alison had plied the strap, Faith whimpered with fear and growing pain as Alison took her in her arms, looking deeply into her eyes the whole time while easing the table away from under her. The young woman gradually lowered the weight until Faith was suspended upside down, her wrists still fastened behind her, her dark mane of hair touching the floor. Even when spread out on her bed that morning, Faith had never felt so helpless and exposed.

She moaned as the pain in her ankles bit first, the pressure of the rope cutting into her. Her hips also protested at the position. Alison waited a few moments, then began to gently stroke Faith's open sex with the pad of one index finger, making her jerk at first before Faith began to groan as the balls settled in an entirely new position, sending shafts of pleasure racing through her body to confound the pain sensors. Alison leant forward and began to run her tongue very gently up one side of Faith's cleft, just outside the inner lips, holding her outer lips open before pulling back on her mound to expose and then lick the distended clitoris which she could see was already swelling.

Faith knew she would be unable to withstand much of this before experiencing an orgasm and, as that was unlikely, knew there was no chance of her allowing this to go too far as she pleaded with her young torturer. Yet why was Alison doing this to her? If she was of Sapphic inclination then she could easily do what she wanted to her without putting her in this position.

'Please. Please!' Faith moaned, hardly knowing what she was doing.

Her mind was sending one message to her brain while her body was delivering quite another. It seemed inconceivable to her that she could experience both these acute sensations at the same time, and produced from such diverse centres, too. But the pain was hardly strong enough to prevent her climaxing, which was the only sensation she could anticipate with any pleasure.

'Please, what, Miss Faith?' Alison asked, completing

another slow lick of the young woman's sex by circling the clitoris with her tongue, allowing herself plenty of time around the aromatic organ. This sweet little pearl would soon be sorely tried. This tiny seed was going to be whipped as hard and as often as those glowing buttocks; and when it was, Faith would be driven into transports of joy. She would do anything, obey any commands, just to have that done to her again. Alison knew, from personal experience, just how pleasant that could be. With luck, Alison would be her guide, and could look forward to making Faith's stay there an utter hell.

'Please let me down. Please don't torture me like this!' Faith begged. 'I can't . . . aaaaaagh!' Her hips jerked in a vain attempt to escape the electric sensations of pleasure coursing through her.

'Do you like it, Miss Faith?' Mrs Marryat asked, entering the room as Alison began to suck the defenceless clitoris, letting her teeth lightly touch the small hard organ.

'Yes!' Faith screamed her anguish. 'Yes. *Yes!*' Her head began thrashing from side to side.

The table was beneath her back 30 seconds later and, after she had consulted her watch, Mrs Marryat looked at Faith with some amusement and said, 'Two and a half minutes, Miss Faith, that's all. What did it feel like?'

'I almost came.' Faith felt drained. Coming so soon after the enema and the strapping, the intensity of the pleasure had struck her despite the pain. It seemed that there was a sharp spear of pleasure pushing out through her clitoris and when it was sucked she was ready to explode.

'That's because of the balls,' Mrs Marryat said. 'They've been priming you since last night. And the phallus I inserted last night. It's something you will have every night. It's coated in a clear, sticky liquid which arouses you. During the day, when you're being trained, you'll learn to look forward to it. It's cumulative, so don't expect too much from it today, but in a few days you'll look forward to the saddle or the standing man.' She began to slip Faith's ankles free, rubbing the skin where the beginnings of a mark showed.

'How . . . how . . . often . . . do you use this . . . this cage?' Faith gasped. The woman looked at her and Faith quickly added, 'Please, Mrs Marryat?'

'That's better.' Mrs Marryat nodded. 'But ask permission to speak next time. It's used when young women can't keep their hands off their sexual organs. I usually smack them for that first. If that doesn't work, then a strapping, I've found, can sometimes manage it. If neither works, then this. But their ankles are wrapped so there's no pain in them and no marks. The only pain is from the hips. And they're licked.

'You said you almost came. You wouldn't; not with me. I wouldn't remove your balls and I would keep you up there for perhaps four or five hours. think of it –' Mrs Marryat paused, her expression almost leering '– four or five hours of being pleasured like that, with only the pain in your hips preventing your release. It would turn your orgasm into a different kind of pain. When it was over, you would be taken to your room, or perhaps just left here, with your wrists and ankles chained apart so there would be no way you could obtain relief by masturbation. If you obtain any sexual satisfaction at all, it's when learning the very necessary lessons of discipline.'

'You're very cruel.' Faith's face paled at the thought of it. To be pleasured past the point of release; pleasured with no hope of satisfaction.

'Yes, it is cruel,' Mrs Marryat answered with a nod.

'I make no excuse for that. But, there are other and worse cruelties; all designed to prevent you masturbating. The only sexual release must be when you're being trained.'

'I wasn't –' Faith began to protest but stopped because the woman was shaking her head slowly.

'Why do you think I spanked you for telling lies? And gave you just a short taste of this, Miss Faith? Because we both know the truth; I smelled your musk as soon as I opened the door. This is to be used if you persist; and you will persist, I know that. Once a young lady masturbates, unless she is broken of it then it will continue.'

'What if my sponsor –' Faith paused sneeringly '– wants me to masturbate?'

'A good question,' the woman said, with a ghost of a smile and a light tone to her voice. 'I hadn't thought of that. Excellent, Miss Faith. I like challenges like that. Come, let's look at some of the other cages.'

Chapter Four

Some were just that: cages. Harsh, welded steel prisons for the confinement of humans. Most were equipped with metal hooks set high up, some with rings at a more reasonable height. All were ghastly to Faith, who had spent less than 24 hours in Marigold's cage. None had anything more sophisticated than a bucket for sanitation, which Mrs Marryat indicated the occupant had to empty each morning.

'They remain there day and night for as long as is deemed necessary. Nothing to do; no one visits them except at mealtimes, and the food isn't up to their normal standard. I had a pupil who lost a stone in weight the week she was in here.'

The woman looked at the far wall, then moved Faith into place against the flat bars. Unfastening her wrists, she placed each of Faith's wrists within a ring just level with her head, then wrapped the chain tightly around the bars. Mrs Marryat then separated her legs, placing the bucket between them. 'For a week she stood like that; waking and sleeping. Unable to turn her head to scratch her nose. Unable to feed herself, and with the stench of her own waste matter constantly with her. I can assure you that the pupil learned her lesson.'

'What had she done?' Faith asked, her horror self-evident.

'She refused to ride when required.'

'Is that all?' Faith asked, surprised. She knew she was going to be released soon, yet already the bars felt as though they were closing in on her.

'That's all,' Mrs Marryat replied, shrugging her incomprehension of the pupil's attitude. As they walked back down the corridor, Mrs Marryat said, 'Room Fifteen for Miss Faith, Alison. Just lock her in there.'

'Yes, Madame.' The young woman nodded while Faith felt her blood chill.

Faith missed lunch. She was alone in the cage in Room 15 with only the bar in front of her and the table on which various straps and canes were kept to look at. The high windows prevented her looking outside but, though she was surrounded by metal, the room was hardly cold, though she found repressing the tremors which ran through her difficult. The half-seen instruments both attracted and repelled her, making her wonder what it would be like to be pinioned somewhere with Mrs Marryat wielding one.

As the light began to fade, the dark-haired young woman in the loose white dress whom she had seen that morning in the yard entered the room ahead of Alison, who carried a covered plate. They ignored her frantic questions and pleas to be released, ordering Faith to retreat to the far end of the cage. When the plate had been set down and uncovered, the two young women quit the cage, locking the small door behind them. Alison immediately left the room.

'What do you expect me to do?' Faith demanded. 'My hands are fastened.'

'You have not been given permission to speak.' The dark-haired woman spoke in an even tone. She was a little older than Faith, but about two inches shorter, and more slender and lithe. Her light eyes and fair skin made a vivid contrast to her black hair, and there was a self-possession about her, as though she was in complete control of both herself and the situation. Even Faith was impressed.

'How am I expected to eat?' Faith demanded, turning to show her fastened wrists.

'Come to the bars to be released.' Again the dark-haired young woman spoke without emotion. Faith's wrists were freed and, while she sat on the narrow bench which served as seat, bed and dining table, the young woman watched for a few moments, before departing silently. Faith looked up from her salad to find herself alone and, unaccountably, felt a loss.

When the woman returned later, she was accompanied by Alison, whose lips tightened into a thin line of dislike as she surveyed Faith through the bars. However, the dark-haired young woman looked amiable enough as she said, 'Up!' sharply and, when Faith automatically rose, 'Come here and turn round.'

'Why?' Faith asked, frowning at her.

For a few seconds the light eyes met her own before the woman said, 'I don't recall giving you permission to speak.'

'Why should I turn around?' Faith asked again, her resolve hardening under the lash of those eyes. They were a deeper blue than those of Alex, yet had the quality of light and laughter which his lacked.

'Wait here,' the woman said to Alison, who nodded her reply as they both moved to the door, the younger woman turning and taking up a position just inside. The dislike on Alison's face seemed to have vanished; in fact, she seemed to be quite pleased with life.

Faith had to admit that Alison stood straight and still; had it not been for her breathing and the occasional blink of her eyes, she would have thought her turned to stone. But what worried her was the slight smile on Alison's cold features – a quiet, impersonal gesture which seemed to contain menace. She asked what Alison was smiling at and what was going to happen, but received no answer until the door opened and Mrs Marryat led the dark-haired young woman into the room.

'What's all this, Susan?' she asked, advancing to the cage, slowing to a halt opposite a surprised and apprehensive Faith.

'Miss Faith won't obey, Madame. She refused to have her wrists fastened.'

'Then she must go to the bar.' Mrs Marryat nodded at once in the direction of the bar between the uprights, her gaze returning to Faith's frightened features. For a moment Faith took a deep breath, then calculated the odds. There were four of them; for Mrs Marryat counted double in Faith's estimation. Between them they could force her anywhere they wanted.

The young woman Mrs Marryat had called Susan unlocked the small doorway into the cage, calling, 'Come out.' She stood back to the left while Alison took up a position on Faith's right.

'I'm coming!' Faith returned under her breath, bending her head, knowing that she was at an immediate disadvantage. Alison grabbed her right shoulder then her upper arm as she emerged, while Susan laid a hand on her arm, tugging her gently in the direction of Mrs Marryat, who stood by the bar.

Alison seemed to have difficulty with Faith's right arm, pushing and pulling it, even when Faith's abdomen was slammed up against the padded section of the bar.

'Madame!' Alison called, an anxious tone in her voice as she looked to the tall, older woman for help. 'She's struggling!' Faith looked at Alison with an amazed look, then at Susan's equally surprised face, for the dark-haired woman had stopped holding her arm.

'Very well.' The incisive voice came from behind Faith. 'Take her to the yard. I shall deal with her myself.'

Faith looked stunned, catching Susan's quick inhalation of breath. Her eyes flickered to her pleasant features, furrowed by doubt, while Faith's right arm was no longer manipulated by the triumphant Alison. What was she doing? From the look of it, she had known that any sign of resistance from Faith would have provoked Mrs Marryat, so she had deliberately made it appear so. Or was this already arranged between the two of them; an excuse for Mrs Marryat to deal with her in the yard? With her wrists fastened behind her, Faith deliberately forced her mind to go blank. Minutes later, she knew the worst.

Her wrists were fastened to the two uprights by snaps which held the bracelets on her wrists and her ankles were secured the same way, her position identical to the young woman she had earlier seen there. Susan busied herself fastening Faith's long hair in a pile on top of her head while from the various doorways, others entered the yard. There were three young men; the two she had already seen, with a young, fair-haired blue-eyed youth in attendance.

The red-headed, muscular young man and Susan both wore white shifts while Alison and two others wore white briefs or knickers, standing in a line facing her. Off to one side, their backs to the bar across which two of them had been bent, were the other two young men and five young women, all naked.

Jackson checked the fastenings, his expression grim as Mrs Marryat came to a halt in front of Faith. Her expression was neutral, yet there was a thick strap dangling from her right hand as her eyes bore into Faith's for several seconds in the sharp, brittle silence. Her loose, plain dress was held with a belt which Jackson loosened, letting the gathered material fall full from her shoulders. Then he unfastened a button at the back, pushing the material from the shoulders until she was naked to the waist.

Martha Marryat carried no spare flesh on her bones, yet there was a supple strength about her. Her breasts may have been beginning to sag, but they were full and still attractive. Her shoulders and biceps looked strongly muscled as the silence lengthened and Faith felt her apprehension increase. Yet something stopped her pleading for another chance; perhaps it was the light in the woman's eyes, the knowledge that it would only waste breath she would desperately need soon.

'I will *not* have disobedience, Miss Faith. This is a lesson you should learn. You will regret struggling –'

'I didn't struggle!' Faith protested, but the sudden flush in the woman's face made her stop.

'You are not permitted to speak.' The woman walked around her, tracked by Faith, who turned her head to the left fearfully. Suddenly, strong hands grasped her face, turning it to the front, and there was Jackson's solemn face, his eyes boring into her.

In a voice only Faith could hear he hissed, 'Don't look round, Miss Faith. It does no good –'

But Martha Marryat had already begun.

In the previous fortnight, Faith had become used to the concept of being spanked, even strapped. Her behind had felt hands and leather on it; even here at the Stables she had seen backsides being tanned, yet there had been overtones of pleasure in what she saw. From the outset Faith knew that this was going to be different; more intense and yet, at the same time, more wonderful.

The first blow from the strap struck just above the outswell of her right buttock, making her cry out as the effect spread through her system. Yet even as she began her second cry following the stroke on the same spot on her left buttock, a refrain passed through Faith's mind, a snatch of conversation earlier that day, when Mrs Marryat had said '. . . when younger, I was trained to whip people.' Whatever happened, this was going to be as good as it got.

Mrs Marryat was standing directly behind Faith, working her way down the soft silky skin of her backside while Faith strained forward against the restraints, as taut as a bowstring, the tendons in her neck standing out like bracing wires. This was unlike the spanking she had previously had at Mrs Marryat's hands; it was harder and hotter on the skin, yet the pain was instantly subsumed in the pleasure of her orgasm. To distract herself from thinking about it, she looked down the yard at the others.

All eyes were turned towards her; Susan's concerned expression standing out from the impassive concern of the remainder. Alison, however, was smiling broadly. Yes, Alison had contrived this, with or without Mrs Marryat's knowledge. Why? Directly in front of her, Jackson stood impassive, his shrewd eyes maintaining a close watch on her, even as her strength to resist began to fail.

Mrs Marryat worked her way slowly down Faith's buttocks then began on the back of her thighs. Each stroke produced another flush of skin as the blood rushed to the surface, hot and angry at being disturbed. The pain sensors clustered in these areas worked overtime, the ripples through the flesh jiggling the love balls to produce the lubricious sensations with which Faith was so familiar. Finally, having worked her way down, Mrs Marryat began to work her way up again, adding another coating of pain on top of the sensitive flesh.

By which time Faith no longer struggled against the bonds which secured her; she hung in their embrace, the pain in her wrists no worse than that elsewhere. Faith no longer cried out, either; her cries had died before Mrs Marryat reached her knees, replaced at first by whimpering and moans as the dreaded pleasure took over. Yet as the strapping continued, the groans of unslaked lust took over and her over-stimulated brain gave up, leaving her in darkness.

Faith became aware of discomfort in several unrelated areas, all at once. Her backside and thighs seemed to be on fire. There seemed to be a glowing heat emanating from her flesh and yet she could feel the liquid warmth between her legs too; the heat and familiar internal and aromatic signs of arousal. There was a ridge of discomfort which reached from just below the throat, down her chest between her breasts and over her abdomen to stop short of her mound. Opening her eyes, Faith discovered the reason.

She was lying astride a wooden bar, her wrists and ankles fastened to the uprights supporting it. By wriggling slightly within her bonds, Faith realised she was actually standing up with her weight on her feet. Her behind was exposed and with it, her hot, open sex. Faith's throat was secured to the bar by the chain attached to her collar. Though she could breathe freely, there was no chance of turning her head more than a fraction; sufficient to show she was in a dark room containing a cage. Whether it was Room 15 was open to conjecture; they had all looked much alike.

Tensing and flexing her muscles as gently as she

could, and hissing with the discomfort of doing so, Faith tested herself. She thought her backside was a mass of damaged tissue which would take some time to recover. Sighing her acceptance of the situation, Faith allowed her mind to wander. Was this what Alex and everyone had meant by 'discipline'? Surely not. If Alex knew how they were ... hang on! She stopped as a thought struck her.

Mrs Marryat said he'd sent others there before her; and they'd lived with him too. Was that it? Is that what he did? Found young women suitable for training, persuaded them to believe they were joining the Chosen and had them shipped off here to be trained as ... what? Victims who could be beaten? Was there a demand for such creatures?

And Alison? Why had she done that? Why had she deliberately tried to make out that Faith was struggling as she left the cage? It could only be in collusion with Mrs Marryat, couldn't it? It looked as though she would have to keep her wits about her if she wanted to survive this. Alex had said she would be out of there in a short time if she obeyed Jackson and Mrs Marryat.

Obey, yes; that was the answer. Do everything they said and they would have little chance to use their whips, would they? They had panicked her in the past, but not any more. Up to then she had thought the pleasure she received was worth the discomfort, but no more. That was what they wanted her to believe, so Faith rejected it. Having come to that conclusion, Mrs Marryat ruined it by coming into the room softly in the darkness to stand alongside her.

Faith heard the door, even recognised the woman who stood there, trembling as she lay inert, unable to control herself. This woman had hurt her more than anyone had ever done, yet she recalled the massive thrills which had swept through her body. The knowledge frightened her.

'Does it still hurt, Miss Faith?' the woman asked, passing a hand over the body in front of her, not touching, just feeling the heat. There was no answer from the nervous young woman. 'Not going to talk to me, Miss Faith?' Mrs Marryat asked in a mild rebuke. 'What have I done to deserve that?'

'You whipped me.' Faith found her voice resentful.

'You struggled when put to the bar.'

'I didn't,' Faith returned, reasoning that as she had been asked a question, she would be allowed, perhaps expected, to answer.

'I saw you, Miss Faith.' The woman spoke quietly as usual.

'Then why had that other one, Susan, let me go?' Faith asked. But Martha Marryat was already moving her hand down to Faith's rear.

With a slow, stroking movement, her fingers lightly found the gaping natal notch between her buttocks, making Faith gasp, and again, as the fingers passed on to the sopping vulva.

'You're soaking, Miss Faith,' the woman said without reproach, then slipped two fingers within her, her thumb slipping into the puckered flesh of Faith's anus.

'God!' Faith gasped, her head jerking up against the restraint of the collar and chain.

'No talking, Miss Faith. Not a sound,' Mrs Marryat said as her fingers began to slip in the mucus-filled vulva towards Faith's button. Faith was about to cry out at that first intimate touch but two things prevented her; Mrs Marryat had told her not to make a sound, and she was restrained in a very vulnerable position. Instead she concentrated on her breathing, trying to damp down the fires which were spreading between her thighs, themselves ablaze.

Faith lost her battle to remain calm, first crooning and then, with gasping cries of delight, exulting in her climax, her limbs straining against the sweet restraints which secured her to the bar.

In the darkness above her, Martha smiled at her reaction, nodding to herself. This one would train beautifully. She could even be trained to the whip. She could take as much pleasure in punishment as most women take in sex.

'Do you want to go back into your cage, Miss Faith?' she asked quietly. 'Answer.'

'How much blood –' the young woman gasped out.

'I'll show you in the morning,' she promised with a smile. 'After you're punished.'

'Punished?' Faith was close to tears, 'Haven't I –'

'You were punished for struggling, Miss Faith, not for disobedience. Susan gave you instructions to remain silent, which you ignored. She tried to get you ready to come out of the cage and fasten your wrists behind you, which you ignored.'

'I didn't know what she meant,' Faith returned in a sullen manner.

'I'm sure Alison explained everything, Miss Faith. You forgot; it's a failing of yours, I believe. One I can cure, fortunately.'

'I didn't know,' Faith stated in a flat tone. 'No one said anything.'

'However, you do now. Tomorrow you will come out of the cage and be punished across the bar, then we can get on with your training. You can ride, tomorrow. And go for a walk; I might even come with you. I'm sure we have lots in common. Now, I'm going to insert the phallus in your bottom, Miss Faith, and return you to the cage.'

The morning brought Faith no pleasure, for her second night at the Stables had been equally uncomfortable. The bench in the cage had been hard

73

and, though not cold, she was unused to sleeping without covers, far less clothes. Naked, her chain connected to a fixture on the bars, she had sufficient movement to reach the bucket in the corner but no more.

Mrs Marryat and Alison, the latter red-faced and sulky, entered when Faith had begun to wonder whether anyone was left alive. The sun had been bright against the far wall; she would have looked at it more had it not fallen on the bar. Under Mrs Marryat's efficient eye, Alison took a stiff, pained Faith to perform her ablutions but on the return suddenly said, 'In here.'

She held open the door to the mirror room for Faith. With some trepidation, Faith followed the shorter fair young woman into the room, surprised when Alison was told not to fasten her to the ring in the wall.

'Look at yourself, Miss Faith,' Mrs Marryat said. 'Do you see the marks of the whip?' On seeing Faith's jaw drop open, she shouted, 'Answer!'

'No!' Faith gasped, wide-eyed.

She had expected to see her buttocks and thighs extensively marked, if not cut. As soon as it had been light, Faith had tried to turn herself into positions where she could examine herself, but without success. Where she had expected weals and bruising, there was a slightly red sheen to the skin, but other than that there was no hint that she had been soundly thrashed the evening before.

'I used a thick strap on you because my purpose was to teach.' The woman paused, her mouth becoming grim. 'Next time you may not be so lucky.' Faith stood looking frankly at her reflection until the woman snapped, 'Posture!' when her head dropped to the required angle.

* * *

74

Back in Room 15, Faith was told to stand at the bar rather than return to the cage and, with a sharp intake of breath to accompany the momentary hesitation, she walked to it, stopping when her abdomen and thighs pressed against the cold wood.

'Spread your legs,' Alison said when Mrs Marryat nodded, moving to the table to collect the snaps. Quickly she secured the anklets to the uprights, then standing close to her said, 'Beg me to punish you for disobedience yesterday.'

'I think we can dispense with that, Alison.' Mrs Marryat obviously recognised the dislike in the girl's voice. 'Just proceed. Six, with the cane.'

'Yes, Madame. Bend over the bar and keep your hands out of the way.' Alison nodded her acceptance, smiling to the wall as she turned to the table to collect the cane. This was obviously something she would enjoy.

The first stroke of the cane, which whistled through the air in a horizontal arc, struck Faith with force, startling even the resident dominatrix with its power. Faith's yell sounded loud in their ears as she jerked her body up in an arc, her hands reaching down to protect her rear from further punishment.

'Shall I secure her wrists, Madame?' Alison asked innocently, looking directly at the older woman.

'Do.' Mrs Marryat nodded.

Without haste, Alison unfastened the bracelets and methodically refastened them again to the other side of the uprights where Faith's ankles were already secured. The young woman's body was bent double and she was able to see between the inverted 'V' of her thighs both Mrs Marryat and Alison. Resuming her position, the young woman paused, then said, 'Six, with the cane.'

'Five, Alison,' Mrs Marryat said in a quiet, determined tone. 'You have already started.'

'Of course, Madame,' Alison answered, as though it had been a lapse of memory. To the watching woman Alison administered the punishment with an even, almost mechanical hand. Each stroke was delivered with speed, power and accuracy; each leaving a welt of white flesh amid a radiating roseate aura before the white turned to a bright red against the background.

Faith writhed helplessly, fastened over the bar, knowing what she had to silently endure before she could be released. Alison was about to land a seventh stroke when Mrs Marryat reminded her again of her first, making her flush and apologise – not to Faith but to her tutor – before being sent from the room.

It was obvious Alison's dislike of Faith approached hatred. Normally a caning like that would have had Faith dripping with lust. Not now. Alison had been taught well; perhaps too well. That was a caning such as would shake a grown, healthy man.

'The time will come, Miss Faith,' Mrs Marryat said, 'when you will bend over and receive a dozen like that, without flinching. Without being restrained, either. Do you want to return to the bathroom?'

'No,' Faith answered as her wrists were temporarily freed and she was allowed to rise before they were fastened again. 'Thank you, Mrs Marryat.'

'Nevertheless, I think you should be sponged down before breakfast. Come.' Taking up the chain she led Faith to the shower where her ministrations were gentleness itself.

After breakfast, which awaited Faith in her room, she was again secured before being taken out into the yard by Alison, where she was left in the sunshine, secured to a ring in the wall to watch what was going on. The short young woman, Hilary, had a young girl of about eighteen brought out and secured backwards over a half-barrel split lengthways, her back to the wood. Her breasts were sagging up towards her chin, but her half-open labia, and her close-trimmed mound were directly exposed to the sunshine. Standing above her, a foot on either side of her head, Hilary had a short strap in one hand and a feather in the other, and looked down at the wide eyes for a few seconds before she said, 'Beg me to begin your training, Jacqui.'

'Please, Mistress,' the girl pleaded at once, 'begin my training.'

'This is called "singing". Prepare yourself. I don't want to hear a word, do you understand?'

'Yes, Mistress.'

A tremor ran through the young woman's body as Hilary walked around to the far side of the barrel. From there, Faith thought, the girl would be unable to see what was happening, just as the first stroke of the strap landed on the exposed mound at the top of her thighs. The young girl gave a yelp of shock, jerking against the restraints which held her in position as she came to terms with the punishment. Hilary paused for a few seconds, waiting for the young woman to relax, then she delivered another stroke of the strap, striking the same spot just at the top of the mound, a fraction from the clitoris.

Again there was a yelp from the girl and a tear burst from the side of her eye to track down towards her ear, but she compressed her mouth into a determined line. When she was settled again, Hilary struck another blow in the same place, stopping with a faint smile before she said, 'Not so bad that time, was it, Jacqui?'

'No, Mistress, thank you.' The girl swallowed her hurt, finding the words at last.

'Remember to put your tongue out when you feel

the pleasure,' Hilary said, then gave her another. This was slightly off-target and it had landed short, on the clitoris. There was a yell as the girl's hips bucked upwards, but to Faith's amazement, this was choked off as she stuck her tongue firmly out.

'Ah! Found it, haven't we?' Hilary asked in high delight, then gently, lightly touched the injured button with the tip of the feather. Immediately Jacqui's hips bucked upwards again until it was withdrawn and the strap brought down on the injured flesh.

Jacqui's hips remained rigidly offered to Hilary, her tongue still sticking out as she fought for breath.

'Do you see?' A quiet voice beside Faith made her start, but it was Susan, who had approached so quietly on bare feet that only her voice betrayed her.

'Why –' Faith broke off as the strap landed again, evoking a croon from Jacqui, though her tongue vanished. Hilary immediately replaced the strap with the feather, tickling her clitoris and drawing the soft tip down the side of her ruby vulva.

'She's being trained to the whip,' Susan answered, 'so she can take her pleasure like that. Soon she won't know which is the feather and which is the whip; won't care, either. They'll both be alike to her. Haven't you heard of that before?'

'That's hideous!' Faith gasped, looking with horror-filled eyes at the young dark-haired woman.

'It's delicious,' Susan returned. 'You'll learn something of it in time. Not perhaps to that extent –' she nodded towards the crooning Jacqui '– but you'll change your mind, I know.'

'How can anyone –'

'Practice. You'll see.'

Up in her bedroom after lunch, Faith sat on the bed while she carefully put her stockings on her feet and rolled them up her legs, then added her boots and finally a short suspender between the top of each stocking, to prevent them slipping down her legs while walking. Then she donned her new brassière, and her still-swollen nipples were eased through the holes, where they bit again. Apart from a grimace, Faith made no complaint. Compared to the stinging in her buttocks, it was nothing at all. Once completed to Alison's satisfaction, she was taken downstairs again where a surprise awaited both of them.

'I'll take her, Alison,' Mrs Marryat shouted across the yard, holding out her hand to accept the chain. Faith was facing the wrong way to see the closed expression on Alison's face when she handed over the chain.

It felt strange to Faith to be walking out of the yard then down a woodland path with her head bowed and dressed as she was – her wrists fastened behind her, her legs encased so tightly in the leather and her sex exposed to the air, her buttocks wobbling enticingly naked. She could imagine the effect this would have on Alex. He was bad enough when she walked in her transparent knickers. This would have him drooling.

Mrs Marryat twisted the collar around to allow the chain to hang down her back and, for almost half a mile, walked a few yards behind Faith before catching up. They stopped while the collar was twisted straight again, the slack allowed to dangle between her breasts, giving the illusion of freedom. As they walked on, the chain swung from side to side, occasionally slipping across her nipples. She gasped at each cold touch, for her teats were as hard as they ever had been.

'I think, Miss Faith,' Mrs Marryat said after they had walked a mile along quiet paths, 'that perhaps I'll try a corset on you. Your waist could contract a little.'

'A corset? I've never worn one in my life,' Faith protested automatically.

'That, Miss Faith, is obvious to anyone who has walked behind you.'

'But why?' Faith asked, emboldened by Mrs Marryat's manner. Faith had begun to work out that she could receive answers to her protests when they were couched as questions so long as she was careful.

'A corset would nip in your waist and, if properly applied and used, make your buttocks appear more plump. More rounded. It is one of the most erotic regions of the female body and you have a nice behind as it is; you should enhance it if you can. The Ancient Greeks – who seem to have known a thing or two about eroticism – built temples to "The Goddess of Beautiful Buttocks", Aphrodite Kallipygos.

'The female buttocks are, relative to body size, larger than those of a male. They have more fatty tissue and, because the female pelvis has a backward rotation compared to males (their backs are more arched) due to the different pelvic construction and leg attachment to facilitate child-bearing, women wiggle their buttocks when they walk; a primitive sex signal. Female apes have buttocks which swell in oestrus while human females can mate all year round, even – should she be so inclined – while menstruating.

'Males, on the other hand, seeing a nicely plump, rounded behind, are filled with desire. Their buttocks are smaller, more angular and harder; built for speed and strength. At least, when they're young. I'm going to put you in a corset to round your buttocks. I don't know if it will work and I may have to ask your sponsor. He may agree to it.'

'What if I refused?' Faith asked.

'Would you?' Mrs Marryat asked, clearly surprised. Faith, too caught up with her own feelings, missed the dangerously quiet tone of the question.

'Of course!' Faith protested.

'I see.' The woman nodded, walking on. Idly she pulled a long stem from a shrub, and walked along the path while peeling off the leaves, her head down, frowning. 'If your sponsor wants it –' she began but Faith was already protesting.

'My "sponsor",' Faith countered, 'can –'

'Right!' Mrs Marryat nodded, her voice sharpening into the tone of command. 'Bend over that fallen tree, Miss Faith!' She pointed with the long pliable stem, now entirely denuded of leaves.

'Why?' Faith asked, surprised at the sudden change of voice and manner.

'If that's what your sponsor wants, then that's what will happen. Bend over!' The voice matched Mrs Marryat's stern expression.

'It's my body!' Faith protested. 'I'm not a slave. I'm free, white and over twenty-one. I can make those decisions for myself, thank you.'

'May I remind you, Miss Faith, that's just what you *are*. A pleasure slave who's been sent here to be disciplined; and showing perfectly why you have been sent. Bend over! I shan't tell you again. If you refuse then when we get back, I shall strap you severely.'

Chapter Five

For several seconds Faith looked at the shorter woman with a mixture of fear and despair, though the rebellious ire was still strong. Yet the calm, almost impersonal look which met her own quelled her. Sullenly and mentally promising herself revenge, Faith placed her stomach against the rough bark, automatically spreading her thighs against the furrowed surface.

'Very good,' Mrs Marryat said, 'you're learning. You should also learn that, whether you like it or not, you have a sponsor who controls your body; its comings and goings and what it does. One!' The thin wand struck across the centre of her buttocks, avoiding the thin red weals left earlier by Alison.

Faith's yelp of surprise and pain stilled the remaining birds, startling them out of their trees, as Mrs Marryat continued in her same calm tone as though presenting a travel lecture to the R.W.I.

'You have no say in what happens to you anymore. You inhabit the body owned, if you like, by someone else. You choose to . . . Two!' The wand struck lower, near the crease which delineated the buttocks and thighs. Faith's second yelp was, if anything, louder and more shrill than the first, dying away while the woman continued regardless. '. . . call this slavery, which it is not; not in the sense of direct ownership. A slave is the legal property of another, and *you* are

82

not property. I agree you are bound to absolute obedience, or the helpless victim of a dominating influence. Both of these are definitions of slavery. If that is how you choose to see yourself, then so be it. Three!'

The third cry rent the still air in the woods as Mrs Marryat looked at the wand. It was still quite fearsome, but her intention was education, not punishment. Faith's red buttocks, still suffering from the spankings and caning, now carried three clear horizontal stripes across them, yet she knew from the sound Faith made that she experienced a good deal of pleasure with the pain.

'There, I've broken it.' Mrs Marryat threw it away before Faith could see it. 'You may rise, Miss Faith. Do you still feel a slave?'

'Yes.' The sobbing reply was hardly audible as the shocked white face rose. The three stripes radiated heat to the other tissues, but were already losing their sting. Faith knew she could expect the first frail fingers of arousal to follow soon.

'Very well.' Mrs Marryat's exasperated sigh became cold. 'You're a stupid young woman who doesn't realise fortune when it stares you in the face. You have become one of the Chosen, with a sponsor willing to invest time and effort in your education. Think of yourself as a slave if you choose; it may even help you come to terms with what is to happen.

'You have been enslaved and are to be trained as a slave in a particular way. All slaves must learn obedience before they are of any use to their masters, and your master is paying me to teach you. You will find, too, there are different kinds of obedience. We shall return to the house. You shall have the corset fitted immediately, then I can deal with the slave as I should have done in the first place.'

Despite Faith's attempts to gain a response from Mrs Marryat on the journey back – completed at a much faster pace which forced Faith to trot to keep up, stumbling over stones and other irregularities in the path several times – the woman made no answer. Once through the large gate, Mrs Marryat chained her in the concrete yard to the chains she had earlier indicated, before vanishing into the house. Left to herself, with the yard empty, Faith looked around and, weak in the legs and unable to bend, collapsed as gently as she could on to her side. Her buttocks were too sore to sit on the rough surface, even though the coldness was welcome, so Faith lay on the concrete to recover both her breath and wits.

Quarter of an hour later, Mrs Marryat returned to the yard. She carried a riding crop in one hand and a bundle of leather and straps in the other, and approached Faith with the command, 'Up, slave!'

When Faith failed to move fast enough to suit Mrs Marryat, the crop was tapped smartly across her left hip, making Faith yelp. Faith tried again, receiving four or five such taps before she managed to stand at last, whimpering in fear before the implacable Mrs Marryat. She struggled to obey because she believed the woman capable of almost any cruelty.

'Face the wall, slave!' the woman insisted, her expression hard and callous. The solicitousness of the morning had vanished in the ire of the afternoon.

First she refastened Faith's wrists to two chains which dangled four feet apart, a foot above her head, each ending in a snap-fastening. Only the length of the chains prevented her having to stand on tip-toe. While Faith waited nervously, Mrs Marryat wrapped the thin leather corset around her waist, settled the lower edge on her hips, then pulled the straps which passed through the leather tight. Satisfied with the tightness of the first, central strap, Mrs Marryat fastened the others, then began pulling them tighter still, operating the same pattern, evening out the constriction.

Faith felt herself being squeezed more tightly than she had ever been, and protested in vain.

'Slaves can have no opinion as to the tightness or not of their corset. They are here to be taught discipline and obedience. It seems I have been too lenient; a mistake I shall not repeat.'

'But please!' Faith gasped. 'I can't breathe. This is killing me.'

'Silence, slave! I expect you'll survive.'

Once Mrs Marryat was satisfied, Faith's wrists were refastened behind her before being led into one of the buildings which looked as though it was still a stable. Faith was led into a straw-filled stall, turned around while a wall-mounted chain was looped through her fastened wrists, then resecured to the wall behind her.

When Mrs Marryat began to walk away without another word, Faith raised her voice. 'I thought I should go to my room.'

The woman stopped, turned, then slowly returned to stand directly in front of Faith, her expression growing even more wintry. For some minutes she looked into Faith's eyes, the leather loop at the tip of her crop slowly stroking Faith's cheek, then her left breast. It was as though she was thinking of a suitable retort.

'This *is* your room,' she finally announced. 'Nice rooms with comfortable beds and hygienic washing facilities are for the young ladies. You are a slave. Slaves are permitted to sleep on straw in the stables, provided they're suitably restrained. And slaves are not addressed politely. They are non-persons. They have nothing. They are called whatever their masters desire. So I shall contact your sponsor's agent, in this case, Mr Pellew, and tell him of your decision to be a slave. He can decide what we call you. I can think of several names, though I doubt whether Mr Pellew would approve.'

As the calm voice laced with icy venom stopped, Faith was aware that by standing up for herself she had made her predicament far worse. But a last vestige of independence flared as she asked, 'How long do you expect me to stay here?'

For some moments the older woman looked hard at Faith, as if allowing her temper to cool. 'Speak when you're spoken to, slave!' Mrs Marryat answered, turning away once more.

Faith's tears flowed before her tormentor reached the door, closing it behind her. Then came the metallic sounds of the bolts being thrown. Sobbing, Faith relaxed, finding it more difficult than ever to make herself comfortable. The chain was not long enough to permit her to lie down, unless she lay on her stomach with her hands held above her back. Yet it was the only position in which there was any hope of rest; her buttocks were still too sore to take any pressure.

Once her eyes accustomed themselves to the light, Faith found the stable a cavernous place. In an adjacent stall was some kind of machinery over which a large horse-blanket had been draped; she could see the rectangular base but through the slats of the stall was unable to make any sense of the other shapes. It seemed to have a high point, then fall away sharply on the long sides of the rectangle; less so on the others. But Faith was concerned with other, more urgent matters.

The straw made her itchy. It prickled her soft skin, and the ends dug into the hot, tender flesh of her bottom, now striped with three long scarlet marks which stood out from the background. As she settled down for a lengthy wait, Faith began to cry again. She felt so alone. This *was* slavery! She was a human chattel, bound to absolute obedience which Mrs Marryat was enforcing. It was her dominating influence which made Faith such a victim. And yet!

Lying in the straw with her chest heaving, Faith felt a thrill coursing through her. She was restrained in a tight-fitting corset, her wrists secured behind her, and had long, tight boots on her legs. Faith's face burned as she realised that she was lubricating again. The churning in her lower abdomen had led to the same conclusion; the seepage of her fluids. Was she fixated on bondage? Or was it that she liked being abused?

It was dark when Faith was roughly awakened by a hand shaking her. She was lying on her stomach in the straw, with wisps of it in her hair. The dark figure above her was so frightening that she screamed, then wept, when she realised it was Jackson. Once he was sure she was awake, Jackson lengthened the chain to allow Faith to lie more comfortably, unfastening her wrists at the same time. Faith lay gritting her teeth as pins and needles swept through her arms. It was several seconds before Faith realised he had not come to release her. It depressed her even more.

'There's food,' Jackson said simply, shining a torch on a metal plate on which was a cold chop and some cold vegetables with solidified gravy. 'Water's here.' He indicated a wide pan, further off. 'Stand up!'

'Why?' Faith asked.

He waited until the temerity of her question had sunk in and died, then repeated, 'Stand up.'

'I can't,' Faith protested, 'I've still got my boots on.'

'You've still got *the* boots on. Slaves can't own

anything, so they're not yours. All right. Lie where you are.'

Lying on her back, Faith tensed while his mouth found her nipples. For a moment she thought he was going to go further, but the soft fleshy teats were soon sucked through the rings. Her wrists were refastened about the chain then she was pushed down into the straw.

'I want to use the lavatory,' Faith said, trying to control her panic with such a mundane statement.

'You're in it,' Jackson answered. He rose stiffly, then walked away, taking the torch with him. The door was rebolted, leaving Faith alone in the darkness.

The callousness was quite deliberate. Most pupils encountered it at some stage in their stay at the Stables. They would rebel, like Faith, at an early stage, which is what Jackson hoped for from them. It showed they were spirited and would be worth something when trained. Each and every pupil had a personal idea of their own worth and, for their peace of mind, required that worth to be acknowledged by the world in which they lived. It was Jackson's task to break that self-view down; to make each pupil see there were other views. Views in which they counted for little.

Each pupil progressed towards that goal at their own rate, conforming or rebelling as their nature allowed, yet each had a sticking-point which it was Jackson's concern to discover. This was the barrier through which they would have to be carefully taken in order to realise what lay on the other side. Once up against the barrier, it often took very little to spill them over into the strange territory beyond; the land most never knew existed.

Once over that barrier, pupils began to accept the

forces at work on them; though their pride in themselves had to be carefully handled. Too little could mean psychological problems. Passing through the barrier usually broke down most of the false and foolish pride, leading to acceptance that someone else knew better. Later, when they had constructed a new view of life for themselves, their pride often returned in different ways. Many were able to achieve far more with this new pride than they ever had with the old pride which had restrained them.

Faith's pride was evidenced by her refusal to accept that anyone – this master to whom she was supposed to be subordinate, her mother, anyone – had the right to decide what to do about her body. Though she had acknowledged Alex as her master, in her own mind that was only a form of words. The only one who had that right, in Faith's eyes, was Faith herself. Now she was being made to realise that her first supposition was correct. She was a slave and would be treated as such. At least, she thought, they've stopped pretending. They're being honest. This is somewhere that kidnapped young women are turned into slaves.

The only reason she could find for this was, of course, sexual. She had been used by the Chosen as they wanted. The men had all entered her; they knew she was a good lay, yes. She could take women, too; which probably made her more valuable. With a weary yet frustrated resignation, Faith wondered where she would end up. A brothel, probably, but where?

For some minutes she lay in the straw wondering what it was she felt, knowing that it wasn't hunger. Far from it. The corset cut into her and she found it difficult to breathe. But at least she could lie on her side, despite the throbbing in her behind, which was on fire, both from the caning and from the thin wand which had marked her skin, though at the time she was unaware of it. All she knew was that she wanted a man as never before. Was this the effect of the love balls, or just the restriction of her flesh?

With difficulty Faith found the water, realising that she had to drink to survive. Sweat covered her hot body; the straw was keeping her insulated from the cold concrete floor. Once she had taken a mouthful, remembering that what went in also came out, she allowed it to trickle slowly across her throat, then lay back again.

It looked like being another bad night; her third in a row. The first had been when she had found herself chained to the bed after two spankings; the second had been in the cage on the hard bench. Now she was lying on straw in a stable. Did they have a dungeon?

It was full morning when Mrs Marryat returned, wearing another plain dress. Faith had been awake for some time, but had no idea of the time, for there was sacking over the windows. She lay on her side when the woman returned to stand over her, a riding crop in her hand, tapping the opposite palm in a gesture reminiscent of Marigold Garland, in whose house her initiation had taken place. Faith thought she would be glad to see the small, neat woman now.

'Not eaten? Lost your appetite?' Mrs Marryat asked finally in a heavy tone. When Faith made no reply, or even changed her expression, the woman nodded. Faith remained calm for, in the small hours when the mice scuttled around the stable doing mice things, she had worked out the situation for herself.

Jackson and this woman, and people like Alison, Susan and Hilary, were perverts who had seized this opportunity to inflict humiliation on her. Well, she would comply. She would do what she was told and she would survive, somehow. They spoke of teaching discipline, so she would obey, and the first thing she must learn to do was discipline herself against speaking or crying.

Mrs Marryat waited for half a minute for an answer but, receiving none, nodded her acceptance of the situation, watching the resolve come into Faith's hardening jaw. There were some like that. It was good when they determined to fight back because once broken, they were easy to manage. It was the weak ones who gave the most trouble. They were the ones who complied; the ones who were ostensibly learning something.

The difficulty was that they quite often succumbed to temptation at the first opportunity. Temptation had to be put in their path so she could measure how much of the training had been absorbed. Mrs Marryat felt that it would be winter before some of them would be ready to leave. Her opinion was coloured by the fact that their families had made no enquiries about their progress in months. They were happy that someone else was containing the problem for them.

'Up!' she commanded. It soon became obvious that Faith, with her hands secured behind her, would never make it. Either the boots would have to be removed, Faith would have to have her hands released, or she would have to be helped to her feet. It was easiest to remove the boots.

Once they were placed at one side of the stall, the command was repeated, this time with a tap of the crop across her buttocks, which made Faith rise quickly, though with difficulty.

'Time for your ablutions,' Mrs Marryat said, releasing the chain attaching her to the wall, before tugging on the chain attached to the collar and pulling Faith out into the yard. With a twinge of memory,

Faith realised the woman was leading her just as she had led horses from the stalls in the stables close to her school. She was less than a slave, now; a slave was a human being. She was being treated as an animal.

On emerging into the light, Faith looked about furtively for some sign of the others, but there was none as she was once again fastened to the wall. Faith looked about her appreciatively, breathing deeply to inhale the crisp morning air while Mrs Marryat walked over to a tap, under which a bucket of water stood. Seeing this, Faith thought her morning wash would be conducted kneeling in front of the bucket but when, four feet away, Mrs Marryat threw the water over her, she caught Faith completely by surprise. Gasping, for she had taken the full force of the water in her face, and shuddering, for the water felt as though it had stood all night it was so cold, Faith was still shaking ten minutes later.

Jackson appeared in the yard, carrying a strange object which he handed to Mrs Marryat, then unfastened Faith's wrists, refastening one of them to the chains on the wall. While Jackson held her other wrist, Mrs Marryat approached, still holding the object. It was a fairly flat metal plate about six inches square, but from two edges sprouted thick, padded straps. One was passed over her free left wrist, which was immediately shackled again and her right wrist freed.

When they began to push her free right hand through the strap, Faith realised what it was, but complied anyway. She was supposed to obey, so she would, but she was held securely, not being given a chance to prove her compliance. Once in place, her wrists again secured to the wall with Faith facing it, Mrs Marryat spent some time adjusting the straps and plate on her back and easing it here and there.

Faith now had the metal plate centrally on her back with two powerful padded rubber rings pulling on her shoulders. As a result, her round shoulders were pulled backwards, lifting her breasts and especially her nipples, to scrape against the wall.

Mrs Marryat and Jackson then turned her around, removing the nipple rings in silence before they stood back. Faith had said nothing. Her silence seemed to irritate the woman.

'Well?' Mrs Marryat asked. 'Is that comfortable?'

'Yes, thank you, Mrs Marryat,' Faith replied, though she trembled. In twelve hours she had acquired not only a tight corset, but a shoulder brace. Part of her felt this was both painful and degrading, yet there was another part which was thrilled with the feeling of constriction and support. The corset only constricted her waist and the upper part of her hips. It flashed through her mind to wonder what a full corset would feel like, thrusting her breasts out while restraining her body. Or a body suit?

A movement off to one side revealed Susan, again in a loose white dress, who came to stand just out of earshot of Faith's turned head, patiently waiting until Mrs Marryat noticed her. While Jackson went off, the two women conferred, looking at Faith every so often so she knew she was the subject of their discussion. After a few minutes Mrs Marryat went indoors while Susan slowly approached the restrained Faith.

'Good morning, Faith. Mrs Marryat has given you to me to train, so we're going to have a good time, I know. Did you sleep well?' Her voice was soft, almost thoughtful.

'No,' Faith answered, her eyes meeting the dark orbs of the slightly older Susan.

'No, Mistress,' Susan said gently. 'I'm going to have to start from scratch with you.'

'No, Mistress,' Faith repeated, responding to the reasoned tones.

'That's better.' Susan smiled. 'Now we'll begin again.'

Susan unfastened Faith from the wall, then took the chain to lead her, still dripping, indoors. When they reached the mirror room, she chained the collar to the wall as before, then crossed to the table while Faith looked at her back and behind. There were three faint marks across her buttocks, but even Faith could see those would be gone within a few hours.

'Stand still!' Susan said sharply as she returned, a thin cane in her hand, making Faith freeze into position. 'Let's see how much you've learned, Faith. Your posture should improve now, so I won't forgive any lapses. You have no excuse.'

Mrs Marryat entered after some time, looking at Faith's proffered back. Across the plump buttocks was a single red line.

'Is she improving, Susan?'

'She is, Madame. Hardly a twitch.'

'She can have a shower and then breakfast in her room. Then you can carry on with her programme after that.'

Susan peeled off her clothes to join Faith in the shower, thoroughly washing the bound young pupil while raising her emotional state by running her hands over her skin. After a solitary breakfast, Susan returned to the room where Faith waited. There was a confident expression on Susan's features as she asked, 'Are you ready to start now?'

'Yes.' Faith nodded.

The young woman looked at her for a moment, then pulled Faith towards her by the chain until she bent her over the bed. There was no hint of the pleasant young woman as her voice ground out, 'This is the last time I shall spank you for that, Faith. You call me "Mistress"!' Then her hand landed squarely on Faith's behind. Desperately Faith put her hands over her rear to protect herself, but Susan stopped at once, waiting until the naked Faith looked round to her. 'Put your arms straight out in front of you, Faith. I'm going to spank you, and I don't want you to struggle.'

'But it hurts!' Faith protested, hoping to avoid telling Susan that it roused her too.

'Of course it does; it's meant to! I'm punishing you for indiscipline, and if you don't do as I say, I'll bend you over the bar. You'll soon know what a cane across the behind feels like.'

Reluctantly, Faith faced the covers, burying her fears in the hope that Susan would hardly be as bad as Mrs Marryat. It was a vain hope, for when Susan began to spank her, her hand rising and falling in a measured, determined rhythm, it was difficult for Faith to believe that she was just using her hand. It felt as though that single stroke of the cane was being endlessly repeated as first one cheek and then the other came in for punishment.

Faith held out as long as she could, steeling herself against the tears, gritting her teeth while hoping Susan would tire first. But Susan was too skilled at the game; she obviously knew from personal experience just what Faith was doing, and kept smacking the bouncing globes which were rapidly acquiring a rosy hue. Mrs Marryat had told her that Faith had to be disciplined, which was something Susan clearly could do.

The first sobs sent a shiver of emotion through Faith's body, wracking it further as the tears began to flow. The spanking was arousing her, distracting from the pain of her burning behind. Her nose wrinkled as she recognised the aroma of her musk, her face scarlet as she realised Susan must know too. Susan kept on smacking, for it was hardly unknown for pupils to cry like that to escape punishment, though not those who usually found it so sexually stimulating. She raised her right knee, lifting Faith's hips to expose the delicate flesh of the join between buttock and thigh, bringing her hand down on that with all the skill she possessed.

When she stopped, Faith lay inert, her breathing shaking her body, moisture threatening to choke her. Susan waited a moment, then placed her hand in the cleft between the proffered buttocks, expecting Faith to tense the muscles. But Faith had other concerns, so Susan's fingers found her palpitating anus, then the moisture on her labial lips.

'You're sopping wet, Faith. I think you liked that, didn't you?' Susan asked.

'No,' Faith breathed through her sobs.

'What have you just been spanked for, Faith?' Susan asked.

'No, Mistress,' Faith answered.

'Better. Are you telling me that you're not roused?' She placed two fingers within the hot, liquid centre of Faith's passion. Faith groaned, her head sagging forward on to the covers again, and surrendered in the slight spreading of her legs. 'You feel wonderful, and why not? It's natural.'

Susan's fingers penetrated more deeply before her thumb pressed and then entered the tighter sphincter, bringing Faith's head up again in a groan of pure pleasure.

'Beg me to spank you again, Faith,' Susan said, clearly confident now of compliance. 'Beg me to punish you with a strap or a cane. Beg!' Her voice sharpened, though only slightly.

'Please Mistress.' Faith halted, feeling the shame of her own desires, yet knowing that unless she gave way to them, she would be tormented in a far worse manner. The unfulfilled longings which Susan had awakened would constantly remind her there were worse sufferings than pain.

'Yes?'

'Punish me, Mistress.' Faith stopped, blushing; unwilling to continue yet unable to stop for long. 'Spank me, Mistress; strap me, Mistress. Cane me!' Faith stopped with her mouth open, shocked at her own outspokenness. Her words had betrayed her innermost desires. Alex had spanked her and she had liked it, but this young woman seemed to have penetrated a completely different part of her body.

'Then we'll go back to the mirror room,' Susan said quietly, 'and you'll stand still and watch while I cane your behind. You won't make a sound, will you, Faith?'

'No, Mistress,' came Faith's breathy surrender.

In the mirror room, Susan made no attempt to fasten Faith to the wall. She picked up the cane and told Faith to bend over with her legs spread wide. As though in a dream, Faith complied, though her limbs trembled stiffly as she bent, the corset inhibiting the movement. She only managed to get her body at right angles to her legs, dropping her head to look between them. Placing the cane against the hot flesh, Susan paused, looking at the trembling limbs, then asked, 'Are you ready Faith? Looking forward to this?'

'Yes, Mistress.'

Faith could see everything reflected in the mirrors – the young woman in white, the cane, her own ruddy buttocks. She could see deep within her natal notch and the labial lips which opened to reveal her betraying sexual orifice. Slowly, knowing the suspense would add to Faith's enjoyment, Susan drew back the cane, building up the tension to increase the sensations Faith would experience. On the third stroke, each of which exploded not only on the surface of the skin but also deep within her, Faith's tears began to drop on the floor. She could see the lines across her buttocks, the physical evidence of her punishment. But she could also see the seepage from her sex, and smell the aroma of her own arousal. Betrayed again by her desires.

When she was finished, Susan returned the cane to the table, then picked up the end of the chain.

'Up.' She spoke as though nothing untoward had happened. Yet when Faith rose to the vertical, Susan kissed her full on the mouth, one hand fondling her right breast. 'There, darling,' Susan almost whimpered. 'You were so good. Does it hurt? It must do, and you were brave, too. But Susan has made you feel very sexy, hasn't she? You'll need to feel sexy for what comes next.'

'What?' Faith asked, then quickly added, 'Mistress?'

'The saddle,' Susan returned enigmatically. 'No talking now, or it's another spanking. Though I know you like it, too much of a good thing is bad for you.'

After leading Faith across the yard, where Hilary was securing one of the young women to the bar, Susan moved into the stall next to the one in which Faith had slept, pulling the horse-blanket off the machinery there. On top of the rectangular box was a saddle, positioned on a steel bar connected to the machinery within the base. Projecting upward from the saddle was a stiff leather dildo, shaped in a parody of an erect penis, but with a thicker ball at the top. Faith stood open-mouthed at the sight, conscious only of her own mixed emotions.

'Spread your legs,' Susan said, and carefully pressed Faith's abdomen to dislodge the balls, having them drop into her waiting palm before she said, 'Up you go, Faith.' Faith stumbled forward, lurching into the machine while Susan steadied her jocularly. 'Steady on! You're too eager. There's no need to rush at the sight of a cock.'

With her hands fastened behind her, Faith required Susan's help to mount the saddle, and was surprised when she was made to stand behind the upright leather. The base of the machine was so close that to avoid the floor, she would have to bend her knees up. Carefully, Susan opened Faith's sex lips as she said, 'Come, Faith, move forward.'

Without thinking, Faith shuffled to a position above the gleaming, polished leather, then on Susan's command, lowered herself slowly on to the cold leather dildo and the equally cold saddle.

Faith winced as the leather touched her hot, delicate flesh, trying to keep her face immobile as she felt it pushing up within her. The dildo was only about four inches long, including the tip, so the intention was never to rupture her. But was that all? Mrs Marryat had said that sexual abuse took place as part of the training, not for the release of the suffering induced by the spankings.

Susan moved around to the far side of the machine to take hold of Faith's right ankle, doubling it up while her wrists were freed, to be immediately secured to her ankles, tilting her forwards. What would she learn here? Was she destined to just sit there, ankles and wrists fastened? The change in position had brought about a change in posture. Now she was upright Faith realised her weight was actually balanced on the dildo and the tiny area of sensitive flesh around and behind it. Her perineum. Mentally Faith pictured herself, swallowing as Susan verbalised what she was thinking.

'You look lovely, Faith. Your shoulders are held back by that brace and your corset is nipping in your waist. Your wrists and ankles hold you just right. But this is another exercise in discipline. Here, you have to learn to control your feelings. After all, you won't be much use to your master if you climax before he's hardly begun, will you? So this is one of the ways we have of getting you used to controlling yourself. I hope you have a good ride. Not long, the first day. We have to get your muscles used to it. Before you know it, you'll be going for hours.' Susan made an adjustment to the machine, then pressed a button and the machine hummed, the vibrations of machinery in the base being transmitted up through the saddle to the phallus buried within her. Then to Faith's abdomen. It was as though her whole insides were being vibrated.

The balls had done their work well for, despite Susan's attentions, Faith could already feel herself liquidising within. When another button was pressed, the saddle began to rock, gently and steadily, back and forth, carrying Faith with it while the dildo rocked back and forth within her.

'That's the gentlest setting to start with,' Susan said above the hum. 'Who knows? Perhaps by the time you leave we'll be on the top setting, where you're bucking and jumping.'

Chapter Six

Once the machine began to move, Faith knew the primary purpose was to stimulate her sexually, though she had been surprised Susan had helped her to sit comfortably. That could have been to ensure there was no damage to her delicate sex, though perhaps she just wanted to hold open her labia. There was more than a hint that Susan enjoyed Sapphic desires.

Unsupported as she was, Faith could only clench her vaginal muscles around the phallus to keep her upright because by having her wrists fastened to her ankles, she was unable to use her knees to grip. No matter how tightly she clenched her muscles, the leather cock moved within; forward as she was going back and back as she was going forward. This set up such unusual sensations that Faith climaxed within minutes, despite trying to conceal it. First came a series of minor orgasms which she managed to control apart from a sheen of sweat on her skin and deeper breathing, but she finally flung back her head, not caring whether Susan knew or not. As soon as Faith had calmed down, Susan switched off the machine then unfastened her ankles, her wrists being immediately restrained. She was then allowed to stand, lifting herself slowly off the leather dildo, but when she reached the ground her legs gave way beneath her. The balls were immediately slipped back into her cervix and, as she was still unable to walk, Susan half-carried her out into the yard, where her wrists and ankles were fastened between the two large posts.

There seemed to be a hiatus in the deserted yard until a few minutes after Susan left her, when gradually the others arrived. Fearfully, Faith watched from the same position in which she had been when Mrs Marryat had used the strap on her, and saw Susan line up with the red-haired young man, while Hilary and Jacqui and the others faced her. Was she going to be punished again? Surely not. She had obeyed. Susan had said she was good.

Anxiously, Faith scanned the faces for some clue as to what was about to happen. Alison looked subdued and there was something different about her. It took a few moments to realise she was naked, her wrists restrained behind her. Yet there was someone missing – the second young man, the one with the fair hair. While she was wondering about that, Jackson appeared from her right, leading the young man by a chain attached to his collar. Mrs Marryat followed behind.

He was a slender, smooth-skinned young man, and seemed to walk in a more upright way than Faith remembered. Jackson wasted no time. With quick movements he spread the young man across the horizontal bar, fastening his ankles and wrists as Faith remembered hers had been secured. Mrs Marryat carried a familiar-looking object which at first took Faith's breath away. The woman obviously noticed Faith's startled expression and stopped beside her while Jackson finished his task, giving Faith a chance to see it properly.

Nine inches long, as thick as Faith's wrist and carved in meticulous detail, Mrs Marryat held a steel phallus, which had a ring in the squared-off end. When Jackson rose, red-faced from bending, Mrs Marryat advanced in front of the young man whose exposed anus and genitals faced Faith. As he began a futile struggle against the bonds securing him, whimpering with fear, she said, 'You know what this is for, don't you, Paul?'

'Yes,' he protested feebly, still trying to release himself.

'First, the phallus will be inserted, then the strap. After which I shall "tease" you a little; you'll like that, will you? Shall I have Miss Faith "tease" you too? Eh? What do you think that would do to your control?'

'No. Please!' His whine was back; his head shaking with the panic this woman instilled at her cold mention of Faith's participation.

'Please?' She frowned. 'We *are* learning manners.'

Fascinated yet horrified, Faith watched as the woman rounded the bound figure, whose buttocks prominently protruded at the height of the horizontal bar. Without wasting time she placed the blunt taper of the end opposite the ring against his puckered ring of muscle, then pushed. Paul grimaced but was silent as he jerked his head up and back, fighting to maintain his composure as his body protested. Hanging his head in bitterness, he clenched his buttocks together.

'You know, Paul.' The woman spoke in an almost conversational tone. 'This hurts you more than it hurts me. Why not accept the fact that you're not ready? Had you taken the phallus, it would be half over by now.'

Paul's cry was softer as Mrs Marryat tried again, pressing the tip to the sepia rose. There was a brief pause during which Faith looked at the others, but they were watching, impassive as statues. The bound young man wept openly, whether from the pain or the humiliation, or just from others watching, she had no idea. Then he half-turned his head, his neck straining round. As his pale bulging eyes looked beseechingly up at Mrs Marryat, both of them still, Faith saw the expression of absolute joy on his thin features.

Mrs Marryat gave Paul no chance. No sooner had he relaxed than the phallus was inserted, further widening his anus. He jerked again but seemed defeated, almost hanging across the bar and accepting what was happening. Faith had to admire the way Jackson and his housekeeper worked as a team, for Jackson now handed a broad strap to her before he unfastened her dress pulling it down to her waist over her naked breasts.

'One!' Mrs Marryat called, her arm cocked and ready, and brought the strap down across the top of the proffered behind.

Paul never cried out, but sighed; a soft, calming sound which barely reached Faith's ears as she saw him sag into the bar's embrace. Again the strap fell, the leather cracking across first one buttock, then the other, raising an instant, ill-defined scarlet weal, soon overlaid with another. Faith was able to see that Mrs Marryat had made no idle boast about her skill. Each successive stroke slightly overlapped the previous one. She was forced to admit her own experience had been typical – an efficient and painful lesson was being administered, yet the young recipient made no sound.

Within minutes, Paul's entire backside was a glowing mass of bright red flesh, and still she strapped. Recommencing from the top, when she stopped, no more out of breath than when she had begun –

though there was a gleam of moisture on her breasts – Paul's behind was a dull ruby-red.

Paul had tears in his eyes, moisture which occasionally dropped on to the concrete, yet he only grunted a little with each stroke, as though protesting, but no more. Stuck out in front of him was a thick erection above a tight scrotum, looking almost obscene. Faith thought that the test, for this was what it *had* to be, had finished at last. Not so. Jackson unfastened Paul's wrists while Mrs Marryat dealt with his ankles, turning him around in a well-coordinated movement which looked practised.

Faith almost gasped aloud when Paul was turned, controlling herself with difficulty, for his erection looked painfully large. The phallus had been pressing on his prostate gland and the strapping had also done its work – both bringing the young man to the desired state of arousal. Mrs Marryat, her dress fastened properly once more, was ready to administer the next stage of the test.

Paul's ankles and wrists were resecured, only bent backward over the bar so that his exposed penis was readily available. Mrs Marryat picked up a short, stiff piece of leather about the size of an insert for a shoe, then with her left hand pinched the bulbous end of Paul's erect penis. He whimpered and gasped as she felt the end, rubbing her fingers together and nodding.

'You're excited, Paul,' Mrs Marryat said in a careful voice. 'I shall have to do something about that.' Then she began striking his erect flesh with the piece of leather.

Again Paul began to jerk vainly against the bonds securing him; head thrown back, mouth open. But no intelligible sounds emerged; not even screams. There were various wails and gasps of shock as Mrs

Marryat struck him up and down, left and right, up and down, left and right again, stopping after half a minute, only to take the end of his erection in her fingers, squeezing hard again.

The stiff red flesh looked painful and the drum-hard skin of his scrotum was filled to overflowing, yet he was unable to release the liquid. But to Faith's amazement, Paul's expression grew more seraphic with each blow. It was as though Mrs Marryat was masturbating him, for his eyes closed, his expression giving way to one of concentration. Again Mrs Marryat struck the same blows, only when she stopped this time, she crouched, taking the end of his hot penis in her mouth.

Paul's groan of pained desire escaped just as she released him to begin strapping him again. Faith wanted to look away, but to her personal shame and aware of her blushes, she kept her eyes fixed on the battered flesh, wondering how much he could endure. The human body could only stand so much, of course. Paul was a healthy young man with an active libido so that his erection eventually spurted over the concrete, Mrs Marryat stepping aside to avoid it. Jackson was ready with a bucket of water to sluice it down the slope to the gutter at the bottom while his housekeeper waited.

'It comes out at about 28 miles an hour, Paul.' She spoke in her same, unhurried voice. 'Yet it takes six hours to enter the womb. Do you think you're ready to leave us just yet?'

'Please.' His chest heaved with the effort. 'Don't. No. Don't. No . . . no . . .'

'Do you think Paul has learned something today?' The woman turned to look at the witnesses to Paul's degradation. There was a pause then a ragged chorus of, 'Yes, Madame!' They acknowledged that *they* had learned, too.

Faith thought she had also learned something, lowering her head instead of speaking. Without a word, Susan released her from the posts, secured her wrists, then walked her down the yard, past the bar on which Paul hung, while Jackson released him. There was no protest from Faith, no opposition, no sound; like the others who were going about what they had been doing in a sombre silence, Faith felt comment was worthless. Besides, she was enjoined to silence unless an answer was required.

Left on her own in her room, Faith lay on the bed – with the shoulder brace and corset, she could hardly do anything else – grateful for the relaxation in tension. The demonstration of their control over Paul, and of Mrs Marryat's ability to provide sexual arousal in an unusual manner, gave her a lot to think about.

After lunch, which was brought by Susan, Faith was again chained to the wall and then allowed to rest for an hour, though she had no concept of the passing time. When Susan appeared, brightening Faith's attitude at once, she supervised Faith in donning her stockings, which she fastened to the suspenders on the corset, and then her long boots. There was something almost sexual in the way that the leather hugged her skin; the boots containing her long, strong legs, the corset her waist and the brace her shoulders. Only her sex, behind and breasts were free and Susan smiled at her as she said, 'I'm going to fit rings to you, Faith. Stand still.'

Bending forward, the woman fastened her mouth around Faith's nipples one after the other, slipping the rings into position but with a difference. Instead of taking up the chain to her collar, Susan held on to a finer chain which had been attached to the rings now encircling the swelling teats.

'There.' She pulled the chain lightly, making Faith gasp both in discomfort and a sudden trickle of lust. 'We'll have to go to the mirror room, don't you think?'

'Yes, Mistress,' Faith answered, knowing that any other reply would merit punishment.

Leading Faith by the fine chain, Susan led the way, keeping the tension constant so that Faith's teats were always being pulled while her body always tried to catch up. Once in the mirror room, Susan led her close to one of the mirrors, letting Faith get a good look at her predicament while she crossed to the table.

'Beg me to strap your behind, Faith.' The doom was spoken in her usual, conversational tone.

'Please, Mistress.' Faith could feel the fear building up, but continued, 'Punish my behind with a strap.'

'Good.' Susan nodded. 'No tears now. You must know I love you.' Then she began, not waiting for Faith to bend over.

With her behind glowing again and the sweet sensations of lust churning within her, Faith was led out of the house and through the yard. It was difficult not to notice the approving looks she received. Gerald had been working a phallus into a small, thin girl's behind but stopped to watch as the proud Susan led her past. Hilary had Roger spread out between the posts, the whole of his backside and legs glowing from the strap. Even the young man's eyes, dulled from patient suffering, took an interest in their passage. Faith's vanity at being the centre of such attention made her hold herself more erect, yet keeping her head inclined at the correct angle.

Once out in the open, out of sight of the house, Susan dropped the chain, bringing no small relief to

Faith, who thought she must surely pull her nipples off unless she had some respite from the strain.

'Did you see, Faith?' the young woman asked, delight in her voice. 'You made quite an impression. Answer.'

'Yes, Mistress.'

'You may talk when we're here, on our walk,' Susan said, not looking at her companion. 'First I shall spank you, or cane you; I may even whip you. After which we shall walk. Then you can thank me.'

'Thank you?' The concept seemed strange.

'Ah.' Susan smiled, turning to look at her. 'But you don't know what we'll do on our walk, do you?'

Faith soon found out.

High in the wood, Susan turned off the pathway on to a small trail through a gap between the ferns where the passage of feet had left a faint trace. Following this, the two young women, Faith being led by the chain again, made their way across the face of the slope until they reached an open space surrounded by shrubbery. To the south the landscape was concealed by trees, yet the canopy was sufficiently sparse to allow bright, hot sunshine through to where Susan stopped.

'Sit,' she said, then helped her companion down. Sitting was out of the question in the corset, so Faith lay flat on her stomach as her behind was still stinging. Her breathing was laboured.

The combination of the love balls, the caning, the strapping and the saddle had all produced a pent-up desire which Faith hoped she could find a way to release.

'Spread your legs, darling.' Susan ran a hand lightly up the back of Faith's left thigh. When she complied, Susan's busy fingers found her heat and, as Faith's head turned, their mouths met. Assaulted in both regions, bound and constrained, Faith could do nothing but remain still, though not for long. Before she knew what she was doing, Faith was kissing Susan as hard as she was being kissed, spreading her legs wider to allow her to enter both openings. Soon Faith spread her legs as wide as she could manage.

'You're a wanton hussy,' Susan accused, though with a laugh in her voice. 'Shall I work on you?'

'Please, Mistress,' Faith breathed, hope flaring in her eyes. The ache in her abdomen was flaring into painful life again.

'You'll do something for me, too, won't you?' Susan asked.

'Anything, Mistress,' Faith answered without hesitation. This was no time to quibble, not with the promise of release so close.

'Anything?' Susan asked. 'What if I want to spank you again?'

'Anything, Mistress,' Faith repeated, lowering her gaze. There was something hypnotic about Susan's dark eyes which sent shivers of trembling desire through Faith. Further desire was something she could do without, yet she felt compelled by internal forces she was unable to understand.

'When we get back, I shall fasten you over the bar in the yard, and you will be strapped.'

'With everyone watching?' Faith asked. Her wide eyes seemed almost to relish the humiliation.

'Only those there already,' Susan allowed.

'Why was Paul . . . is it Paul? Why was he punished?'

'He's lucky "Mad Martha" didn't geld him.' Susan snorted a laugh. 'He thought he was ready to take responsibility . . . to leave, in fact. He hasn't made enough progress.'

'It seemed . . . excessive.'

'Excessive?' Susan's fingers were working slowly and she was smiling as she considered this. 'If "Mad Martha" had got Juliet to "tease" him she'd have ripped his cock off with her teeth. She hasn't got much time for Paul. Alison's been demoted; she was the one who proposed testing him. Did you notice her? It'll be a couple of days before she'll sit comfortably.'

But it was too late for Faith. The gentle marauding fingers within had caused sufficient pressure to bring on the release Faith had sought. Jerking her head back, her body rigid, the young woman strained as she experienced the welcome sensations of sexual satisfaction.

Lying inert afterwards, trying to control her breathing, Faith made no resistance when Susan rolled her on to her back, her languid eyes looking up at the woman who had brought her such pleasure. For a moment Susan hesitated, then moving slowly, began to unfasten the buttons at the neck of her dress.

As Faith watched in silence the dress was opened to reveal her firm bosom, then it was pushed over her hips until Susan wore only her white panties. These too were slowly slipped down her thighs as their eyes locked, the young woman keeping her smile in place.

Faith's pupils enlarged, she swallowed visibly, and her increased breathing kept her large, firm breasts heaving. Faith was being aroused despite herself.

'Spread your legs, darling.' Susan spoke softly, running a light, smooth hand over Faith's left breast, hesitating for a moment at the swollen nipple and sending shivers of fire through the recumbent figure.

Despite herself, Faith's legs spread a little and, as Susan remained still, watching her eyes, they gradually slipped wider until she was satisfied. Placing herself between the smooth, abused thighs, still smarting from the strap, Susan carefully placed her clitoris against Faith's button, resting there for a moment. The upper slope of her bosom rested against the lower slope of Faith's, her weight taken on the hands on either side of Faith's head. But that was less important than the lower stimulation, for already Faith was beginning to hyperventilate, her mouth opening and closing as she desperately sought air.

Gradually, Susan began to move, rubbing her hairy mound against the comparatively bare protrusion beneath her, occasionally slipping higher, dragging her own clitoris across the stubble that remained of Faith's pubic hair. Though Faith felt aroused, she could see the flush come to Susan's features as the transformation she was beginning to recognise as lust took control of her. More and more Susan was pressing her own clitoris against Faith's mound, pressing savagely downwards to increase the abuse of her own flesh.

Gasping, her hips moved faster, ignoring Faith's whimpering desire as she fed her own needs; taking her pleasure on the body of her charge. Suddenly Susan's arms collapsed as she fell forward on to Faith, moving up the last few inches to fasten her mouth on Faith's, her tongue pushing between Faith's lips.

From beneath, Faith could still feel the working hips on her abdomen, and realised that Susan was continuing with her own sexual stimulation and rubbing her clitoris frantically. She found the sensations of Susan's abdominal contractions strange; it was something Lillian had never allowed her to feel. Her own desires.

When she was spent and lying exhausted on the taller woman, heedless of the pain and discomfort she was causing Faith's fastened wrists and back, Susan raised her head to look into Faith's eyes. 'You're mine, Faith,' she whispered softly, urgently. 'Do you know that? *Mine*!'

'Yes Mistress,' Faith answered unhappily, only too aware of the discomfort in her wrists.

'When we get back to the house, I'm not only going to punish you, I'm going to shave your motte. You don't have much, but I'm going to take that ... and I'm going to oil you there; and your teats. Everyone is going to look at you and desire you, but you're mine. Do you understand?'

'Yes, Mistress.' Faith felt the slow coiling of desire stirring again. Unlike Susan, she had not climaxed though she had been aroused, and the picture being presented to her increased the sensations of desire and humiliation within her. Secured as she was, with her sex and breasts glistening with oil, Faith knew that she would present an erotic sight.

'You'll be restrained,' Susan said slowly, knowing the effect it was having on Faith. 'You'll beg me to shave your motte, and punish you. Won't you?' Her soft voice thrilled through the recipient's frame.

'Yes, Mistress,' Faith answered obediently, another notch in her surrender being taken up, her eyes dropping.

Entering the yard behind Susan, being led by the chain attached to the rings around her teats, Faith groaned inwardly. Mrs Marryat and Jackson were both present, supervising most of the other pupils, and all eyes turned to watch as Susan almost strolled to a wall, where she secured her charge, whose long-legged gait drew more than one admiring glance. Left alone while Susan vanished indoors, Faith stood secured by the chain at her throat, head downcast while she waited for the inevitable. She heard footsteps then saw Jackson's and Mrs Marryat's feet stop in front of her. A hand took her chin to raise her head so that she looked directly at the woman.

Mrs Marryat's expression was cold and composed as usual, yet there was an acknowledgement in her eyes that progress was being made. 'Are you being good, Miss Faith?' she asked.

'Yes, Mrs Marryat,' Faith answered, looking her in the eye.

'We'll see, shall we?' the woman asked, after a pause which added nothing to Faith's self-confidence.

When Susan returned, she brought a high stool and a bowl of water and, while the couple watched in silence, she positioned Faith's behind on the stool two feet from the wall, telling her to spread her legs wide. Her wrists secured behind her and fastened to the wall by her throat, Faith's body was held at an angle which enabled Susan to work easily.

'Tell Madame what you want me to do, Faith,' Susan stated.

'Please, Mistress –' Faith swallowed '– shave my mound.'

'And afterwards?' Susan's light voice held no trace of menace.

'Please Mistress –' Faith hesitated, closing her eyes '– punish me with a strap.'

'Good.' Mrs Marryat nodded to Susan. 'Carry on, Susan. You seem to be getting somewhere, but remember to be severe with her. It's what she needs.'

'Yes, Madame.' Susan's head nodded imperceptibly, though her eyes remained on Faith's fearful features.

Though she kept her eyes cast down, Faith was aware of the interest as Susan shaved the remaining hair from her mound, then applied the oil with smooth, cold hands as one of her fingers penetrated her, making Faith inhale deeply to control her reaction. When the oil had been applied all over her breasts, Faith knew the inevitable had arrived. Taking her down off the stool, Susan's easy manner vanished.

'You want me to punish you again. Not before time, too. Spread your legs.'

Faith did as she was bid, trembling as the dark-haired young woman left her for the bench on the far side of the yard, returning almost immediately. In her hand was a broad, thick, black leather strap, shiny with use, the deep, dark surface looking as though oiled. She recognised what had been used on Paul's buttocks so effectively. At one end was a narrower piece with a long loop through which the woman placed her hand, holding the thinner section. She brandished it before Faith.

'This is a strap.' Susan still spoke quietly yet with some menace, holding it where Faith could see it. 'This strap is going to be used on your behind. You shall carry it to the place of punishment, and you shall carry it back again.'

Yet instead of the woman going behind her, she sank to her knees before Faith, her smile still in place. Suddenly Faith began to tremble with horror as she realised what was intended. Carefully parting Faith's outer lips, Susan pushed the handle into her vagina like a thick leather dildo, seeming endless as it was thrust upward, filling her as even Alex had never done. What made it worse was the fact that Faith could feel her excitement rising.

She was lubricating! Her abused body was betraying her, even as the instrument of punishment was being pushed into her, easing its passage. When it was as fully home as Susan wished, the woman rose, ordering in a sharp voice, 'Legs together! Come, you can't stay there for ever, and if you drop it on the way to the place of punishment . . . or on the way back . . .' Susan left the threat unspecified.

Faith trembled as she felt the hard outlines of the strap on the back of her knees and up her thighs, the hard, smooth leather filling her passage. All movement in the yard stopped as Susan led Faith by the chain attached to her nipples to the long bar, where Gerald stood beside Jacqui's naked, scarlet buttocks, the brown staining leading to her anus clearly defined.

At the bar, Faith was secured as best she could be with the corset, then the strap was removed from within her, Susan commenting to the red-headed young man as she wiped the handle, 'Faith *is* looking forward to this; soaked the strap already with her love-juices. Wet her, would you? I think it's time she found out what a strap means.'

'Sure,' he agreed. His accent reminded Faith of the West Country, though more polished.

Gerald took a sponge of cold water from the bucket beside him, and applied it to her buttocks, soaking them, and allowing Faith plenty of time to think about what was going to happen. The water would make the noise greater, of course, and it would moisten and soften the skin but, stroke for stroke, it would not make them worse. Where it did succeed was in allowing the recipient to endure more strokes.

When he was finished, and had worked the sponge into her hot, trembling vulva too, Susan placed the strap against the young woman's lips, instructing her, 'Kiss it. Kiss it now and it will kiss you later.'

Faith closed her eyes and clamped her lips together, feeling this would be the worst ordeal she could ever endure, but the strap was briefly placed against her dry mouth anyway. Deep within her Faith knew that, despite her refusal, this was another sub-mission; she had kissed the strap.

Faith heard the familiar whistling sound instants before the strap exploded against her buttocks, jerking her head back as the pain spread through her, driving her breath from her body. Even had she wanted to, she would have been unable to cry out. There was no need for Mrs Marryat to tell Susan to strike harder; Susan was using the strap harder than she had before. The second stroke followed not long afterwards, before Faith had recovered, her head jerking again as the tears started, flooding her eyes instantly.

Her quivering lips failed to conceal the whimper at the third stroke, or the gasp at the fourth. But on the fifth, Faith lost her fight with silence, for her throat unhinged to deliver a cry to the four walls of the building which was music to Susan's ears. She had swung the strap hard, for this was the pupil's first public strapping across the bar and should be properly delivered.

The protest let Susan know that, for all her apparent progress, Faith was a normal young woman with normal tastes. She did not like pain, so it was safe to proceed with their routine of gradually introducing her to the incremental aspects. Pain had to be administered, but too much too soon would teach her nothing. She had to be shown the pleasure to be had from it too.

Faith had to understand what was happening and why. By gradually increasing the severity they not only prepared her but maintained her internal tension. She would never become used to pain, for the acceptance of pain was corrosive – the more inflicted the more desired. Faith would always find that until she left the Stables, the next lesson would always be more painful than the last – more pain, more humiliation – until finally she would accept anything without protest. Once she had that poise, that ability to surmount the apparently insurmountable, she would be fully trained. But alongside the discomfort would be the wonderful feelings that the teaching was designed to evoke.

Chapter Seven

Once completed, her buttocks glowed like fire, yet because of the water Gerald had applied there was less discomfort. The handle of the strap was then pressed against Faith's lips again, with the injunction to kiss it. Again Susan inserted the handle into her vagina, and Faith noticed that her discharge had soaked her thighs. Released from the bar, her wrists were fastened behind her immediately before she was taken to the stable where the strap was removed. On mounting for her second session on the saddle, Faith quickly slipped herself over the upturned dildo, welcoming the cold kiss of the smooth, polished leather as her hot flesh slipped easily over it.

Wriggling and settling herself into position, Faith ignored Susan but looked straight ahead instead, keeping her face pointed meekly downward and avoiding her eyes. Susan fastened Faith's wrists to her ankles in silence, and a soft, heartfelt groan of pleasure came from her charge as the pressure of her weight was applied to her sex.

When she was done, she asked, 'Do you think I was too cruel to you, darling?' There was no answer. 'You'll have worse before you leave here, darling. All I'm doing is preparing you for the future. One day, Gerald may use that whip on your behind; the one he was using on Jacqui. That's far worse than I did to you. You'll look back on this in a couple of days and feel ashamed that you thought so badly of me. Never mind.' Susan sighed. 'Unfortunately, though I love you, I also have to train you. You'll thank me later. Enjoy your ride, darling.' Susan pressed the button to start the machine.

As before, Faith was unable to grip with her knees to reduce the strain on her vaginal muscles, her only anchorage. With her hot skin cooling on and warming the leather, her lubricious sensations were being sated on the upstanding dildo. Faith's only hope to avoid humiliating herself by the intensity of her climax was to ignore the young woman who stood watching with folded arms. Climaxing too soon, or too violently, would have confirmed to herself as much as Susan that the strapping had aroused her.

Yet Susan refused to allow Faith to ignore her. Planting herself directly in front of the rocking saddle, she unfastened the buttons of her dress to the waist, peeling back the material to expose her breasts. While Faith rocked, Susan openly fondled her breasts in front of her.

When Susan stopped the machine half an hour later, Faith was covered in sweat, her hair falling about her face and her features heavy with desire. Faith had taken as much pleasure from the dildo as she could, squeezing her sexual muscles hard as the pressures within had overwhelmed her. Her reasoning was that it was the one part of a day not devoted to discipline, to which she could look forward. Again she was sponged down then returned to the posts in the yard, spread out as before. Susan went indoors, leaving her to watch as Gerald, Hilary and Juliet, now wearing white briefs, went about disciplining the others, the two overseers watching patiently.

Faith was not ignored. When bringing some of the

others to the bar or one of the devices used to secure them, the trio would stop by Faith, examining her closely. While their charges stood patiently waiting, heads cast down, the principals would comment on the effect of the strapping, or pass a hand over Faith's hairless mound, tickling her sexual flesh lightly, watching for a response.

The bound young woman thought it would be best to make no response, for spread out as she was, they could do what they chose. Hilary's light eyes were full of mischief when she led Alison away by her collar, her behind marked by the application of a four-stranded whip. Alison's tears disfigured her face and her sobbing shook her chest, but Faith could find little in her to pity. She remembered how Alison had made it appear that she struggled, earning her the strapping in the yard.

'Been on the saddle, have you?' Hilary asked, ignoring her charge.

'Yes, Mistress,' Faith answered, not taking her eyes from the ground before her.

Hilary was short and stood directly in front of Faith, her trimmed pubic mound visible through the thin material of her briefs, a reproach to the hairless Faith. Even so, the shorter young woman stood spread-legged so that Faith could see her clitoris and the raw red line of her labia, from which she detected the familiar musk.

'See how you like this.'

Hilary crouched in front of her, spreading her legs wide. She wore a leather harness which constricted her breasts, thrusting them out ahead of her, and her teats looked painfully swollen, the skin shiny. A rivulet of sweat trickled down between her breasts and her face was covered in a fine beading of it. With contemptuous ease she produced the carved phallus she had just removed from Alison's behind, inserting the tip into Faith's sexual passage.

'Ah!' Hilary smiled, delighted as it was sucked higher with the muscular contractions of Faith's trembling abdomen. 'You like that. I'll have to tell Susan; she'll be interested.'

'Yes, Mistress,' Faith breathed, thankful that it had not been her behind.

'No one told you to talk!'

Hilary's humour vanished instantly as she rose, and quite deliberately she delivered two open-handed slaps to the outer aspects of Faith's breasts, smiling at her grimace. The heat from the slaps on her flesh added to the churning within Faith, who suddenly wondered whether Hilary could bring her to orgasm by that means alone. The thought added to the churning, so Faith tried to think of something else.

'I don't think Susan is being severe enough with you. If you were mine you'd get a lot more of that. I'll suggest it.' Turning away, she tugged the chain attached to Alison's throat, pulling her in the direction of the stable containing the saddle. Faith wondered how Alison would be able to endure it.

In the smart King's Road restaurant they made an attractive group, Alex Pellew's tall, fair figure towering over the others while Max Hawes, older by at least five years than the others, looked squat and dark by comparison. Twenty-nine-year-old Lillian Brampton, slim and elegant, had hair almost as fair as Alex's and eyes slightly less icy blue, but alike enough to be his sister rather than his guest. The other young woman was very slightly heavier than Lillian, but wore her naturally bronze hair like a flag. Helen Pellew was Alex's half-sister and, at 22, the youngest of the group.

Alex looked up from the food in front of him into

the amused expression of Lillian Brampton's eyes. To his right, his sister Helen sat facing Max, on his left. Both women wore black ribbons at their throats. This sartorial embellishment meant nothing but a fashion accessory to the other patrons of the expensive French restaurant, though all four knew it was at Alex's hands that they had been earned.

'You're very quiet, darling,' Lillian observed for the third time in as many minutes, aware from his blank expression that Alex's mind had registered only that he was being spoken to and not the content.

'Yes.' He sighed. 'Sorry.'

'Business?' Max asked quietly. 'I know the markets are in a bit of a mess these days.'

'No, not really.' Alex shook his head, then changed the subject to one of more general interest. 'When do you want to take delivery of Lillian? And who do you want as a witness?'

'Your choice,' Max reminded him quietly. 'I'm not bothered who it is –'

'Just so long as you get her. I know.' Alex smiled at the man, then transferred his attention to the woman opposite.

Lillian's expression was neutral for she knew that, though she was keen to be given to Max, it seemed strange to be parting from Alex after all this time. In a way, she resented their ability to pass her from one to the other. Yet there was something comforting in the knowledge that Alex had thought long and hard about her future. His, of course, was bound up in Faith.

'Not your people, I take it?' Max asked, nodding towards Helen.

'God, no!' Alex exclaimed. 'They'd have forty fits unless I explain it properly. Helen's the only one who knows, and she knows better than to tell them.'

'It could be painful for her, yes.' Max nodded.

Helen had been brought up in the Chosen ever since, five years before, her half-brother had taken her virginity and begun her training. On many nights she had lain, tightly secured in her bed, wondering what all the fuss was about, enjoying the restriction as much, if not more, than Alex's ministrations. Yet she knew it was for the best. Her half-brother treated her almost as an equal, which was a rarity in the Chosen. She hoped he would be equally considerate when it came to choosing her husband and future master. Keeping quiet about this deception over Lillian was one way to show her responsibility.

'Julia?' Max asked.

'Julia means Harry,' Alex answered, nodding as he looked into Lillian's eyes. She looked back with an expression of indifference, as though all men were equal to her. 'Julia it is, then.' Alex nodded. 'Tell me where and when.'

'Give me a couple of days to think about it, would you? I have to go abroad again and this time, it may take some time.'

'No rush. Faith's in the Stables. We don't need to worry about her return for some time yet.'

'How is she getting on, Alex?' Lillian asked, biting her lip at her outburst. From his expression, Alex was annoyed at her asking about her replacement, so she had to think fast. 'It's just that, having found her for you, I have an interest. I spent quite some time in her preparation, too.'

'Yes.' At once Alex's irritation eased at the memory of how valuable her assistance in finding and training Faith had been. He could understand her interest and wanted her to continue helping with Faith. 'You did. She's only been gone a few days; hardly time to settle in.'

'No word?' Max asked. 'Usually Martha gives you some idea.'

'Not yet. I might see about going down there, actually. See how she's doing.'

'Would Martha allow it?' Lillian asked. 'She was never one to welcome visitors in my day. Said they put the pupils off. Knowing an outsider was watching them made them skittish.'

'I'll talk to her,' Alex agreed.

At the flat in Cheyne Walk, Alex made his preparations while Helen relaxed with a drink and a magazine. He placed the pillow centrally over the brass rail at the foot of the bed, checked that he had everything to hand, then went through to the drawing room.

'Helen!' he said sharply, attracting her attention at once. She had been listening to the sound of his preparations and was ready, rising to her feet. Without speaking, she swallowed convulsively, then walked past him down the corridor to the familiar bedroom where the walls were mirrors.

Watching her reflection, and that of Alex who stood off to one side, she removed her dress then laid it on the chair beside the bed before she started on her underwear. Naked, her head bowed as he approached her back, she steeled herself for the cold caress of the plain steel collar with the four equidistant rings, unable to suppress her excitement when it fastened about her throat with the familiar, metallic click. No matter how many times this happened, even knowing and welcoming what was to happen, Helen still felt a shiver of apprehension at this point. She revelled in that first cold caress, gooseflesh covering her spine and arms, raising her breathing rate in anticipation.

Alex carefully fastened the bracelets around her wrists, allowing her the freedom of not being properly secured yet. If Helen had her way, Alex would have fastened them just above her elbows, then joined them with a short chain to pull her shoulders uncomfortably back. She delighted in discomfort.

'Over you go, Helen.' He watched her as she went to the foot of the bed, holding the top rail as she stepped on to the bottom one; then laid herself across the thick pillow, moving slightly to balance herself properly on the rail which, despite the thickness of duck-down, she could feel through the material. With her head resting on the bedcovers, she needed no instruction to place her wrists crossed on her rump, making it simple for Alex to snap the spring-loaded protrusions together.

Last of all, Alex stooped to fasten similar anklets to her, drawing her legs apart before securing them to the frame. From where he stood, Alex looked at the smooth pink flesh of his half-sister's exposed behind and the deep ruby-red of her open vulva. Putting out a hand, he stroked his fingers lightly down the smooth skin of the plump, gaping labial lips, making Helen wince and hiss.

'You're very hot, Helen,' Alex observed softly, then added, 'and wet, too. How long has it been since I last fucked you?'

'Three weeks, I think ... or maybe four. Before you found that ... was her name Faith?'

'Faith, yes.' Alex nodded, placing a finger directly into her vagina, slipping it deeply and easily to the web. 'Tighten.'

Helen at once contracted her muscles about his digit, which he tugged gently towards him, testing her. The strength of her response confirmed that Helen needed release. She needed him to mount her, but she also wanted a spanking, as though without one her pleasure would be diminished. Perhaps the spanking was more important to her than the sex.

'Are you going to go through with it, Alex?' Helen asked, distracting him for a second.

'Go through with what?' Alex asked, applying more pressure, and slowly withdrawing his finger from the slippery passage, while Helen tightened herself against him. Withdrawal like that drove her wild with lust; already he could hear her breathing growing harsh. Three weeks was a long time for someone like Helen to be without sex.

'Giving Lillian away. Doesn't she mind?' Helen managed to gasp as she concentrated on keeping his finger within her vagina. Her harsh panting added to Alex's understanding of her state of arousal.

'She's going to a good home, Helen,' Alex responded as he watched the oily secretion ooze from her orifice. He waited until it reached her urethra before scooping it up with a finger, then began to work it on to her perineum as he continued. 'After all, she's going to Max. Who better? After all, he trained her in pleasure. She thinks the world of him, and he of her. It's an ideal solution.'

'Daddy won't like it. He's set on you and Lillian –' Helen stopped talking as he tapped her perineum with his finger, jerking her head up. Alex could bring her off with that alone, but she wanted more than that. What did she have to do to get it? Ask?

'Father will agree once Lillian is Max's,' Alex said, stroking the back of one finger down her taut, inner thighs, making her shiver even more. 'What do you want, Helen?' he asked. 'You're becoming tight as a drum.'

'Spank me, Alex. Please?' There was a catch in her throat as she spoke, a hesitation she knew was involuntary but inevitable. Alex was the only man who had spanked her and she knew the delicious effect it had. She had been well trained. Helen had done the 'pillar dance' more than once and had always been thankful that Alex had been there with his hot, welcoming erection, to satisfy the lust it provoked. But he was distracted these days, so would he agree to spank her? It was the most severe that she thought she could expect from him. A strapping would have been wonderful, but too much to hope for here. It would mean he would have to gag her, for she always loudly voiced her appreciation of a strapping. She always appreciated being properly gagged.

'A spanking?' Alex sounded amused. 'You haven't had a spanking in a while, have you?'

'No, Alex, and I need one. I've been so beastly to Mummy. Aunt Frances says I should do the pillar dance again, but she never got round to it.'

'I'll gag you, then. I don't want the neighbours complaining.'

'Thank you, Alex,' Helen breathed happily as she felt the moisture building up in her eyes at the prospect. A spanking from Alex could set her alight, and when he drove himself into her, she would have no inhibitions about yelling.

When he returned, Alex was stripped and ready, but she stopped him by asking, 'Have you spanked Faith, yet?'

'Yes, of course. Why do you ask?' Alex sounded surprised. Helen had never asked about any of the other women he had been with; not even Lillian. Though delightful, his half-sister was curiously self-centred when it came to sex. Or perhaps incurious would be a better way of putting it, he thought.

'Did she take it well?'

'Yes.'

'As well as I do?' Helen persisted. She knew she was irritating him, but that was the idea. Now that he had agreed to spank her, she wanted him to put plenty of power into it. Ideally, she would have liked him to take a strap to her labia and clitoris, but that was too much to hope for.

'She can yell louder than you,' Alex answered.

Alex sat on the bed beside her and pinched her cheeks together. In the Chosen, it was never done for the woman to willingly open her mouth to a gag; social etiquette demanded that she be forced. As Helen allowed the gag to be forced between her teeth, she noted the size of Alex's erection, thinking that within a few minutes, despite the pain in her rear, that would be bringing her such a wonderful release.

As he composed himself for the spanking, Alex checked over everything in his mind again. He chose to spank in the bedroom because it occupied the top corner of the building, with only deaf old Mr Delaude beneath him. Because of this, the gag was hardly needed but he knew it increased Helen's pleasure to be further restrained. Which brought his mind inexorably back to Faith again. Even as his hand began to address the soft inviting flesh of Helen's buttocks, his mind went back to Faith's pert rear on Harry's boat, and her obedient anguish. The look in her eyes when he had asked her to strip and take a spanking because he loved her told more than she intended.

Faith's response had been exquisite; obedience and passion mingled to such a degree that he felt she would be perfect for what he had in mind. He could picture her, silently hanging from straps in the ceiling in the theatre at the club, while one of the members did his best to penetrate her. But that was a long way off yet.

After removing the gag when the spanking was

over, Alex stepped up behind Helen to the wide open labia, now a deeper ruby shade than the glowing buttocks on either side. The spanking had stimulated Helen, for her juices soaked over the hot tissue and turned the soft skin of her inner thighs shiny. He placed himself at her entrance then slowly inserted his erection into her hot, liquid, welcoming orifice. Helen whimpered with pleasure as her head was thrown back.

He remained still for over a minute, waiting while Helen's muscles squeezed him as tightly as they could, trying to crush his erection. It was an old game they played and one she had never yet won. Despite her best efforts, Helen's muscular movements only increased his desire. Afterwards, with increasing speed, Alex began to move within her.

Ridden to a limb-shuddering climax, her groaning cries stifled by the covers which, in her passion, Helen bit as hard as she could, the young woman was finally released from her position, though her wrists were still restrained. Taking her into the shower, Alex gently and thoroughly washed her from the roots of her hair to the tips of her toes, telling her when to spread her legs apart or bend over to gain access to her more intimate places, arousing her again in the process.

Tucked up in bed afterwards, a feeling of peace stealing over her, Helen asked, 'Is there anything I can do, Alex? I mean, at home? Talk to Mummy, or something.'

'Why?' he asked.

'Do you want to be Faith's master?' Helen asked.

'I *am* her master,' Alex answered quietly in the darkness. 'She's ridden the three-horned god and the only thing I haven't done is shave her. Lillian got most of it off.' His hand dropped to her depilated mound, sending another thrill through Helen's tired body.

'What . . . what are you going to do?' Helen asked, shocked at the admission. She knew her half-brother had had relations with women in the past, though he never brought any of them home. It was accepted in the family that these young women lived with him, performed with him, and went the way of such casual relationships. This sounded different, though; much more serious.

'I'm going to marry her, Helen,' Alex said soberly in the darkness. Helen's legs parted to allow him greater access. Helen hadn't had sex for three weeks and was trying to get as much as she could. Whoever became her master would have to have either a strong constitution or take a strap to her backside pretty often.

'Marry . . ?' Helen halted as her own moist out-pourings soaked her half-brother's fingers.

'Serious, isn't it? Now you see why I had to give Lillian away.'

'Does Lillian know?' Helen asked. She turned on to her back, spreading herself wider, for she could feel the heat from Alex's erection. Soon he would mount her again, so she readied her wrists beside her ears. Would he fasten her to the bed? She hoped so; he knew how much she liked it.

'Of course she does.' Alex clearly recognised her gesture and rolled between her knees.

'She's Faith's mistress.'

He was already reaching down to open her sex lips again. Before she could think of a reply, Helen felt the tip enter her and all thought of Faith and Lillian and the rest of the world deserted her. All she knew was that she was in Alex's bed, with Alex's erection slipping into her passage with the prospect of another successful mounting in view. That was sufficient.

* * *

Mrs Marryat sat in the high-backed chair looking at the three members of her staff. On the opposite side of the room, Jackson was busy with the accounts, making sure the Stables continued to be both profitable and well run, thus making her efforts worthwhile. If they ever lost their reputation for efficiency, their standards would inevitably decline.

Gerald, Susan and Hilary were all naked, each of them having been attended to prior to the usual evening meeting. The system for the day was simple. The meals were taken to the pupils in their rooms by those members of staff not directly involved with the training. After the evening meal, the dishes were removed and the pupils locked into their rooms for the night.

Mrs Marryat dealt with the promising pupils first; finding the weak links in their technique and awarding suitable punishments. For some like Alison, who had been so negligent that Paul had been tested before he was ready, demotion and a sound whipping in the music room was the answer. Bent over or stretched out, their mistakes were pitilessly examined and punished. It would take some considerable effort for Alison to merit wearing knickers again before her training was complete.

If indeed the girl could be trained, for part of that involved the ability to take responsibility. Susan had confirmed that Faith had put up no struggle and it was only by a close reading of her notes that Martha discovered the girl had been turned down by the Chosen. Jealousy? Was that it? Once the junior members of the Stables had been examined, they were returned to their rooms, where Jackson would have left their evening meals, while Martha got to grips with the business of dealing with her three senior staff.

Susan had opted to remain at the Stables after her

own training, and was doing a good job too. She seemed almost to welcome Mrs Marryat's attentions after a day's teaching, going willingly to the bar or rack and stripping herself naked to have her punishment, be it five strokes of the cane or a sound thrashing. Most days, Susan's performance merited none at all.

Gerald too had opted to remain. He had been sent by his guardian, who had little interest in him beyond getting him a good education. Beaten at school, he had soon appreciated the benefits of the training at the Stables; his muscles were such that he was second only to Martha herself in the severity of his ministrations.

Hilary, the most junior of the three, was a small, wiry girl who found maintaining a cold, impassive demeanour difficult. But that would come in time. It was the least difficult trait to inculcate. She had been too lenient with Miranda that afternoon, allowing her to escape with only two strokes of the whip.

The girl had almost finished her training! Five? Ten would hardly have been enough to test her. So Hilary, of the three, had been given the other eight, and now sat on the cold metal plate placed on the seat, thankful for the mercy of the cooling heat sink. Even after her shower, the aroma of her musk lingered in the air.

One by one Mrs Marryat went through the pupils, discussing their progress, nodding when observations were made. It was the most informal of the meetings, for with them, Martha could relax a little. They had been tested and punished if found wanting; now she could meet them on a more intimate basis.

When she came to the newest pupil, Susan was ready with her comments as Martha said, 'She's got a good brain and she's used to making up her mind.

Most of the girls here are fluff-heads; wild but basically weak. It's just a matter of time to eradicate their weaknesses and make them obey. This one's disobedience is very, very different; I haven't come across many like her.'

'Which is why I like her. She's a challenge,' Susan commented. 'She should pick up pretty quickly now.'

'What's planned for her?' Hilary asked. 'I stuck a phallus in her crotch today and she didn't twitch.'

'She's a new pleasure slave who needs training. I thought she was someone's daughter until they sent those notes,' Martha observed.

'She's right then,' Susan observed sadly. 'She *is* – or at least *will* be – someone's slave. What a prospect.'

'None of our concern, Susan,' Martha said quietly and their eyes met. 'Our job is to discipline her, that's all.'

Mrs Marryat willed the concern from her eyes and voice at Susan's bleak expression. She had noticed it before, but never so much. Susan liked women, yes. She used that liking, which she thought amounted to love sometimes, to bring them out of the fugue into which some of them slipped when they were first at the Stables.

Some young women gave up thinking for themselves, reacting like cattle in a market, obediently being pushed hither and yon until they were returned to the outside world little better than they arrived. Often the only benefit was that they were inured to the vagaries of life and had a capacity for enduring suffering. Sometimes, Martha thought, it was the best they could hope for, given that the girls were what she had called them: 'fluff-heads'.

As the light went out, Faith felt herself sigh with contentment. She was back in the peaceful haven of the bed again, secure and warm, without having to share her water with mice – or rats. It was only now, in the crisp white safety of the bed, that Faith allowed herself to think of the possibility of there being rats in the stable.

She hardly knew what to make of the attitudes of Jackson and Mrs Marryat; they had been fierce to her – had hurt her in fact – yet she felt they were doing their best. What that best consisted of, Faith was unclear. Was it that they were curing her of her rounded shoulders, or were they just giving her the pleasure of the saddle?

Faith had survived her first few days now; she knew what to expect, except . . . what was she to do about Susan? The young woman had been kind at first; had spoken to her less sternly than Mrs Marryat did, and yet there was the undoubted fact that Susan had made radical alterations in her regime. Since she had been put in charge of her, Faith's pubic hair had all but vanished, though she had to admit that, once she was used to it, the feeling of cool air on her hot organ was very pleasant. Yet she had been led around like an animal with that chain attached to the nipple rings.

Faith took a perverse pride in being the centre of attention, even though she knew that the reasons were that she was on display. With her bosom thrust out by the brace and pulled out by the chain, the corset nipping in her waist and the boots encasing her legs, naked mound only added to the salacious picture she presented to the others. But there was still the problem that the constriction of the leather excited her, as well as the pressures of the spankings and strappings. She relished the effect she had when displayed to the others, though she knew it was the perverse sense of being humiliated in that way. Sighing her bewilderment at the new experiences, Faith fell asleep.

The following morning when Susan awakened her, Faith lay rigid for a few terrifying moments, unaware of her location and having to come to terms with the change in scenery, but the sight of the young dark-haired woman prompted her usual response. She rolled on to her right side, tucked up her knees, then rolled upright, head inclined forward, her wrists automatically reaching behind to be shackled together. The rings had not been removed from her wrists or ankles during the night, so it looked as though they were permanent.

For a moment Susan seemed taken aback but when she regained possession of herself she said, 'Sit up, Faith.'

When Faith's head rose, Susan bent first to kiss her mouth, putting her hand on the young woman's back. She examined the swollen nipples critically, nodding to herself. They were quite large, very close to the optimum and, if they swelled any more, would be too big.

'Do you want to use the lavatory?' Susan asked, her tone light and friendly. Part of her success was the way in which she could remain calm and pleasant, even when subjecting her charges to physical pain.

'Yes please, Mistress,' Faith replied in an eager voice, her head lowering again to the usual position. She was a pleasure slave being trained, so it was right that she adopt the correct posture of one at all times.

'That's right,' Susan complimented her. 'Manners. Let me look at you. Are you feeling better than yesterday?'

'Yes, thank you, Mistress,' Faith answered.

'Come along, Faith. Chin up and let me look at

136

you.' Faith's head rose, her features still while the young woman looked long and intently at her. Her eyes were clear and there was a fresh tension about her. 'After breakfast,' Susan said, unfastening the chain, 'I shall take you to the mirror room but, after that, would you like to ride for an hour, Faith?'

'Yes, I'd like that; thank you, Mistress.'

'First we'll go to the mirror room and see what progress we've made. Then to the standing man. I'll introduce you to him. I think you should shower afterwards, and I'll massage you before lunch. Would you like that? I can give you a very pleasant massage.'

'Yes, thank you, Mistress.' The same even reply. Faith was coping with the new regime by being unfeeling until she had tested it out. Only when she knew what to expect would she begin to invest some emotional capital into her attitude. Already her head was again bowed, looking at the carpet in front of the door to the corridor.

'And a walk after lunch?' The young woman felt that with all the other fixtures, this was pushing the girl fast, but at least she would get some idea of her disposition. 'Do you feel up to that? The weather's improving so it should be very pleasant out-of-doors this afternoon.'

'Yes please, Mistress.'

'There! That's the day planned.'

The session in the mirror room followed the same procedure with the only variation being that Faith was asked which she wanted; spanking, caning, strapping or 'the paddle'. Not knowing what she was letting herself in for, Faith chose the last alternative as she faced the wall, her expression revealing her shock when she realised her mistake.

Susan returned from the table with a long piece of

wood resembling a canoe paddle, being about two feet long and six inches wide on the flat blade which tapered to a long round handle which could be used by both hands. The surface of the thin, flat blade was covered in black, shiny leather, looking as if it had been well used.

'Stand still!' Susan said sharply as Faith's head turned slightly towards her. Deliberately she swung the paddle, striking Faith directly on the tensed buttocks, making her yelp with the pain of it. 'Don't be such a baby!' Susan snapped. 'This is far better than the cane; it just looks worse, that's all. Now stand still! Posture!'

Chapter Eight

Faith froze in an upright position, more used to remaining still for minutes at a time, willing herself to remain silent despite the pressures on the love balls. In the darkened room on the other side of the glass, Mrs Marryat nodded her appreciation of Susan's handling of the new girl. The paddle was like the strap in many ways; it delivered a stinging blow yet produced only a reddening of the skin which vanished quickly. It taught lessons which had to be repeated over and over without undue harm to the subject.

Standing straight, Faith did her best to remain still. She suspected on a few occasions that Susan struck for no reason, but agreed with Susan that it was preferable to the cane. Susan had already given her a demonstration of the power of the cane and Faith had no desire for another. When Susan was satisfied, she brought the paddle over to her with the injunction, 'Kiss it!', waiting stern-faced while Faith reluctantly leaned forward to press her lips to the handle. 'Good.' Susan nodded. 'As your teats are the right size, I'm going to stop using the rings.' Her voice drifted into silence, watching the anxious young woman's reaction.

Faith's smile broke through her impassivity, but some quality in Susan's face or voice brought the expression of wary apprehension back again. She remained wary, knowing that the change would hardly be for the better, waiting to hear what new device would be used for her humiliation. Learning to bear humiliation was, after all, part of learning discipline.

'I have some small clamps on a chain: nipple clamps,' Susan said carefully. 'We'll try them.'

With trembling limbs, Faith waited while the young woman returned the paddle, then took two small clamps from the pocket of her dress. They looked like the business end of the clutch pencil she had bought Albert for his birthday, the one with such fine lead. He had complained about having to sharpen pencils all the time, but though he stopped complaining, he never even thanked her for it. Odd what her memory could do at times of stress.

What Faith's mind was doing was displacement activity; thinking of something other than the horror she could foresee. Without hesitation, Susan operated the clutch, pushing out the three prongs to surround the swollen, coral tissue. When it would distend no further, she released it. Instantly a shaft of pain sank through the sensitive nipple which made Faith gasp, thankful she did no worse. Faith had learned that the pain would soon turn into a warmth which would generate other, less traumatic sensations. From Susan's expression, had she cried or protested, the paddle would have returned to her stinging behind.

Without waiting, Susan fitted the other, allowing the length of fine chain between them to dangle, as it had from the rings. Another convenient bridle with which to lead Faith about; further proof the young woman was accepting the discipline.

'That looks nice, doesn't it?' Susan turned Faith towards the mirror so she could examine the result. 'You may thank me, Faith.'

'Thank you, Mistress,' Faith returned dutifully, wondering whether she was going mad. Was this the same young woman who took her into the bushes, and who rubbed their most intimate parts together? Was this the same woman who seemed to understand her suffering?

'Now, perhaps, we can get on with your training.'

Unsure of what her training was to consist of, Faith followed in trepidation on the end of the chain as Susan hurried her across the yard, where those terrible poles stood, making her shudder at the sight. No one was strung between them, though Hilary was spreading Alison across the bar, the phallus already deeply embedded in her anus and a whip protruding from her sexual organ. Passing into the 'clinic', where she had been given the enema and spanking, Faith found herself seated once again in the familiar chair.

'Do you know what this enema is for?' Susan asked. 'You're to have them every other day until your skin is clear.'

'Yes, Mistress.' Faith's head hung. There was no point in protesting for she was aware of the growing sensations in her abdomen. The nipple clamps had begun the work, but the thought of being fastened to the chair, upended, and given an enema, completed it. She felt ashamed of what was happening to her; ashamed too of her resistance to the paddle and spankings. Ashamed, if she thought about it, of enjoying the sensations they produced within her. All this shame combined to bring her face to the same red as her buttocks when at last Susan tilted back the chair.

Martha Marryat listened to the male voice on the telephone with a mixture of apprehension and eagerness. She disliked people coming to the Stables to watch the progress of their protégés. It was easy for the pupil to have a bad day and make a mockery of

141

what they were trying to achieve. Yet there was no denying that Faith was already much improved. If done carefully, it would go a long way towards establishing mutual trust.

'I should be pleased if you *would* visit us, Mr Pellew,' she said carefully. 'My only objection would be that it would upset Faith to see you. Some young ladies become tearful when family or friends see them.'

'She wouldn't have to see me, would she? I mean –' Alex hesitated '– she could be blindfolded, couldn't she?'

'She would still know someone was watching her,' Martha returned. 'But if you don't mind confining your visit to the mirror room . . ?' She paused. 'It's a bit restricted, I know, but it would be the easiest to arrange.'

'If that's it, then fine,' Alex agreed. 'When?'

'The morning after tomorrow? Early; eight o'clock. Faith is usually there with her guide at that time.'

'Yes.' Alex decided at once. 'I'll be there. Thank you, Mrs Marryat.'

As she replaced the telephone, Martha thought that it would do no harm to make sure that Susan showed Faith off to advantage. Of course, the girl had hardly begun her training, and the mirror room was ill equipped to indulge in an extensive demonstration of control, but the spanking and paddling would suffice; perhaps a caning too. Faith should be able to take all three before then. Susan would see to it she was prepared.

Cleaned up after the enema, Faith exited by the other door into a corridor from which she was led into a long narrow room. Against the far wall was a thin strip of aluminium bracket which reached from knee

142

height to the ceiling, pierced at two-inch intervals by a shaped hole into which fitments could be secured. Above her head, one such fitment supported a hook, the sight of which immediately sent a spasm of terror through Faith, who shrewdly guessed its purpose.

'This is the standing man,' Susan said calmly. 'It looks terrible, doesn't it? But in time, you'll come to love it.'

She led Faith to face the bracket. There were two cleats sunk into the wall about four feet apart at floor level, to which Faith's ankles were secured by snaps on the end of the short chains.

Susan had to push and pull the unwilling legs into position, chiding her gently. She had worked her hard the previous day, even giving her another half-hour on the saddle to compensate for the severity of the strapping in the yard.

Releasing Faith's wrists to fasten them in front of her, Susan raised them high above her until the hook engaged them, holding the lean body taut, almost flat against the bracket.

'You'll have to move away, Faith.' Susan's voice sounded silky smooth behind her as a soft hand gently pressed on her stomach, pulling her away from the wall. As Susan crouched in front of her, Faith was unable to see what she was doing, but when she rose again, the trembling began throughout her body.

Susan had fixed a large, upright leather phallus to the bracket in the wall so that it pressed against Faith's sex lips, the tautness of her body pressing them open. Yet that was not enough. She carefully took the delicate labial flesh in her hands, moulding it around the smooth, polished roundness of the leather.

'Can you feel, Miss Faith?' Susan asked. 'How your hungry little button is pressing it? I've placed it

143

high, so there's no chance of you mounting it, but you can rub yourself against it if you like. Go on; try. Up on your toes; that's it; just a little. Now down again; that's good. See? Nice, isn't it?'

Faith made no answer, for the feel of the smooth leather on her clitoris was strange. She had received no stimulation there that morning, or indeed since Hilary's fingers had brushed her button the previous afternoon. The saddle had filled her passage, but did nothing for the little pearl above it.

As she felt the delicious kiss of the leather, Susan asked, 'This *is* nice, isn't it, Miss Faith. Won't you answer? You should answer; or perhaps you want me to use the whip? We don't really want that, do we? We're good girls.'

'Yes, Mistress, it's nice.'

'Of course it is. You like that; rubbing your little honey-pot against that nice, big dildo. Does it give you pleasure? Answer.'

'Yes, Mistress,' Faith replied, her head lowering in shame. Her legs were aching already, but obedient to the orders, she kept on moving that inch or two up and down.

'Do you know what goes with pleasure, Faith?' the woman asked.

'Yes, Mistress,' Faith answered, the tears already starting in her eyes. She knew only too well, for Susan had taught her well.

'What?' the gentle voice cooed in her ear, pleased with the reaction.

'Pain, Mistress.'

'Pain, yes. But there *is* no pain, is there? So we shall have to add some, won't we? We shall have to spank you. The only question is, with a hand or the strap?' Susan paused, waiting.

It mattered little to her which Faith chose, for if

Faith chose the hand, her training would take a few days longer. If Faith wanted to start with a spanking, then she would deliver a severe spanking on those taut buttocks which were already losing the marks of the paddling. If, on the other hand, Faith chose the strap, it would be a breakthrough; an indication that Faith was beginning to learn something about discipline. And herself.

It had been Susan's experience that the young women who claimed loudest to abhor being hurt were the ones who, in the end, embraced it most fervently. She herself was a case in point. Her own experience fitted her very well for teaching discipline to these pampered young women, imposing some order on their lives.

'S-s-s-strap, please, Mistress,' Faith breathed raggedly.

'Clever girl!' Susan approved, smiling. 'The strap, of course. Because spanking with the hand is too intimate, isn't it? You can feel the balls working, can't you? And the ointment we put on the dildo last night. We'll gradually use larger dildos until you're comfortably able to take a man in your bottom, as you did at your initiation. But you'll have to keep your bottom oiled, in case someone wants it. You're Chosen, so you must be able to satisfy anyone's wants.'

'Yes, Mistress.' Faith was hardly aware of what Susan said. She had known the familiar sexual ache between her thighs since awakening, but to be first paddled, and now strapped; how could she endure it? How could she be so calm about the thrilling prospect of being held straight and strapped?

'We'll talk about it later on our walk,' Susan said. 'For now, I have to strap you only a very little. You're having so much pleasure there that a little pain would hardly be noticed, would it?'

For almost twenty seconds she waited for any kind of answer, then asked, 'Miss Faith? Would you notice if I used the strap?' Her quiet, confiding voice reminded Faith of the vicar who had comforted her mother after her father's death.

'N-n-n-no, Mistress.' Faith suspected that should she answer 'yes', then Susan would deliver a spanking that would hurt for hours. To avoid that, Faith was willing to compromise. By volunteering for the strap she hoped to avoid a worse punishment.

'Good,' Susan cooed. 'But it won't last long. I'll only strap you until you come. While I do, move your little button up and down, yes? The sooner you come on that lovely leather, the sooner I'll stop. Do you understand, Miss Faith?'

'Yes.' Faith felt a gleam of hope. She had been working herself off on the leather for some minutes, rocking her hips gently, and could feel the orgasm building up. If she could hurry it along, then she would only get a few of that terrible strap.

'Good,' Susan said as she stepped away. 'I'll start.'

Susan had noticed the movement of Faith's hips as she had spoken and understood what was passing through her mind. She had been introduced to the standing man in the same way and could remember the delicious feeling of besting her instructress, thinking the sadistic woman would be upset she had come too soon. As she now appreciated, the woman had been as glad that she had reached her orgasm quickly as she hoped Faith would. It would make subsequent visits much easier to handle, especially when she began to use the whip.

'One!' she called, swinging the strap hard.

The strap was a thick, yet pliable one (Martha reserved the thin straps for *very* special occasions which required severe discipline), cracking against Faith's

146

still reddened buttocks, driving her on to the leather, where her clitoris felt as though it was exploding, pressed tight between the opposing pressures. Faith opened her mouth to cry out in pain as the sudden heat surged through her, drowning the flaring pain in a tidal wave of pleasure.

Susan had timed her single stroke well. Any blow would have produced the same effect. The erupting cry as Faith's pleasure was delivered brought forth another, as she realised that one stroke of the strap was all she would get. The twin reliefs brought a smile to her features, thinking that she had outwitted this otherwise knowledgeable young woman.

But a shock of knowledge ran through her. One of the strap! One was all it had taken to bring her to orgasm. The relief which pounded through Faith's mind held elements of wonder and relief at the lightness of her penalty, yet deep within was the truly dreadful thought that she was obtaining sexual release through the pain. The strap was less of an evil than she had ever imagined.

Susan smiled to herself, thinking it was lucky she struck when she did, otherwise Faith may have climaxed before the strap touched her, invalidating the whole point of the exercise. She consoled herself with the thought that within a few days Faith would be impaled on the leather cock, writhing in pleasure as she used her vaginal muscles to work her orgasm while she was steadily strapped. It was a stage she should have reached days before, but better now than never. It was time, though, to comfort her.

'There; that wasn't so bad, was it? Just one? I wish I could get *my* orgasm that quickly; you must be quite practised. Do you want to rest or ride?'

'I should like to ride, please, Mistress.' Faith could feel the sweet stinging in her buttocks as Susan unfastened her wrists from the hook, refastening them behind her. It had been a lot better than anticipated and, after the number of times she'd had the strap across her backside, one stroke was never going to make much of a difference.

There had been times when she had felt the hot flesh of her backside, wondering why there were no raised weals and no stiffness when she moved the following day. Even though she had been shown her own reflection after the strapping in the yard, she had hardly dared believe it. When she felt more confident, she would ask, but for now, she was learning what she could.

This new experience had set her mind whirling again as she thought about the paradox. Her pleasure would have been delivered anyway, Faith knew that, but the pain of the single blow had intensified it somehow. Jamming her clitoris against the leather had helped, of course, but to Faith's mind, it was the strap which had done the work. Why?

Faith rode the saddle, uncaring that Susan stood alongside her, watching her abandonment in the pleasure it provided. Already, Jackson had reduced the size of the dildo to make Faith use her muscles to maintain her balance. Knee pressure and the use of her vaginal muscles were the only supports against the swaying movement, which had also been increased.

She was shining with sweat as she was helped down, her expression delirious for a few moments as Susan checked the position of the balls in her body. It was already difficult to push them home, so her passage was tightening. Soon they would have to reduce the size of her balls and perhaps increase the number. Susan knew the advantage of Faith being kept aroused at all times; it was her refuge from the harsh reality around her.

After a quick shower, Susan returned her to the room in which the enema had been given, where a couch now replaced the chair against the bar. Her wrists were first released then fastened to the sides of the couch at her head, while the chain at her throat was fastened there too, giving her very limited movement.

'There.' Susan smiled when she was satisfied that Faith was secured. 'Time I massaged you. In a bath-house in Japan, I'd be called a "*yuna*" and be wearing a tiny costume which showed almost everything I had. Can you imagine that?'

'No, Mistress,' Faith replied quietly. She actually thought that beneath the plain white dress the woman wore, she had quite a good figure, but her clothes gave no indication of it.

One after the other, her wrists were released from the couch, feeling odd after being imprisoned for so long, but there was no other way to remove the plate from her spine. Lying out naked on the flat leather couch, secured again, Faith was massaged by Susan's experienced hands. It was done lightly, but oil was introduced into her anus, being massaged well in by her long, strong fingers.

Lunch followed the same routine, Faith remaining in her room afterwards, then obediently donning her corset, stockings and boots to precede Susan through the woods. When they were well away from the Stables, Susan drew alongside her, asking, 'You said you knew something about the Chosen, Miss Faith. Is that true, or were you just teasing?'

The younger woman shook her head, 'I don't know much; not that much anyway. The Chosen. Odd name, isn't it? Chosen by whom?' she mused. 'For what?'

Faith thought Alex and the others had been very

careful in their choice of words about the Chosen. It was as though they were retailing a standard line; an innocuous, glib description which described nothing, or very little.

'For . . . service,' Susan said carefully. 'That describes it best.'

'Slaves,' Faith answered with grim finality. 'Pleasure slaves. Bound to obedience to their masters; to provide whatever sexual favours they require.'

'Yes.' Susan nodded. 'In a way; though not the slavery you think. If you want to split hairs and call it slavery, then I can understand. I suppose it must seem like slavery to you; coming new to it, so to speak.'

'If it's not slavery,' Faith asked, 'then what is it? What is this place if not a slave-training school?'

'Young men and women, often from excellent families, some with dangerous propensities, are sent here for training; in obedience, mainly, like yourself. In discipline and obedience first, because later they're trained in pleasure. Once you accept the pain and pleasure here, you're ready for the more refined, more advanced, pleasures, later.'

'More advanced . . .?' Faith stopped, her mind whirling.

Those were Alex's very words when he was first telling her about the party. That she might find it very advanced. Was that the purpose of the Chosen? Was he trying to make her a whore?

'Are . . . are all the others . . . volunteers?' she asked, provoking a sudden laugh from the woman at her side.

'No!' Susan gave vent to a derisive reply. 'Only a few and, oddly enough, they're not the best. The best are the . . . the wild ones; the difficult ones, if you like. They have an individuality the others lack; people like yourself. I'd rather have three or four like you, darling, than a dozen others. I know where I am with you.'

'Are . . . are they . . . treated like . . . whores?' Faith asked, ignoring what she took to be flattery.

'Whores?' Susan stopped, and when she came to the end of the slack of the chain, so did Faith, almost pulled off balance. 'What made you ask that?'

They looked at each other across the warm path, flies and bees filling the air with the sound of their vibrating wings while, further off, some birds chirped joyfully to the sky. Yet the air was cold between the two of them.

'I wondered whether I was being trained as a whore,' Faith answered. 'Bent over that bar and strapped like that; getting on that saddle every day; rubbing myself on that leather cock this morning.'

'Miss Faith,' Susan sighed, shaking her head and smiling. 'You will *mount* that cock eventually. You'll strain against the strap so it'll slip inside you; and later, you'll be mounted directly on it, with your feet dangling free. You may howl as I strap your behind, but you'll want it; you'll run to that room within the next few weeks. Do you understand what I'm saying?' Her expression was anxious.

'No!' What little colour Faith had fled at the description. It sounded a nightmarish regime.

'Later, I'm going to use a slightly different strap on your breasts, on your vulva and your anus. All of them will tingle, I can promise you, and you'll beg me not to stop. Does *that* sound as though I'm training you to be a whore?'

'Then what *are* you training me for?' Faith's lip trembled. The thought of having a strap applied to her more delicate, more intimate parts seemed too horrible to contemplate.

'I told you: service. When you leave here, you'll be further trained in pleasure. I don't know who'll do it; probably your master. It's his job to train his own pleasure slaves and anyone who makes a bad job of it in the Chosen risks their reputation. My job . . . *our* job, is to prepare you.'

'Slavery!' Faith gasped. 'Sexual slavery.'

'If you like to call it that, then do. It isn't. I believe that where you will go when you leave here, there is at least one young woman related to your sponsor. Do you think they'd pass their own flesh and blood into slavery? No, that's ridiculous. But your training will be in sex: sex, pleasure and pain. You'll learn them all so that when you marry – and you *will*, believe me – you'll provide an excellent sexual relationship with your husband. Your husband may even be your master, or your "sponsor".

'The important thing to remember is that pain, like pleasure, is transitory. It hurts, yes. I've experienced far more of it than you ever will, but it can be borne; even enjoyed. But just enduring pain isn't a measure of your training or your ability. Anyone can, if they put their mind to it. What sets people apart, what makes them truly trained, is the manner in which they endure it – a stubborn acceptance isn't enough.

'To start with, we fasten you to teach you about pain, but gradually, the bonds are removed until you accept the whip without them. You go to the place of punishment and eagerly accept the whipping; you already understand the importance of not crying out. I admire that. It's a lesson not everyone learns, but you have a predisposition towards that side of things as you must already know.

'When you leave here, if your master tells you to prepare for a whipping, you don't break down in tears or flee; you go to where he directs and you wait for him. You accept what is to happen.' Susan paused, nodding for a moment as their eyes met. 'And ... in an odd way, it elevates you above your master.' Her voice was hushed almost to a whisper. 'Because you're able to do what he may not. You saw Paul being tested; how he struggled when he was fastened. Not you.'

'But he'd ...' Faith stopped, her head dropping again as she remembered the scene.

' "Mad Martha" made him accept the phallus to remind him there is pleasure to be had, even there. A phallus is an impersonal thing; cold and sexless, but effective. The purpose was to shame him because his penis became erect and stayed that way by providing manual stimulation of his prostate gland.

'Paul still finds it difficult to accept being buggered by a phallus *and enjoying* it. That humiliated Paul in his own eyes far more than anything else would have done. He likes being buggered, you see? "Mad Martha" forced it into him without him accepting it; shaming him *to* himself. Paul learned the lesson of obedience.'

'How did you learn all this?' Faith gulped, forgetting to add the obligatory 'Mistress' – but there was a look in Susan's eye which suggested this was one time she would not be too severe.

'Because I *was* a whore,' Susan said before she fell silent.

Susan led the way to the concealment of the shrubbery in the stiff silence that fell between them, helping Faith to lie on thick, dry grass, then rolled Faith on to her front. The shorter, dark-haired young woman idly drew her fingers lightly over Faith's buttocks. The traces of the paddling were vanishing and the single broad mark of the strap was already fading from the skin, if not from Faith's memory. Her agile fingers quickly found the sensitive crease between the bouncy globes, and Faith spread her legs wider to admit the fingers into her hot, moist depths.

For some moments she hesitated, sighing as she looked at the glowing pink skin in front of her, then began, 'I'm from Essex; Colchester, actually. I don't come from a privileged background. This accent isn't mine really. I went "on the game" as an amateur when I was about fourteen or so.' Susan paused, then shrugged. 'Local boys, you know the sort of thing. When I left school I didn't have many qualifications, but London was the only place to work, so I went there. Pretty soon I found that fucking was the only thing that paid well enough to keep me the way I wanted.

'But it's a dangerous business. There's pimps who want forty and fifty per cent of the "take" – more if they can get it – and they know if they threaten to slash your face apart, you'll give it to them.' Susan stopped again, shuddering. 'Then there's the "clap", and AIDS. I was lucky, in a way. Just when I thought I'd have to find something else to do, a client made me a proposition. He didn't want straight sex, he wanted me to use a belt on him. Really spank him.

'I'd heard about blokes like him, of course; who hasn't? But he was genuine and he liked what I did, so he told his friends. Pretty soon, I had more clients than I could handle, and I avoided AIDS too – but I had limitations. I knew how to use a strap or a riding crop on their cocks and I could flay the skin off their backs if that's what they wanted, but I didn't know *myself*, do you see?'

She looked down at the gasping, fish-like young woman who, under the manual and aural stimulus, was already well into her orgasm. Susan mercilessly drove her thumb into the sensitive spot on the inside of Faith's thighs, cutting off the supply of lust as though turning off a tap. Shocked, Faith lay recovering, licking her lips as she concentrated on the sensation of the fingers which had never left her body, while Susan continued.

'One of my clients told me about this place, and I managed to arrange an interview with "Mad Martha". At first, I thought she was just a crazy fool who liked whipping people. She showed me around, showed me what they did, then suggested I try it out. I thought, What the hell, and she told me to strip, so I did.

'She chained me to that couch in the "clinic" with my legs hanging off one end, then raised it until it was about five feet off the floor. Then she got a very thin cane and started using it on me, vertically, crossing my backside from one side to the other. Of course, going that way, I took several directly on my fanny, and if you've never known the lovely pain you get, you *will*, I promise you. It's a real treat.

'Before I knew what I was doing, I was begging her to fuck me, do anything. All I wanted was release from the desire, and the pain.' Susan stopped, withdrawing her fingers while Faith turned her head, sorry at the loss but intrigued at the story.

'What happened?' she asked.

'She didn't, of course,' Susan answered. 'She told me that if I wanted to learn more about it – and myself – I should agree to come for training. Told me how much she charged, too. I could afford it and I knew I wanted more of what she'd dished out, so I agreed.

'I went back to town, closed up my flat and my "business premises", then came down here with a suitcase, thinking like a fool that I'd need clothes. That was over a year ago and I've never regretted not going back. "Mad Martha" taught me more about myself than I ever thought possible, and I like it. One day, perhaps, I'll go back to London, but not as a whore – not in the strict sense of the word, anyway. But I've been rewarded here; as you will be. Probably more rewarded than I ever was.'

'What?' Faith asked, frowning at the older woman in complete astonishment.

'Trust me, Faith.' Susan looked at her with a mixture of command and pleading, willing the younger woman to comply.

'What would you say if I did?' Faith asked, fearful and yet thrilled at the same time. Surrendering control like that was a dangerous step.

'I'd say –' Susan paused, then smiled '– I'd bring your orgasm on again, strip off and enjoy you the way I know you like. Then on our walk back to the house, I would have you bend over so I could test you. I'd smack your bottom with my bare hand, or use a switch; perhaps I'd come to your room, later tonight, undress and put you across my knees and smack you then. Would you like that?' There was a lascivious insinuation in her tone.

'Why?' Faith asked, shaking at the very thought of a smacking under such circumstances.

'Because, as I think you understand now, smacking with the bare hand is more intimate. Putting you over my knee – especially on your own bed – with both of us naked, would make it more intimate still. I know from your notes that you enjoy sexual relations with women. That's nothing to be ashamed of, Faith,' Susan said quickly as the younger woman blushed. 'And I would love you. I'd do all that, then place the dildo in your bottom again, and leave.'

'Would you unfasten me?' Faith gestured with her wrists.

'No.' Susan shook her head. 'You'd be pleasured with your "jewellery" in place. I can't remove that even though I'd like you totally naked. When you move on, you may lose them; some don't. You –' She paused, sighing and shaking her head. 'It's difficult to say. If I was your lord and master, I'd keep you in chains until your dying day.'

'Why?' Faith gasped, impressed, despite herself, with the utter honesty of the woman and thrilled by the prospect of being kept semi-permanently secured.

'Because you look beautiful in them,' she answered.

'Chained? Beaten?' Faith's shock was profound. 'Is that all the future I have?'

'Don't think like that, Faith.' Susan covered Faith's mouth with her hand. 'I love you.' Then she began again the manipulation of Faith's vulva.

Chapter Nine

Having both reached a climax as Susan rode Faith as
before, Susan donned her dress then helped Faith to
her feet, retracing their steps to the path in silence.
There was something strained between them, as
though the subject they discussed had been greater
than either could comprehend. Abruptly, Susan began speaking in an absent tone, as if to herself, yet
clearly taking up the conversation from where their
sexual relationship had interrupted it.

'You're an intelligent woman, Faith. Some, like
Jacqui and Amanda, always fight against the whip;
against the restraints; they see them as degrading.
They can't see that if someone has taken the time and
trouble to do this – to care for them in this way –
then they must be worth something. The discomfort
passes in time; it can even be useful. You know that
bending over the bar and being strapped only makes
your sexual desires greater. You should see the men.
Paul, for example. Five or six with the strap and he
has an erection that looks as though it'll explode.'

'You . . . you do this to *them*?' Faith gasped.

'We do this to those who are sent,' Susan answered
firmly, starting to move again. 'We don't pick and
choose. Men, unfortunately, always take longer.'

'Why? Why should –'

'Pride. You're like a man in many ways, Faith.
Your pride won't let you surrender yourself to obedi-

ence; you only obey what you understand, instead of obeying what you're told. You don't trust us and your pride won't let you succumb.'

'You want to destroy my pride?'

'No!' Susan shook her head quickly. 'Not destroy it; that would be ... terrible, a crime. A crime against humanity, even. I don't even want to humble your pride for I'd abase you in your own eyes. That's worse still.'

'What then?'

'What I'm trying ... what *we're* trying to do, is teach you to control it. Keep it, by all means; use it, but surrender yourself to obedience too.'

'And what is this ... obedience?' Faith could hardly take her sarcasm from her voice.

'Service. Service to others; service to yourself. Keep your emotions under control.'

'What's the point?' Faith asked, curious as to why Susan should divulge such detailed knowledge. There had to be a reason, for this confiding manner was totally different from how she had previously known her.

'The point is, you're a very proud young woman. You feel you have ... worth; a position, of sorts; a place in the hierarchy of society, yes?'

'A lowly place but ... yes, we all have a place,' Faith answered.

The woman smiled, nodding her acknowledgement. 'Your worth ... your "place" ... is dependent upon others, not yourself. You could be as clever as Einstein but if you were disliked and despised you'd get nowhere. Obedience means a willingness to learn. When you went to school and university, you entered a new world with strange customs, where new girls had little worth. You had to learn the ropes. Obedience.'

'But I knew the rules,' Faith protested.

'You know the rules here. Obey.'

'Obey or be punished!' Faith protested.

'Those are the rules *outside*,' Susan said with a smile. 'Here we say "obey *and* be punished".'

'Why though?'

'Punishment isn't something terrible, as you've discovered. Fear it, but mix it with pleasure too. Today you were spanked against the cock, and tomorrow you'll be spanked there again. There'll be other delights until you regard it for what it is; nothing more than a test of your willingness to obey. Once you have learned that, you can proceed to learning about pleasure. *Real* pleasure.'

They reached the fallen tree where Faith had bent over to be punished with the wand. To Faith, in the state of peace within herself, it was all just countryside, until Susan pointed to the fallen log.

'Abase yourself over that, while I fetch a wand. Spread your legs out wide, because I shall want to see the fluid run from your love-lips as I mark your buttocks.'

Without waiting to hear her answer, Susan turned to walk back the way they had come, searching for a plant to provide a suitable instrument. She found one about 40 yards along the path, stopping to break it off and shredding the leaves to provide a serviceable switch. Faith watched her go in silence for a few moments, thinking about what she had said. When the dark-eyed dominatrix returned, Faith was leaning over the rough bark of the tree, her eyes on the ground on the other side. The toes of her boots were pressed to the soft earth about four-and-a-half feet apart, the tension in the soft skin of her thighs visible above the top of the boots.

'Very good, darling.' The woman nodded. 'You're

learning to accept. One!' Susan brought the wand down across the centre of her buttocks, marking them immediately.

Faith jerked and yelped as the stinging seared her skin. By the fifth, tears were flowing, but Susan continued to twenty, leaving a series of parallel lines across her buttocks. She would have cried out, but was only too aware that her pain was being subsumed in the rising desire, unslaked despite Susan's earlier ministrations. Susan was right about her desires, Faith thought. The stinging heat of the switch was arousing her again.

When it was over, and the mucus flowed down each thigh, Susan reached over to Faith, pulling her gently to her feet, a smile of pride on her face.

'My darling, you were magnificent. I only wish Mad Martha had been here to see it; or Clive. Never mind; next time, he will. You've no idea how humiliated you'll feel when you spread your legs wide in that position with him looking at you, and you know by now how thrilling that can be, I'm sure. Up to now he's always stood in front of you, but he'll stand behind now and, like me, admire your charms.'

'What?' Faith turned towards her, eyes widening from the pain and desire.

'You'll only be abasing yourself to obedience, my darling. Besides, don't tell me that you don't get a thrill out of being humiliated.' Susan looked at the shock in Faith's eyes at her knowledge. 'Don't worry. You'll want him behind you; you'll even plead with him to satisfy you.' She nodded sadly. 'Yes, you will. You'll feel so passionate. Now –' Susan wiped the tears from Faith's face and kissed her mouth softly '– we should get back. Mad Martha'll be pleased to hear how well you obeyed.'

After dinner, taken as usual in her room, the rings

were replaced and the dildo – the one previously used – emplaced without the least quibble. Faith was not to know that Susan put more aphrodisiac ointment on it this time. Once done and between the sheets, Faith's eyes closed on the world and she was asleep within moments.

Saturday morning began early for Alex. He was up before dawn, driving down the M23 towards the Stables and fighting for space on the road with workers heading for Gatwick and Crawley and tourists trying to leave the country on charter flights to the Mediterranean. Off the main road, using more gentle country byways, he was happier, though his progress slowed to a crawl at times.

Martha was waiting when he pulled up at the front of the house, travelling slowly to avoid disturbing any of the household unaware of his arrival. Since most of them had been up for almost an hour, it was a useless precaution. She escorted him upstairs to the door to the small room which most pupils thought was a locked cupboard, making sure no one noticed his arrival.

Though the house hummed with activity and a certain amount of noise, there was an orderly pattern to it. Faith was being bathed by Susan while other pupils received similar attention by their personal attendants. Though Martha despaired of finding adequate staff, she managed to maintain the important one-to-one relationships pretty well. Occasionally, two instructors would work on one pupil while the other pupil kicked his or her heels, but this was avoided if possible.

Sitting in the darkened room waiting for Faith's arrival, Alex appreciated the excellent coffee which Martha brought, and when she showed no signs of wanting to leave, asked, 'How *are* things with her? When will she be ready to leave?'

'It's difficult to predict,' the woman said. She took the only other seat. 'Some learn quickly to begin with and tail off later, while others are slow starters and catch up. Some proceed at their own steady pace. I have to say I've known only a few with whom I was satisfied in under eight weeks.'

'Middle of July.' He frowned in the darkness, nodding. There was a certain amount of light coming from the other side of the glass screen separating the rooms, but insufficient for either to see the other's expression.

'Anything less would, in my experience, leave certain areas ... incomplete.' Mrs Marryat tried to be helpful and polite for Alex had supplied her with a number of pupils and had recommended more to her.

'I'm not making a criticism,' Alex returned quickly. 'Just trying to get some idea of the timescale. Two months; I see. That would give me time to make suitable arrangements. Less or more and I would make different ones, that's all. How is she otherwise? Content?'

'Faith has settled at last. Being an intelligent young woman made it ... difficult, to start with. She took nothing on trust. You'll see the result, though. I think you'll be pleased.'

Quarter of an hour later, the door from the corridor opened in the larger mirror room and the lights were snapped on as the white-dressed Susan led Faith inside, startling Alex with the changes he saw in her. She seemed to stand taller – certainly straighter – because of the brace. The corset nipping her waist had been tightened since her arrival. His interest rose at the sight of her oiled, naked crotch, looking defenceless framed beneath the solid leather of the corset and suspenders.

Yet it was the sight of Faith being led in by her nipples which provoked the most surprise. Martha, realising she had said nothing about them, quickly explained. 'Her teats are the right size now, so we're using nipple clamps attached to that chain. With those long boots and the other appurtenances, it makes her look quite delightful, doesn't it?'

'Yes.' He looked thoughtful.

Though the two occupants of the mirror room could see and hear nothing of Martha and her visitor, a microphone relayed the sounds from the mirror room to the waiting pair as Susan led Faith to where Susan had placed a high stool. Seating herself, Susan said, 'Lay across my lap. Spread your legs wide.'

That morning, Susan had been told by Martha that in the mirror room she should run through several disciplines with Faith, and she would try to look in on her. She wanted to see whether the girl was, at the end of the first week, becoming as good as Susan claimed. From where he sat, Alex had an excellent view of Faith's exposed genitals, and of Susan's hand as she began to smack the exposed buttocks.

There was no rushing Susan; she used a smooth, tireless action, and apart from the gasps and cries of pleasure from Faith, the cracks of skin on skin were the only sounds in the mirror room. After several minutes, during which time Faith's tears flowed only slightly more copiously than her musk, Susan told her to rise, then to lie on her stomach on the top of the stool.

While Alex watched, his features impassive, Susan began first with the paddle, then the strap, adding further layers of pained, rosy heat to the inflamed tissue. Faith's cries grew louder, but containing the lurking hoarseness which everyone listening, including Faith herself, recognised as desire.

Finally Susan told her to remain still while she fetched the cane and, like the other implements, had Faith kiss it before telling her, 'Six this morning, and I don't want to hear a sound. You've been good up to now, but one sound and I'll give you another six.'

'Please, Mistress.' Faith spoke for the first time. 'Please use the cane.' She felt she needed the pain to suppress the internal longing.

The six strokes were delivered in a slow, almost lazy fashion, each reaching the selected target; six evenly separated lines across the hot, inflamed buttocks facing Alex. Faith gasped a few times, and he saw the reflection of her pained grimaces, but she swallowed the cries in her throat before they emerged.

Susan helped Faith to vertical again. 'We should start with the standing man,' she said, looking indulgently at the taller female. 'But you've been so good, Miss Faith, I think you should have the saddle first. Would you like that?'

'Yes, Mistress,' Faith answered tightly, willing herself to remain civil and controlled, when her whole being cried out in protest. 'Thank you.'

'Come,' Susan said. Picking up the chain and pulling Faith's nipples painfully out, she led her from the room.

Alex sagged back in the chair when they had gone, silent for a moment before asking, 'Who's that young woman? She seems quite good.'

'Yes,' Martha agreed with a smug expression. 'She's a former pupil who stayed on; some do. Faith is her sole responsibility. As you can see, she's benefited from it.'

'Yes,' Alex agreed, rising abruptly. 'She has. Thank you. Middle of July, you said?'

The woman knew no answer was expected, waiting quietly while he turned over the matters on his mind.

He had to juggle things around, both at home and with Max and Lillian. Lillian Brampton, his pleasure slave, former lover and Faith's friend, should be given to Max before Faith returned; which meant he could attend to Helen's needs too. Were her mother and aunt available?

'Shall we carry on, or do you wish –' Mrs Marryat turned as the door from the corridor opened again, admitting Hilary and Amanda, the latter naked save for a black leather brassière which tightened the flesh of her breasts towards the centre, making them appear shiny and swollen, with huge nipples. Taking the opportunity, and turning off the sound, Martha asked, 'Would you want Faith restricted in one of those? They're exquisitely painful, and it would look well with that corset.'

'No.' Alex shook his head at once. 'Inflicting pain to serve a purpose is one thing. If it's to discipline her, then yes. But not just as a matter of course.'

'She would come to love it,' Mrs Marryat suggested, then seeing his jawline harden as he watched Hilary prepare the blonde with the mass of hair for a strapping, added, 'but you're right, of course. If she isn't going to learn anything from it, why bother?' Alex returned to town happier in his own mind now that he had seen Faith disciplined. She looked as though she would train beautifully, too. How could he persuade his family to accept her?

By the end of the second week, Faith was still reserved; lowering her head or her eyes, looking only briefly at anyone who spoke to her and answering quietly and politely, even when it was one of the other pupils.

Susan was trying to break Faith of the habit of thinking about the world outside, knowing such behaviour hindered rather than helped pupils. If they thought the Stables was not the centre of their world, then mental friction arose. They had to put everything out of their minds other than the need to be alert at all times and to obey instantly.

Faith accepted the few changes in the routine without comment. Changes such as the substitution of three smaller '*rin no tama*', for the two '*hari go*' previously used. These had been known for centuries in China as 'Burmese bells' and were originally reputed to have contained the saliva of a mythical Burmese bird, also claimed to be an aphrodisiac with a low boiling point. So low, in fact, that they were supposed to boil even when held in the hand; when they would emit a soft, ringing sound.

They were, in fact, small silver balls containing either mercury or a small piece of copper and, like the '*hari go*' with which she was familiar, were free to move, providing stimulation to the user within the cervix. They were also left in place during intercourse for, being smaller and lighter, they added pleasure to the master when the tip of his erection came into contact with them.

One morning, when led to the standing man, Susan deliberately lowered it a couple of inches before fastening Faith's feet to the snaps and her wrists to the hook above her. She was equally careful to open Faith's lips around the tip of the polished leather, smoothing and stroking them into position. The young woman was taking twenty or thirty strokes before she climaxed, so it was time to change the rules again.

Faith watched in horrified awe, knowing what was intended. Susan intended her to rise up on her toes, push forward and allow herself to sheath the monster within her. This phallus was a flattened cylinder of

167

almost six inches circumference – about the thickness of her wrist – and the sight filled her with thin rivulets of fear and eager anticipation. As she looked down at the light brown sheen of her lower abdomen, her old apprehensions rose again like ghosts. Without warning, the strap cracked against her buttocks, a slight upswing delivered to the underhang, in the soft flesh where the thighs met the buttock.

Deliberating in the peace of her bed, Faith had come to terms with the strap and paddle. She appreciated the point made by both Martha and Susan, that although they brought her buttocks up in a rosy glow, there were never any marks and the stinging was usually gone by morning. The realisation had made her reconsider the pain, but this sudden assault startled her and made her jump upward and forward in an effort to escape.

Before she knew what had happened, the end of the phallus was embedded deeply within her. Faith's toes were barely touching the floor, though as she slid down on the smooth leather she gained purchase and some measure of relief now that the initial move had been made.

The sexual aching deep inside, from which she never seemed to be free these days, made her groan with delight as she felt herself envelop the smooth thickness of the polished leather. Her gasp of satisfaction was drowned in the second stroke cracking on to her behind, but such was her desire that she hardly felt it. Something within her had exploded and her breasts were still glowing from the thrashing Susan had given them the previous afternoon with a small, suede strap.

Faith had been bound to, but facing away from, one of the posts in the yard, her wrists above her head, body stretched as usual, taut as a bowstring.

Once she was satisfied with the arrangements, Susan had produced the thin, broad, suede strap, drawing it slowly through her fingers, allowing Faith plenty of time to see its pliant strength as she explained, 'Your pride is still strong, Faith. You believe yourself to be beautiful, and you are. You have a wonderful figure, one many would envy; lovely breasts with gorgeous teats. Yes, those delicious teats. How proud they are, don't you agree?'

'No.' Faith had half-suspected what would happen when she was fastened in this way after being massaged.

'Disobedience; lying *and* not addressing me properly.' Susan pouted, tutting softly. 'That will mean more punishment, not less.'

Before Faith could change her mind about her answer, Susan drew the strap sharply across her right breast, just above the nipple, making Faith cry out in pain and surprise.

'Hush!' the woman said in a surprised tone. 'Why are you crying when all I've done is stroke you? There's worse to come, believe me; far worse. I'll tell you when you can cry. Now, shush! Not another sound until I tell you. Do you understand?' Her eyes bored into Faith's own. Despite herself, Faith clamped her lips together, nodding desperately. She knew that she would be unable to comply, that she *would* cry out. And so it proved. The suede strap was whipped across both breasts, each square inch of skin being leathered, flushed and rosy with the blood brought to the surface. The nipples, already sensitive from the rings and clamps, came in for particular attention, blood suffusing them until they too swelled, like the remainder of her breasts.

Occasionally Susan would stop, feeling them as though they were tomatoes and pinching the nipples to make Faith wince with the different pain. Yet through that pain there was a deep glow of pleasure which, to her surprise and self-disgust, Faith was beginning to recognise. It was more apparent when her buttocks were abused, for however she denied it, the pain was directly related to her sex organs. But there was a component of it in her breasts. Faith felt herself half-fainting with the sheer pleasure. When it was over, Susan soothed the nipples with her mouth, laving moisture on them while Faith thought they were large enough to fill the whole inside of her mouth.

Now with the residual stinging from her previously ignored bosom adding to the pleasures of her abdomen, Faith felt her control slipping. She was able to use her toes to spring herself up and down on the phallus by pushing on the floor, working with frantic speed on her orgasm.

'That's no use, Faith,' Susan said in a pause in the strapping. 'Vaginal contact for orgasm is almost worthless. Remind me to tell you about it sometime.' She then began again to ply the strap.

Faith eventually cried her release to the wall as the elemental force within her moved again, releasing the pent-up fury of her sexuality. Behind her, Susan brushed away a tear at the sight and sound. Faith was making progress. Tomorrow, the phallus would be raised a foot while there would be blocks for Faith to stand on to impale herself, her wrists securely fastened behind her. Once in position, the blocks would be removed, leaving her suspended on that single point of contact. She would then have to use her vaginal muscles as her feet would clear the floor.

Much as she hated it, Susan thought Faith would have to take between twenty and thirty strokes before she achieved her release. But it was vital that Faith learn this skill of milking a phallus to achieve both her own release and that of the man wedged within her. This was merely obedience, and when Faith showed a willingness to endure it, they would pass on to other things.

By the end of May, after the departure of Alison and the arrival of a new girl, who spent her first week screaming that she was Lord Pratman's daughter and they would all pay for treating her like this, the routine varied again. Every other day she was placed in the yard to have her breasts lashed with the suede strap, her high keening whimpers of pleasure her only response.

To Faith's surprise and Susan's pleasure, Faith was crying out less in pain than in lust. Instead of fastening both her hands above her on the same pole, Susan now spread her between the two large ones, stroking the back of her hand up and down her growing fleece as she worked.

Where before Faith had twisted and struggled to ameliorate the blows, now her mind was diverted to her seeping sex, which felt as though it was on fire. The dildo was no longer inserted, for she had shown her ability to accept a large, thick one without discomfort. A suppository now administered the drug which aroused her. Faith was beginning to acquiesce to the strictures of the Stables; immersing herself in the pain and using it to protect herself.

Paul too had improved, yet there were times when he was missing, and others – usually every few days – when Faith would be present to witness him being further tested with the phallus and strap. Faith wondered why it was, unless Susan was telling the truth that he enjoyed it, but he would never consent to having the phallus inserted. Martha Marryat always had to force it in, leaving him limp over the bar, his head

171

hanging before the testing began. Faith found she could line up with the others to watch the performance with similar impassivity, looking across to where Gerald stood. There were times when she caught sight of Roger's expression when the phallus penetrated Paul; the longing in his features came as a revelation.

Susan carefully shaved her pubic mound every few days, keeping it as smooth as possible, and when she was left in the yard to wait for Susan, or after the standing man, Faith found she had no inhibitions about adopting a position which allowed everyone to look at her organs. Though Roger was never in a position to do so – and, she suspected, had no interest – Gerald would walk across, a smile on his face, his fingers gently tweaking her sex lips. But Faith knew that should she show any interest in his touch, she would be spread over a bar for punishment.

The afternoon walks continued, with Faith's buttocks free to move as they would while her thighs were closely constrained, yet it produced a long, graceful gait which the length of her legs enhanced. Every morning the brace was removed from her shoulders for her shower. Slowly but surely, Faith's shoulders were regaining their proper place and with that came the other advantages to her posture.

She stood more upright, which pulled her diaphragm up and her hips forward, making her appear far more erect yet – with the new walk – more relaxed than she had previously been. Faith could feel the changes both within and without, noting the lustful looks directed towards her by Hilary.

One afternoon, as soon as they reached the centre of the secluded shrubbery, she unfastened Faith's wrists, standing slightly uphill from her. Surprised, Faith paused, trembling as she waited for the next order, yet when it came, she was more surprised than ever.

'Turn around, Faith, and unfasten the buttons of my dress.'

Trembling even more violently, Faith turned slowly, to find Susan facing uphill, away from her, presenting her back. Faith hesitated, yet Susan waited patiently, a contrast to her normal manner. Reaching round her with hesitant hands, Faith's fingers found the four buttons one after the other, resting lightly on the yielding breasts. When the bottom one by her navel was undone, Susan said, 'Remove my dress, Faith.'

More confidently, Faith took the material and slipped it from the young woman's shoulders, letting it fall to the grass around her feet. Susan turned round to face her. 'Now my panties. Take them off . . . slowly!' Susan's tone was sharp as Faith reached for them. Faith had to step back a pace as her corset refused to allow her to bend and her boots prevented her kneeling, but she managed to remove them. 'Thank you, darling.' Susan smiled at her, then helped her to the grass, where Faith automatically spread her legs to allow Susan to mount her. There seemed to be something bothering the woman, for her expression was almost pained as Faith lay beneath her, watching her closed eyes as Susan ground her clitoris against Faith's mound to obtain her release.

At first, Faith had been glad none of the men, including Jackson, had bothered about mounting her, but as the days turned to weeks and the aphrodisiac worked, she found herself dreaming of sex and, to her horror, of Jackson. She dreamt of his penis working within her, imagining the sensations again. After three weeks without normal sex, being stimulated every day by both chemical and biological means, Faith's system was priming her for another lesson.

* * *

Faith awakened earlier than usual one morning, lying back while the pearly light filled the room. She had drifted into an idle languor when she became aware that Susan was standing over her, her sharp eyes missing nothing. The covers were down around Faith's widely parted knees, her outer sex lips gaped, and from her honey-pot came the unmistakable scent of female musk. Her fingers were conveying the liquid seepings from within her up around her inflamed and slightly swollen clitoris.

She paled at once, her lips trembling as, with a scramble, she shot into her normal kneeling position, her head bent, face flushed with fear and humiliation, arms behind her, waiting for her personal Götterdämmerung. Faith expected shrieks of rage and abuse, possibly physical assault on her unprotected back, but instead Susan paused, making Faith even more nervous, wondering what unspeakable punishment was being devised.

'Sit up, Faith.' Susan temporised, clearly wanting to see what attitude her charge adopted before she made any comment. Faith complied at once, her wrists remaining crossed behind her and her behind resting on her ankles while she looked at the foot of the wall ahead.

Faith had paled considerably from her embarrassed flush and was visibly trembling.

'You were masturbating, Miss Faith,' she accused sternly.

'Yes, Mistress,' Faith answered in a quiet, hesitant voice, and as the silence continued, the tears began to plop from her eyes to dribble down her cheeks, though without any sobs.

'Why are you crying, Miss Faith?' Susan asked.

'Please, Mistress.' Faith swallowed heavily. 'Don't ... don't whip me. Don't put me in the cage. Please! I'll be good, I promise. I *will*! I won't do it again.'

'You're being most difficult, Miss Faith!' Susan said sharply at once. 'Masturbating, indeed! Don't we have a nice time out on the hill? Don't you ride the saddle every day? Isn't that enough for you?' But it was in vain. Faith had the twin visions of the whip and the cage in which she had hung upside down, her ankles held apart. Mrs Marryat had been explicit about what happened and had given her actual experience of it.

'Please. Don't whip me, please.' The tears were flowing even faster as a frightened Faith impressed Susan with her sincerity.

'You *shall* be punished, but not whipped,' Susan promised. 'Or put in the cage. Much as you deserve it.'

It was that which broke Faith's control. The relief in the promise that she would not have to endure the savagery of being whipped or sexually tortured in the cage brought her to sobbing.

'Come,' Susan said briskly, as she removed the chain from the housing. 'You should shower.'

Chapter Ten

At breakfast Faith's composure had returned, though she detected a stiffness in Susan's behaviour. They then progressed through the mirror room briefly before heading for the clinic. Eventually, Faith was taken to the saddle, after which, when she stepped down, sweaty as usual, Susan broached the subject which Faith had been trying to forget.

'It's time you were punished for masturbating. Are you ready?'

'Yes, Mistress,' Faith answered warily, unsure how she would be punished. She was uneasy at Susan's calm solicitousness for, when she had been on the saddle, Susan had quit the stable, obviously to make the arrangements.

Taking a long, thin leather thong from the pocket of her dress, Susan tied it to the loop at the front of her collar, making sure it would be difficult to slip. Letting the other end drop to the straw at their feet, she moved around behind Faith, instructing her in a cold, stiff, impersonal manner.

'Part your legs, Faith.' When Faith obeyed, Susan drew the thong between the smooth thighs. Rising to her feet with the leather held loosely between Faith's legs, standing behind her and speaking in a confiding tone, Susan said quietly, 'We're going for a short walk and you'll be entertained at the end of it. But, to punish you for being so disobedient as to masturbate, I'm going to do . . . this!' As she said the last word, very harshly in Faith's ear, she pulled the thong sharply upward between Faith's buttocks.

Faith gave a gasp as the leather thong was snapped against her clitoris, lifting her on to her toes. The thong caught between Faith's buttocks while Susan bent and examined its precise location. Faith had drawn her legs together, but too late; the thong led down her body from the collar, between her mobile breasts and across her abdomen, until it vanished within the fleshy folds of her naked pubic mound, pressing directly on the sensitive clitoris, whose shielding flaps of skin now failed to protect it.

Susan gently teased Faith's sex open with her fingers to check that the thong also passed between the inner lips, having to tease one out from beneath it with a fingernail, and smiling at the sound of Faith's breathing growing harsher as the juices began to flow.

Clearly satisfied that the thong was central and pressing on the delicate organs, Susan rose, looped the remainder around her hand, then lifted it gradually, allowing the pressure to build up until the young woman rose up on her toes to mitigate it.

'Ah!' Susan said in a light tone. 'Are we dancing on air, Miss Faith? Good; that's what we like to see. Now, forward, and don't stumble over your chain, otherwise this will cut more deeply into your clit. Up on your toes.' Susan put more pressure on the thong until Faith began to bend forward, then relaxed it again as she had found the optimum position.

Faith tiptoed out of the stable, her breath catching in tight, almost frenzied spasms as, still with bound wrists, she led the way out to the yard. Susan steered her towards the posts, where she wound the end of the thong around one, tying it off and maintaining the tension so that at no time was Faith able to get down from her toes. Her clitoris was on fire, as were her openings, for the thong's rough surfaces had rubbed against the soft flesh of her cleft. It had even rubbed the sensitive skin of her anus to provoke an itching which was maddening her. It seemed that every part of her lower abdomen was irritating her at the same time.

Their arrival brought a temporary halt to the proceedings in the yard, where Gerald was bending Juliet over the bar, smiling at their arrival. By slightly turning her head, Juliet could see Faith's predicament, made worse when Susan strung another thong through the rear loop in her collar to secure her loosely upright to the post. With the muscles in her calves beginning to tremble with the effort of supporting her weight, Faith was beginning to appreciate the full horror of what would happen.

Should her muscles relax, then she would lower herself on to the thong, cutting directly into the soft flesh. If she stayed on her toes, then her ankles and calves would suffer. Was 'diddling' herself worth it?

'Right.' Susan stepped back, putting her hands on her hips and standing in front of Faith. 'That's better, isn't it?' Her voice was loud enough for the others to hear clearly. 'You don't feel much like masturbating at the moment, do you?'

'No, Mistress.' Faith groaned, feeling that the punishment so far was sufficient to deter her. But clearly the lesson had hardly begun.

While Faith watched, feeling the first stirrings of lust inside her abdomen – despite the discomfort and knowing that the pressure and her humiliating position were conspiring against her – Gerald ran a hand over the taut plumpness of Juliet's buttocks, letting his fingers stray between them. His fingers found her sopping opening, parting the lips to reveal the dull ruby hue within, looking every so often at Faith's wide-eyed amazement. Already stimulated, Juliet groaned breathily as Gerald tested her bottom with his fingers, first looking round to check that Faith was still watching, and smiling when he saw that he had her undivided attention.

Faith had ridden the saddle for an hour, which was always stimulating. Her '*rin no tama*' were working within her. Her clitoris was on fire, as was most of the rest of her, so the sight in front of her made her body respond. As Susan stretched her arms over the bound young woman to grasp her buttocks, pulling her natal notch open, she looked Faith in the eye. *This* was the whole point of the exercise – the forcible assault on Juliet's rear, just in front of the roused and bound young woman. Giving a groan of unfeigned pleasure, Juliet was penetrated in the way she preferred – '*per anum*' – and as Susan released her once she had Gerald within, it was time for her work to begin. Clenching and unclenching her muscles, tensing and flexing her legs alternately and slightly moving her body against the leather, she brought him to a sweating climax in about five minutes, while he stood with his hands kneading her soft breasts.

When his squirmings had ceased he withdrew from her and walked off to one side, leaving Juliet, red-faced and gasping. With her eyes closed and a smile of contentment on her pleasant features, Juliet hung unresisting where she was fastened, lacking strength to do more. It was obvious to Faith that the young woman had been pleasured in the most exquisite manner possible.

After a few moments, Susan found some tissues and, advancing to stand before Faith, carefully wiped her, watching her charge all the time.

'Now you know, Miss Faith, why you must endure

the standing man each morning,' Mrs Marryat said quietly. 'To enable your muscles to squeeze an erection to climax. Though you're not being trained as Juliet is – to take it in your bottom – you should be prepared for even this. In case you haven't been told, it's called "the Master's Right". Only your master can take you there without your permission. Anyone else has to have *his* permission. Not yours, *his*.'

Faith had almost had an orgasm watching the display of sheer eroticism. Now that it was over the discomfort of her position, temporarily forgotten, was returning. Her ankles were weakening and if they gave out, she might suffer serious physical damage. Mrs Marryat watched closely as Susan unfastened the thongs from the post, starting with the one causing the pressure on her sex. It was allowed to fall heedlessly to the floor as Faith gratefully relaxed on to the soles of her feet, gulping air into her lungs. Without hesitation, Susan knelt in front of Faith, telling her to spread her legs wide, but even when Faith did, her thigh muscles shaking with the tension, the thong remained adhering to her sex.

The outer lips had tightened around the thong and, with the sticky seepings from within, had been sealed inside. Gently Susan touched the closed sex lips then, wetting her fingers with spittle to run along the join, tried to insert her nail delicately between the thickened lips. Faith's sex was hot, aromatic and distended with blood; the combination of the pressure and the scene before her and, of course, the after-effects of the ride and the balls within her, had almost been too much. Mentally she was shaken by the realisation that the discomfort to her leg muscles had been worse than to her sex. There the discomfort had been overwhelmed by the arousal of her lust.

After several applications of spittle-soaked fingers,

Faith's lips parted to release the thong, dropping it free from her sensitive area. Her clitoris stood out almost a centimetre.

'Did that give you pleasure, Miss Faith?' asked Susan.

'Yes, Mistress,' Faith replied, biting her lower lip and unwilling to elaborate, her head meekly bowed. She was aware of Mrs Marryat's interest, standing close to observe and listen to the exchange. If she hesitated, the chances of being punished, she thought, were high.

'Which? The thong or Juliet's pleasures?' Mrs Marryat asked.

'I don't know, Madam.' Faith's reply was honest, if not informative. 'I've ... seen ... that before, but –'

'How do you feel, Miss Faith?' Mrs Marryat asked.

'I ... I ... I ache, down there, Madame,' Faith answered.

'Do you want me to stimulate you?' Susan asked.

'No thank you, Mistress,' Faith answered, rapidly recovering her composure.

'Why not, Miss Faith?' Mrs Marryat asked, smiling at her.

'I've just been punished for that, Mistress,' Faith answered, her head still bowed like a dejected child.

She desperately wanted something; anything. A tongue; a finger; a hairbrush; anything. Anything rubbed against her sex would bring her to orgasm now, yet even as she spoke she could feel it diminish. Faith had learned her lessons well, preferring to avoid being hurt than to court being pleasured.

'Excellent.'

Waiting until Mrs Marryat had moved over to where Gerald was releasing Juliet from her confinement, Susan released Faith's throat from the post. Checking the position of 'Madame', she said softly,

'Tonight, I'll come to your room to spank you, darling. Though you learn quickly this was only half a punishment. Would you like that?'

'Y-y-yes, Mistress.' Faith's eyes dropped again as her heart sank like a stone.

That night, with her throat still tethered to the wall, her body spread across Susan's naked thighs, her legs spread wide, and her buttocks glowing from the smacking, Faith found herself aroused by the soft fingers which delicately explored her. With one hand holding her full left breast, Susan tantalised her with her touch, tracing lightly the varied curves of her body, following the crease between buttock and thigh, making daring little pecking forays into the deep hollow leading to her anus. For a time Faith was made to hold her buttocks apart while Susan invaded her in this fashion, steeling herself to the intimacies, her face scarlet as she felt the dreadful humiliation.

Faith was convinced Susan was right about spanking with a bare hand being the worst, for it *was* such an intimate touch. She had learned that first at Alex's hand on Harry's boat and now felt herself becoming aroused long before Susan had stopped. Her musk had filled the air long before those fingers had slipped within her labial lips. The worst came when Susan finished her explorations. She began, as Faith knew she would, to gently stroke the soft flesh of her pubic lips. First her finger was gently drawn down the outer lips, lightly touching, making the flesh twitch under the torture of her touch; bringing a smirk to Susan's face.

Then light, surprisingly cold fingers separated her outer lips to allow air to reach the hot inner cleft, so richly red, a groan of pleasure escaping Faith as she lay inert. She knew that she was revealing more of herself than she intended, but the intensity of her emotions prevented concealment. As she trembled beneath Susan, aware that every movement was transmitting a message of desire to the woman, Faith felt Susan begin to caress her.

She was sobbing quietly into the covers as Susan expertly caressed her stiff inner lips, flipping those delicate flaps this way and that, watching them stiffen slightly as the blood suffused them. Her outer lips were already painfully swollen and when Susan exposed Faith's love bud with her fingertips, Faith felt she would swoon. Thrills were coursing through her body like tidal waves of pleasurable pressure, threatening to engulf her. A few gentle caresses to her clitoris were sufficient to bring on her orgasm, a violent back-arching climax during which the older and more experienced woman held Faith securely across her naked thighs.

When she was finished, lying inert, the woman said quietly, 'Tomorrow, darling, you'll receive your strapping on the standing man, from Mr Clive. I do *not* want to hear a word from you, do you understand?'

'Yes, Mistress,' Faith answered in almost a whisper, lowering her face to the covers. Jackson. The man would see her; watch her try to climax with that phallus within her; punish her as she struggled.

'Do you love me, Faith?' Susan asked, bending at the waist to kiss her shoulder.

'Y-y-yes.' The admission was torn unwillingly from Faith's chest.

Susan aroused a variety of strong emotions within Faith, from hatred to love; and desire. Faith had watched her help Gerald sodomise Juliet that morning, and now she had provoked an orgasm such as Faith had rarely known in this place. Her touch, even when spanking her in this intimate manner, was always sure, and her fingers always cold, as if she had no emotion. Yet now and then Faith saw deep within her dark eyes a fire which was often hastily concealed.

'Then you will be trained in silence tomorrow, won't you? For me. I'd be ashamed to have Mr Clive think you have learned so little control that you cry out, even momentarily. You'll do this for me, won't you?'

'Y-y-yes, Mistress.' Faith then began to sob quietly, her tears being soaked into the thin blanket.

'Hush.' Susan put her arms around Faith's shoulders. 'Why are you crying? He won't use a whip; just the strap I used.'

'Wh . . . wh . . . why?' Faith bleated into the covers, not turning to face her. 'Why is he –'

'Why is *he* going to strap you?' Susan almost whispered. 'Because your training has reached that stage. After breakfast we'll go to the standing man; you *will* go willingly, won't you? Eagerly? Lightly? You have been so good lately.'

It was true. Over the past few days, Faith had found herself looking forward to the sessions on the thick leather phallus. The ache in her loins on awakening seemed to grow more urgent with each passing day; emotions which the saddle only intensified. She had found that with her vagina sleeving the upright, even with the strap turning her buttocks cherry red, the desperate urge was assuaged. Susan had predicted that she would come to love it.

'Yes, Mistress.' Faith's shoulders slumped as another increment of surrender took place within her. She knew she liked being fastened. Her wrists being secured behind her were as nothing. She remembered fondly when Alex had spread her on that bed, secured her so that she was hardly able to move before he made love to her. They seemed impossible days of childish innocence compared to what she now endured as a matter of course.

Now she was finding she was coming to welcome the strap across her buttocks for the feelings it provoked. If she was unable to have a real man inside her to scratch the itch she felt, then the leather phallus would have to do. She knew now what Lillian had meant about liking women, but there was nothing like a real man's erection.

'I shall be there, darling.' Susan tried to sound encouraging. 'Helping you.'

'Helping . . .?' Faith half-turned her body to look up at her with a frowned question, but the woman pressed her head back down again.

'There are many ways of helping. Oh, you'll cry; you'll sob. That lovely face will be soaked in tears, which is right and as it should be. But you won't protest; nor will you complain or beg to be released, will you?'

'No, Mistress,' Faith answered, though the dread in her chest made her pray that this was just a nightmare.

The nightmare began even before they left the house, when Jackson made her kiss the strap before he inserted the handle of it into her sexual passage.

'You'll carry that with you.' That had been a surprise. Susan rarely made her do that. He was looking at her flushed features with no sign of amusement. Perhaps, she thought, it was the fact of Jackson crouching in front of her, holding her sex open while he slowly inserted the leather within her, his eyes on hers, passing the message that he wished it was another, similar object which he would like to push into that hot, aromatic tunnel. Kissing the strap seemed to be a fetish at the Stables, for she was made to kiss it afterwards as well. As if that expiated any ill feeling she may have harboured towards him. Thinking about it, she was surprised to find she bore him none.

They reached the long, narrow room where the blocks stood beneath the upstanding leather dildo, walking in single file; Susan first, then Faith, trying to hold herself comfortably upright. Somehow the phallus looked larger to Faith as she halted before it. The man tugged at it as if to make sure that it would not come off the wall, then after tugging the strap out of her, gestured towards the upright member.

'Position yourself.' He spoke curtly, sending a wave of fright through her. Up to then, she had imagined him to be a more avuncular character.

Carefully, Faith stepped up on the blocks, wrists still secured behind her. Susan opened her sex lips to allow an easy impalement. It would never do for their pupil to be hurt, especially in *that* area. Faith eased forward on tiptoe, the point of the leather dildo brushing into her cleft until she found the spot she sought, then lowered herself on to her soles again, gasping as the cold leather slipped within.

'Up!' Jackson said sharply, accompanying it with an almost playful upward swing of the strap which ended on the underside of one buttock, making Faith react at once, standing again on tiptoe. 'Down!' She stood flat on her feet again, trembling. Twice more she rose and fell, each time accompanied by a soft strike from the strap, before she realised that what he was doing was stimulating her passage into lubricating the leather.

Once satisfied that there should be sufficient slippage, Jackson kicked the blocks away, allowing Faith to slide down the leather until her sex lips met the flared base, preventing further movement and taking her weight on it. Faith sighed deeply at the familiar pressure and tried to compose herself, already tightening her vaginal muscles ahead of time and feeling the beginning of a sexual thrill at the prospect. Susan was beside her, a cold, soft hand delicately feeling the skin on her abdomen.

'Mr Clive! Feel.' Susan ran her hand over the slight distension of the soft abdominal skin. A rougher hand was placed there, separated from the firm cylinder within her by her warm flesh. 'Well bedded in.' Susan said. 'And the balls are prominent too.' Her soft fingers found the smaller, more rounded swellings.

'Let's see how she performs then, shall we?' Jackson asked as his hand withdrew.

Faith groaned quietly, her mouth trembling with the horrified anticipation. She was completely at his mercy, her buttocks towards him, with no defence possible. Then Susan moved her hand, running down from her slightly bulging abdomen to the delicate flesh of her love bud. With flaring hope, Faith swivelled her eyes towards the woman's amused expression as she heard the familiar slight rush of air just before the strap exploded on to her buttocks.

Susan had administered a greater dose of stimulant the previous night so there was already an almost agonised lust building up within Faith's abdomen, not slaked by the '*rin no tama*' being left in position when she had mounted the standing man. As the pain swept through her, more fierce than anything Susan had provoked, the dark-haired young woman caressed her clitoris with her thumb, sending a shaft of sheer sexual ecstasy upward through her body. It was a race between the sensations of pain and pleasure to be the first to reach her brain. Pleasure won by a distance. Her mouth hung slack and her head jerked back to look up at the ceiling. She gave vent to a gasping sob which was a mixture of pain and pleasure as the second stroke of the strap was laid across her buttocks.

On the fourth stroke, Faith's orgasm was procured, her squirming body hardly required to induce it; her groaning, gasping, wracking sobs the only sound. Her sexual muscles, trained for weeks on the saddle in the stable, had clenched the phallus so tightly that she hardly moved her abdomen at all, yet her climax sent rivulets of liquid down the leather shaft and the supporting bracket.

'Well done!' Susan enthused quietly, her voice almost a whisper. 'I knew you wouldn't let me down.' She began kicking the blocks back beneath Faith's feet.

Gratefully, Faith placed her feet on them, her legs weak, but just about able to support her weight. The transfer of weight from her abdomen to her feet allowed her to rise a little, yet she was still impaled on the leather. A rougher hand than Susan's felt between her thighs, then a voice she recalled through the mists of lust which were slowly clearing from her mind, said, 'Damned wet. I think she likes it.'

'Miss Faith is a good girl, Mr Clive,' Susan said primly. 'She obeys.'

'Then let's see her obey again. Remove the blocks and let's see how she does a second time.'

'Don't let me down, darling.' Susan evinced no surprise that Faith be required to endure this a second time.

Almost in a dream, the blocks were removed and Faith slipped down the leather shaft, landing with almost a bump, and a sliver of discomfort shot high within her.

'Don't stimulate her this time,' Jackson instructed. 'She must learn to do it herself.'

188

'Of course, Mr Clive,' Susan's quiet voice agreed, 'but I'll remain where she can see me.'

'Do.'

This was worse; far worse than the strapping she had endured at the bar. Though he was strong, Jackson knew just how hard to deal each stroke. He began high on her buttocks, gradually moving the point of contact downward as Faith writhed, flexing her muscles. She could feel the desire shooting through her again, but insufficient to bring about the quick release she sought. Several times she almost begged for the woman to stimulate her, yet the quiet, almost reposed and yet interested features which stood alongside her, watching her agonised writhings, prevented her. Faith was on her own with the pain and desire.

The first strapping had released the pent-up sexual desire which the drug had induced, so that this new sexual ache was constructed purely of the strapping she was receiving. Yet it was not powerful enough to bring about her climax on its own because of the earlier release. So Faith was forced to squeeze her muscles tight about the shaft, putting so much effort into it that, despite herself, she writhed under the pressures of her own muscles and the strap, which was turning her buttocks a deep red.

Under Susan's injunction not to speak, Faith relapsed into sobbing incoherence; wails of pained frustration as, despite her best efforts, the passion mounted within her until, at last, she felt the rush of pleasure sweeping over her. Her face illuminated as she felt the first pangs of the delicious release; it seemed that even the strap ceased to pound on her buttocks as, with a cry of pure joy, she threw back her head again. Faith climaxed. With that climax, Faith understood at last that pain no longer had the

189

ability to subdue her. She was free of that tyranny at last.

Faith had no memory of how she was removed from the standing man; one moment she was exulting there, working her hips back and forth in mid-air, the delicious pleasure within her being released despite the numbing ache in her buttocks; the next she was lying on a blanket in the sunshine of the yard, her wrists and ankles spread wide and secured to the bases of the posts.

She could feel someone bathing her hot, flushed skin with cool water and, opening one eye, found it was Susan. There was no sign of Jackson, but she knew he was unlikely to be far away; not with her legs wide apart like that. Down the yard, Roger was being put through his paces by Hilary, in whose hand the strap was bringing a beautiful blush to his willing buttocks. There were times, Faith thought, when despite his predilection against females, Roger loved Hilary and her ministrations.

'That was very good, Miss Faith.' Susan bent forward to kiss her mouth. 'You did very well.'

'Did ... did ... did I ... cry ... too much, Mistress?' Faith gasped out, feeling the emotion in her chest was too much to contain. She had tried very hard not to let her distress show, but knew too that in her incoherent ravings she could easily have pleaded for release; or mercy from the terrible strapping.

'You cried, of course.' Susan's mouth moved down to her right breast. 'But I said you would. Anyone would have cried with *that* strapping. You were very good.'

'Was ... was ... was it ... bad?' Faith asked in a tremulous voice, hardly wanting an answer, yet she had to ask.

'Your behind looks like a Morello cherry,' Susan

replied with a sad, rueful smile. 'And tomorrow, you'll have the same again, only I shan't be there to help you. Tomorrow you have to do it for yourself.'

'You won't?' Faith's expression looked agonised, for she trusted this strange woman in a way that eluded her understanding. This woman had caused her more pain in a few short weeks than anyone else had ever done, yet she had also shown her kindness; love, almost. For some unfathomable reason, Faith trusted her.

'I shall be there, of course. But you won't see me. All you'll see will be the wall ahead. You must learn to bear this alone; you must learn obedience. So tomorrow, after breakfast, you'll have the strap inserted as today, and you'll lead the way to the standing man as willingly for Mr Clive as you do for me. You must love Mr Clive's touch, as you do mine.'

'Will . . . will he . . . touch me?' Faith asked, the panic flaring in her eyes at the thought of Jackson's fingers on her delicate sex lips.

'He'll open your sex to the standing man, yes. If he wants to caress you, he will. Do you object?'

Faith thought about this for a few moments, then realised that to object would be disobedience, for Susan had already told her what would happen. She took a deep breath as their eyes met, trying to relax her limbs in the restriction of the restraints on them, and answered in a dull, expressionless voice which was her only defence against the panic filling her. 'I'll obey.' She lowered her head and eyes in submission.

'The time may come when you must taste the whip. Hush!' Susan placed her hand over Faith's trembling mouth. 'Not today; not soon, either. Perhaps not for some time yet; but it *will* happen.'

White faced, Faith looked up at her, unable to conceal her alarm, but knowing that deep down she was excited at the prospect.

Chapter Eleven

It had been the subject of a long discussion between Susan and Mrs Marryat, on the relative benefits of telling Faith what was to happen in advance. With others, they were put across the bar and whatever implement was desired to produce the effect was used. With Faith this could provoke panic. Susan knew she would accept what was being done without fuss, both for the practical reasons of making less disturbance and subjecting herself to the discipline of others.

Yet so sudden a step could panic her into struggling, and there were others who watched, and feared. If Faith knew in advance – if she came to terms mentally with what was to happen – then she would be calm in the face of the punishment.

'Why, Mistress?' Faith asked anxiously in a broken voice as their eyes locked, feeling the fear within her mounting. 'I've obeyed; I've been good. Why must I be whipped? Am I not sufficiently obedient?'

This was the other side of the coin – the intellectual justification for what was to happen. Susan thought that if she could get this point across to Faith, the whole experience would be far less traumatic. It was worth trying, for she knew that she loved this tall, beautiful young woman.

'Because, my darling, you must. You must experience all these things to achieve obedience, for only when we can honestly tell your sponsor how you behave under the whip can you be released. It's part of your training, I'm sorry.'

'I have obeyed. I don't want to be whipped,' Faith sobbed quietly, slumping back on the concrete, despair wrecking her composure.

Susan knew that telling Faith so soon after the standing man had been a risk. She could see the turned heads further off, where Gerald and Hilary were looking. Even some of the pupils were breaking their concentration to turn their heads. If either of the two guides saw them, she thought, they'll get warmed backsides for that. She knew that it was the sight of Faith, usually so composed these days, breaking down like that, which was causing the problem.

'Don't let us have any of this nonsense, Miss Faith.' Susan's voice hardened slightly, but was still reassuring. 'The fact we've come this far shows that you *can* obey. At one time, we thought you'd be our first failure. You came very close, Miss Faith.'

'What would have happened if I had?' Faith asked, swallowing her tears, looking up with the liquid still filling her eyes. Part of the problem was that she had gone so quickly from ecstasy to despair; the sudden shift overloading her mind with emotion.

'I don't know,' Susan confessed with an embarrassed smile. 'It's never happened before, to my knowledge. Normally the young women we get here haven't got your intelligence; they rebel, but they haven't the wit to put up an effective mental resistance. They soon learn the lessons of obedience because they don't have the intelligence to outwit us, and pain soon overcomes them. You think too much. You have pride in your intelligence, as you *should*, but –' Susan sighed, shrugging her bewilderment '– pride is what we're trying to control, isn't it?'

'I've got no pride left,' Faith returned, shaking her

head, feeling she was the most miserable creature born.

'Oh, you do, Faith,' the calm woman answered at once. 'You do. You take pride in your appearance and you always make sure that long, dark hair looks lovely.' Susan stroked the lengthening mane. 'You take pride in your posture, even without the brace. When you can look me in the eye and accept that you're to be whipped, then I'll be sure that you control your pride, and not the other way about, as it was when you came. Once you control it, then you can be trained to use it.'

The following day after breakfast, Faith led the way down to the yard, ignoring the others who were beginning another day's training. Jackson was waiting for her, the long strap dangling in his hand. With a determined step, trying to ignore the fluttering of desire in her abdomen, she forced herself to walk up to him and, as Susan had dictated, knelt awkwardly, head bowed. Quietly she asked, 'Please, Master, may I have the strap?'

Jackson was silent for a moment. His eyes met Susan's, nodding his acceptance of her efforts. Martha had been right again, of course. Faith was becoming used to the strap, though she was nervous of it, as anyone with any sense would be. But she no longer feared it quite so much; from the faint aroma in the air she was looking forward to it. Progress indeed.

On his command she extended her lips to kiss the strap then rose, with Susan's help, and spread her legs to accept the cold embrace of the handle. When it was lodged securely. Faith followed his gesture to walk ahead of him. Holding her head bowed as decorously as she could, her wrists secured behind her and shoulders back, Faith walked calmly to the standing man, even stepping up on the blocks without having to be told. She was shaking with nervous tension, but thought that she alone knew how much she actually wanted this release. The tensions of the preparations were making her desire it more than the morning before. Whether she knew it or not, whether she was disgusted by the concept or not, Faith was becoming partly trained to the whip.

The pain of the strap she would endure would be quite incidental to the release of desire, the pain of which, Faith now felt, was more terrible than that of the leather. The knowledge that her desires lay in that direction subdued her, but she swallowed the humiliation of having that secret shared by the others. After the massages Susan gave her, the rides and the walks with their attendant pleasures, the burning in her buttocks was a minor feature of her life. It was reduced by having other things to take her mind off it. She thought that should she be fastened in the yard with nothing to occupy her mind after the strapping, it would indeed seem as terrible as it had at first. With nothing on her mind but the stinging flesh and her own humiliation, Faith knew she would have to come to terms with the feelings she dreaded.

As Susan had told her, Jackson's fingers opened her sex with surprising gentleness while Faith looked directly ahead, not allowing her mind to dwell on what was happening. She bent her knees carefully to insert the phallus, crouching lower until it was fully sheathed. Jackson kicked the blocks away instants before the first swing of the strap, catching her unawares so that her yelp was part surprise. Yet by the time she had taken ten strokes, her welcome climax had been reached, her hips jerking against the restraint within her, her crooning pleasure leaving neither Jackson or Susan in any doubt about her orgasm. Fortunately for herself, Faith was unable to see the look of relief they exchanged. Another milestone had been successfully passed.

After the saddle and a relaxing massage, Susan led her out to the sunshine of the yard, where Jackson was positioning what looked a little like an executioner's block. It was about five feet square and three high, but there the similarity ended, for it was covered in soft, pink, long-haired sheepskin. Surprised at this reminder of her initiation, Faith had no premonition as she was led by her taut, clamped nipples towards it.

Standing beside it, Faith was relieved of the long, black, leather boots, feeling the breeze as a refreshment on her skin again. Though she liked her boots, was used to them and even found them a support, being deprived of them on a warm spring day was a rare treat.

'Kneel on the block, Miss Faith,' Susan said in a firm tone, holding her arm to steady her as she mounted.

Down the yard, Paul hung from the poles again – he was in trouble for some misdemeanour or other – while Jacqui sucked in her breath as Hilary, with more than usual care, cracked the strap across her buttocks. Everything seemed normal as Jackson folded a flap of the sheepskin aside to remove a plate from the top, revealing a depression within. Susan moved the kneeling Faith until both her feet were positioned within the depression, then Jackson placed the plate over the top of her heels, adding the sheepskin on top of that, concealing the plate to provide a soft surface.

'Now –' Susan smiled winningly at her '– spread your knees apart, Faith, as wide as is comfortable, and when you're done, sit back on your heels.'

It took less than a second for Faith to understand the importance of the position in which she would find herself but, gulping, she complied. Moving her knees well apart and resting back against the sheep-skin, the long hairs tickled her sensitive pubic lips, reminding her of the gentle approaches Alex had made with the chinchilla mitten, lying face down on his bed. He had gently tickled her pubic hair, not touching her skin, allowing the tendrils to send the messages back to her skin.

'Lean back as far as you can.' Susan smiled as Faith began to obey, finding that with her ankles fixed beneath her, yet still able to turn slightly, she was able to rest her shoulders and back flat on the sheepskin.

Faith was now even more aware of her position. Her body was drawn backwards in a straight line, her flattened breasts pointing upwards and the open legs exposing her most intimate parts to the air. There was pain in her thighs where the tension was greatest, the tremors spreading through the rest of her body as she thought about what might happen.

It would take no effort on Jackson's part to mount her, but would that be so bad? After all, she had been mounted by several men, one after the other. Perhaps Susan had avoided telling her the truth. Perhaps she *was* destined to be a whore? Perhaps that was what they were doing – teaching her to be a whore and training her to accept whatever her clients desired, whether it was sex or being whipped. She had made the suggestion to Susan and never received a satisfactory answer.

Susan checked that Faith's shoulders were securely placed on the sheepskin, then had her rise again to a more comfortable position. She was ready to proceed with the lesson in obedience, yet felt confident Faith would accomplish this too. The young woman had come a long way from the sulky, defiant pupil who had refused to strip on her first evening. Perhaps it might have been better to have taken her down to the yard that evening, once she had undressed, and bend her over the bar. A strap across her buttocks then might have saved a lot of trouble.

But things were better now. Much better; though unless she did this right there could still be difficulties. Momentarily she considered fastening Faith's collar to the block, but that would hardly help Faith exercise control, would it? She had to be free to rise, even at the cost of taking more severe punishment. Only by accepting the choice and remaining would she demonstrate her self-discipline. Susan thought it might be as well to remind her of that before they started, otherwise Faith might not understand and make the mistake she feared most.

'Miss Faith,' Susan began in her soft, silky voice, reaching up slightly to kiss Faith's lips in a passionate caress, her tongue pushing deep within Faith's surprised mouth. She held it until Faith, in spite of herself, responded.

After removing the clamps from her teats, Susan rested a hand on Faith's right breast before she pulled away, looking at her fondly with a smile which suggested passion.

'As you were such a good girl this morning, I'm going to whip you.' She put her other hand over Faith's mouth to still her instant protest. 'Not with one of the whips you've already seen; quite a small one. Just this; the same suede strap, really. I call it a whip for convenience, that's all.'

Removing her hand from Faith's mouth, she produced from her pocket the small length of suede leather about six inches long and half an inch across, attached to an ivory handle. Holding it up in front of the young woman's frightened eyes by the tip of the handle, she gave her fifteen seconds to see it and get used to the idea.

'You'll find that, administered properly, a whipping with this can stimulate you wonderfully.' Susan paused, looking directly at her. 'Do you know where I shall apply it, Miss Faith?' Her eyes passed the message to Faith.

It was such a small whip, and having already experienced its use already, Faith knew there could only be one location sensitive enough to receive such a build-up, yet her vocal chords refused to admit what her mind accepted.

'No.' Faith's reply was more an exhalation than a protest, but the woman smiled at her apprehension.

'There's no need to be afraid. I'm going to whip your sex and bottom mouth. I'm going to separate your lips and whip the inside of your cleft, your inner lips and the entrance to your vagina, and your clitoris. And do you know something, Miss Faith? It'll sting for a short while, but then you will feel the most *amazing* sensations, I promise you. You'll feel that your whole sex is on fire, and you will beg me . . . yes, beg me, to put out that fire.'

The woman paused to give Faith, who thought Susan had missed her vocation in selling, time to absorb the information before she continued. 'And there's only one way I can put out that fire, isn't there? I could fasten you on the block – there are ways of restraining you – but I want you to obey me and lean back as you did, and accept this. Give yourself to the whip. Would you do that for me? Would you?' Her eyes were fixed on Faith's face.

For some moments they looked at each other before Faith asked, 'Does it matter if I refuse, Mistress?'

in a voice which gave no indication of her answer. In truth, Faith was such a welter of emotions that she had not yet considered her response to this outrageous suggestion.

'No,' Susan answered. 'If you refuse, I'll just secure you. I'll still whip you, no more, no less, but your obedience will mean that this isn't a punishment but ... an act of love. And, when you beg me to put out the fire, as you have been so good, I shall.'

Faith looked at her for a few moments longer, then swayed backward until her shoulders were pressed to the sheepskin. Her eyes closed, waiting for the torture to begin, trying to maintain a neutral expression.

'Remember; I love you, Faith. I want you to be the best pupil I've ever had here. Difficult, but by far the best.' For a few moments she hesitated, then brought the suede strap down on one of Faith's sex lips.

Susan was right, Faith thought with a savage intensity. Each stroke on her outer lips produced a stinging which was not unbearable, though far from pleasant. Not having been stung by a bee or wasp, Faith was unable to compare it with either, but she imagined it must be something on those lines, for it was certainly less than the strapping she had at the standing man. Yet the cumulative effect of the rapid tattoo of blows was to produce a hurt. A hurt which seemed to press deep within, churning deep within her abdomen.

She felt the strap entering her sexual recess yet knew that Susan had not used her fingers to open her up. As the whipping on the outer lips proceeded, Faith's legs drew apart almost of their own volition, splitting her labia apart and exposing her inner cleft. She was opening herself up to this torment without being able to help herself, and revelling in the sensations produced. The suede found her urethra, her inner lips and the entrance to her vagina open to the world. Ah! The pleasant agonies she endured as this delicate flesh was subjected to the abuse; an abuse that was rapidly transferred after a few strokes up to her clitoris.

The little love bud seemed to swell under the sharp cracks of the suede, the surrounding, protective shroud of her mound held well back out of the way by Susan's left hand. To her shame, Faith could feel her breasts swelling and she began to pant as the effects of the violent message reached her brain. This was more arousing than she had imagined. If Lillian had done this on that first night, she would have disgraced herself by screaming for more.

Frantically, Faith tried to raise her hips towards the suede, but her body was tightly tensed in that position. She tried to turn her shoulders, writhing in the delicious warmth, while Susan, one hand on Faith's abdomen to pull back her mound and steady herself, began to minister to the tiny pink ring of her anus.

As the tip of the whip exploded on to that secret orifice, Faith believed she would pass out; not even when the whip had licked her perineum had she felt so abandoned. She was moaning and gasping with the effect of the heightened feelings which flooded her, crying as the twin sensations of pain and pleasure mounted higher than she thought she could bear. Faith knew that she was seeping fluid; even *she* could smell the aroma from her hot, flushed sex.

She could hear the different sounds as Susan directed the small whip on to the moist flesh or scooped it up to wet another part of her hot vulva. Release from this *had* to come soon or she would burst into tears, but when she *did* begin to cry, Susan redoubled the speed and force of the whipping, seeming to know that Faith needed prodding to greater heights.

Faith was sobbing when the whipping stopped, the tension of her body now gone. She lay there inert, trying to regain her breath, her tongue poking out as the woman's face appeared beside her, the usual urbane calm still present. For a moment the woman looked at her, then kissed her mouth, imprisoning her tongue for a moment.

'Now,' Susan said in a slow, menacing tone, 'I'm going to whip your breasts and those delicious teats for a few moments and I want you to tell me whether you have enjoyed it and are enjoying it, Faith. Don't feel afraid or ashamed. Tell me how you like it. Cry out . . . let everyone in the yard hear you.'

As the suede began to crack against her rigid nipples, Faith began to writhe again, her voice raised in a hoarse, passionate cry, scarlet with the shame but oblivious to everything but what Susan was evoking from her.

'Yes! Please! Please, Mistress, I like it! I *love* it! Please! Please!' The tears were flowing freely down the already stained cheeks as Faith fought with her desires, and lost.

'Do you want more, Miss Faith? Tell me,' Susan asked, just as though seated beside her on a park bench.

'Please, Mistress, more!' Faith demanded, trying to swallow to force moisture into her burning throat.

'Do you want me to whip your sex again?' The question was asked in the same conversational tone.

'Yes!' Faith screamed, crimson with the shame of self-knowledge that this woman had roused her to ecstasy by whipping her most private of private parts, generally abusing her most erogenous zones. Even had she been aware that all activity in the yard had stopped – that even the most cowed pupil was watching her writhe under the sweet ministrations of the suede lash – it would have counted for nothing. Faith was taking her pleasure, heedless of shame or decorum.

Susan obliged Faith, cracking the suede all over her sexual organs again before she carefully took a sponge from the bucket of cold water beside her and began to bathe the skin she had struck, cooling the tissue. Faith had no energy to lift herself into the kneeling position so she lay still while the water trickled down between her thighs, luxuriating in the coolness which still did nothing for her desire. The woman continued bathing her for some time, pressing the water into her sex and anus, and wiping the sponge over her breasts occasionally, before she asked, 'You see? I was right, wasn't I?'

'Yes, Mistress,' Faith agreed, quietly hoarse, defeated by the depth of her passion and her self-knowledge that she found this treatment pleasurable. A few weeks before she would have considered it hideous torture. Now she knew herself better.

'Let's get you back on your feet,' Susan said as the bustle in the yard recommenced, moving to the young woman's shoulders and placing a hand beneath her. 'I think I'll have to massage your legs again to get them working.'

'Please, Mistress, please.' Faith turned her head to look into the woman's calm eyes. 'Release me, please. I should like to be released, and you promised me release if I obeyed.'

'You're not restrained, Miss Faith,' Susan replied.

'Release me . . . my . . . my pleasure,' Faith said.

'What do you say, Miss Faith?' Susan asked quietly.

'Please, Mistress, please.' Faith thought it was the quality of her begging that was at fault, so she put as much sincerity into it as she could manage.

'Unless I know what you want me to do, Miss Faith . . .' The older woman shrugged her helplessness.

Faith composed herself for a few moments, her mouth trembling, gulping as she thought of what she was about to ask. She was as aware as Susan of the semantics. If she asked this woman to deliver her orgasm, which was turning rapidly to a pained tension within her, then she was abasing herself further. But the alternative was to touch her sexual organs, which would probably mean a strapping at least. A dilemma, with both alternatives equally painful.

Flushing as red as when she had been pleasured, Faith asked, 'Please, Mistress, I . . . I beg you. Release my pleasure.'

'Bring your orgasm on, you mean? If so, say it. I'm not offended by the use of the term, so why should you be? It's a perfectly ordinary word.'

'I beg you, Mistress.' Faith's breathing was becoming more laboured as she thought about it. 'Bring relief for my orgasm.'

'Certainly, Miss Faith.' Susan smiled.

To Faith's surprise she extended her hand towards Faith's thighs, looked carefully at them, then pressed her index finger on to the familiar sensitive spot on the inner aspect of her left thigh. At first Faith could only feel the slight discomfort of the pressure, but suddenly she felt the pent-up pressure of her desire flooding down between her thighs as though a tap had been turned. Yet there was none of the passion she had experienced when her orgasm was released on previous occasions. It was a release, rather than a sexual fulfilment.

Susan looked at her fondly for some moments, then said, 'One orgasm a day is quite enough, Miss Faith. Had I touched your clitoris, you would have exploded. You also have to learn the discipline of release.'

'What?' Faith felt almost depressed as the woman helped her to resume the kneeling position again.

'There will be other times when you'll have sexual satisfaction from that; tomorrow night, perhaps. I'll visit you. But you have to learn that desire such as you felt just now can be released without the debilitating orgasm you've known. Now let's massage some feeling back into those lovely legs of yours, then take a walk. Would you like that?'

In their secret hideaway on the hill – the 'nookey nook' Susan called it occasionally – Faith found herself responding more to Susan's advances, rocking her hips to rub herself against the woman's clitoris. Already stimulated twice beyond desire that day, she thought the fact she could still find the ability to respond somewhat surprising, though her partner only smiled fondly at her.

'What's wrong, Mistress?' Faith asked suddenly as she realised the slightly distracted Susan was trying to conceal something from her.

'Paul has been masturbating again,' Susan said quietly, 'so he must be punished.'

Yet there was something odd about the way she spoke, as though it was more serious than his usual sin. Paul was caught masturbating every other day and was punished for it, yet he persisted with a determination which Faith thought verged on monomania. If she wondered about her own predilection for masturbation and where it would lead, the example of Paul before her provided a warning.

'Why, Mistress?' Faith asked quietly, her eyes on the scenery, not looking at her companion. Having established, or re-established, a relationship with her, it was a privilege she wanted to retain. One which she thought may be withdrawn as a result of her nervous question.

'Why?' Susan asked, frowning at her, clearly surprised at the question.

'Yes, Mistress.' Faith gathered a little more courage when the blast refused to come. 'I thought masturbation was only frowned on by the Church. The "Sin of Onan" and that. I didn't realise they were religious here.'

'Ah!' Susan gave a brief smile, nodding her acceptance of the question while Faith breathed a sigh of relief. 'We don't object on religious grounds, Miss Faith, but on practical ones. The pupils we get here are usually immature in some way or another; probably why we're able to do so much with them, I suppose. But they've got to learn that masturbation, in *this* context, is counter-productive. Once you're clear of here you can do what you like, or in your case, what your master likes. That's up to him.'

'You're not one of the Chosen,' Faith broke in with a protest. 'Nor is Paul. What's he here for, anyway?'

'Paul raped a thirteen-year-old girl.' Susan spoke in a harsh tone, bringing a flush to Faith's face. 'He's a nasty piece of work, really; only his family connections have saved him from prison. He says she asked for it; lay down and begged him to do it. It's his standard whine whenever he's in trouble; as though people will believe him!' She sighed and shook her head. 'As I was saying, here we try to push your sexuality into positive channels, so if you masturbate, then we can't – or at least, not so efficiently – do what we have to do, which is why we discourage it. There's some that won't learn, though, no matter how you explain it, which is why we must punish every so

206

often. You know what happened when you were caught masturbating. The effects of masturbation aren't so serious on you as they are on Paul. You can have orgasms all day; he needs time to recover, and in a busy training programme, it's something that can't be tolerated.'

'But why are you so sad, Mistress?' Faith asked, wishing she understood that one, central fact; the one piece of information Susan seemed reluctant to impart.

'Part of everyone's training here is in learning to accept pain; dealing with it and so on. But there's also the infliction of pain.' Susan paused. 'I got into this by that route, remember? I was "Miss Whippy", before I ever set eyes on Mad Martha, but you've never done it before, and Madame has decided it's time she taught you. You're the one who's going to punish Paul.'

'Me?' Faith's jaw hung open.

'Yes. She wanted to try it before, but you were too new. You're grown up now, Miss Faith.' Susan looked her in the eye. 'You're going to whip Paul.'

Faith's colour left her as she thought about the suggestion. Punish Paul? She knew the business end of a strap and that was all.

'I ... it ... it seems so ...' Faith sighed, shaking her head as she looked off over the sylvan countryside, so peaceful in contrast to her own heaving emotions. When Paul was punished, like the rest of them, Faith was made to watch, as much for his humiliation as her education. When she was punished, he was usually missing; Susan, Jackson and Mrs Marryat suspected Paul would derive pleasure from the sight of Faith, or any of the females, being bent over the bar.

'It's necessary, Miss Faith,' Susan began, smiling

thinly, glad the approach had ended and she could go on to the business of instructing her. 'That's what's going to happen today, when we get back. *You'll* administer the punishment. It won't be much … probably like his test.'

'Me,' Faith sighed, looking wide-eyed into the serious face beside her.

'You must learn how to wield a whip, Miss Faith. One day you may be required to use one, either in punishment or to arouse someone; perhaps someone you love. You can practise on Paul. Come!' Susan was imperious, commanding Faith to her feet, fastening her wrists behind her before donning her own clothes. Unwillingly, her heart pounding within her chest, Faith followed Susan out of the shrubbery, pulled along by the clamps, letting her mind settle on the pained sensations within her glands rather than the prospect of what they would find on their return.

The yard was silent when they reached it. Paul was already secured to the bar, his expression sulky rather than fearful. Everyone appeared to be waiting, heads turning in their direction. They had stopped out of sight where, to Faith's surprise, Susan had removed the chain from the clamps on her nipples – though she left the clamps themselves in place – then freed her wrists.

Still braced, corseted and thigh-booted, Faith looked the picture of a 'bondage queen' as she entered the silent gathering. She felt a fraud, for what did she know about administering discipline? Receiving it, yes – she could write a thesis on that – but dishing it out? She hoped Mrs Marryat and Jackson, and more importantly Susan, would realise that, not having done this before, she would require coaching before she could perform adequately.

Martha Marryat turned from Paul, letting her eyes

scan the flushed young woman who looked about to faint at any moment. Funny how it took some of them. Hilary had been only too eager to get her hands on the straps and whips, as had Alison. Faith was a different type; a reluctant young woman who looked as though she might be just the thing. She certainly looked the part of a dominatrix.

As the two women waited slightly up the slope from the bar, Jackson overcame Paul's resistance, provoking the familiar smile from the young man. While this was happening, Faith kept her eyes on the wall ahead of and above Paul's back. Mrs Marryat let her eyes roam around the assembled 'school'. It was this constant attention to detail which ensured the continued success of the Stables.

The new girl looked white, so she had warned Hilary to be ready to catch her if she looked like fainting. Roger, of course, looked longingly at the preparations, wishing no doubt that he could change places with Paul *or* Jackson. One of these days, Roger would mature into a wonderful exponent of the art, so long as he confined himself to women. She would hardly like to vouch for his impartiality with men.

Chapter Twelve

As usual with Paul, the young man clenched his buttocks against the large, cold, metal phallus which Jackson offered to his rear. Jerking his head up, his mouth slack, Paul whimpered as Faith was guided by Mrs Marryat to stand alongside her in front of the young man, a reminder that he was being closely observed. To Faith's mounting shame at being forced to be such a reluctant participant, she watched as a smile appeared on Paul's features. Then, to her surprise, he gave up the struggle.

'He's beginning to enjoy it, Mr Clive,' the woman beside her said sharply. 'You'll have to stop. We don't want him using this for sexual gratification.'

'No.' Jackson stopped at once. A scowl replaced the look of pleasure which had decorated Paul's pallid face. Mrs Marryat, Faith had already learned, was an acute observer; it was a lesson Paul had apparently forgotten.

The two women moved behind the young man until they were beside Jackson, who had a whip in his hand. As they stopped beside him, Faith saw Mrs Marryat's head nod once, realising that he was being told that she had been primed.

'You're in for a rare treat, young Paul. Miss Faith's going to deal with you.' It was only then, when faced with the imminent prospect of using the whip, that Faith realised this was as much a test of *her* obedience as *his* punishment. If she refused, would she take Paul's place? Possibly. It was an option she declined.

'No!' Paul gasped as he tried to struggle, confirming to everyone that he had learned little since his arrival. From Susan, Faith knew he had arrived in early April, at least a month ahead of her; yet still he struggled against the restraints as though he could free himself. While she felt irritated by the irrational behaviour, Faith wondered whether she would have been silent and unprotesting had their places been exchanged. Probably not, even in the best of times.

'Here!' Mrs Marryat held the carved phallus towards Faith, willing her to take it.

To Faith, who gulped audibly when it rested in her hands, it seemed even larger than those she had previously seen inserted into his rectum. Larger too than anything she had taken in either of her openings, the standing man and Alex included.

'Miss Faith's going to fit you with the phallus, Paul,' Jackson's voice carried to the others, for whom this was as much a lesson as for Faith and Paul. 'You know what'll happen if you resist. More of the same.'

'Mr Clive has oiled his bottom so well,' Mrs Marryat cooed. 'You could get a rolling pin in there without any trouble. One push and it'll be over.'

'I ... I ...' Faith began, but Mrs Marryat was already steering her to Paul's naked buttocks, angled in their direction. Paul moved slightly as he strained against his fetters.

Jackson turned, his powerful hands spreading Paul's buttocks apart, displaying the pink anus within the brown staining which spread deep into the recesses of the inner cheeks. Faith had seldom seen this before, though she had often wondered about it. The phallus, mostly guided by her mentor, was placed on the puckered pink ring of muscle, making Paul jerk and whimper at the touch. She thought it must have been cold too. Faith was about to tell them that she was unable to do this when suddenly some primitive desire took hold.

With a sudden grimace and hardening of her jaw, Faith pressed the rounded end of the phallus against the ring of muscles which had already been weakened by previous intrusions. It was the memory of his smile on other occasions after insertion of the phallus which hardened her heart, despite the abuse he yelled at her.

'Aaagh! Stop it, you stupid bloody cow!' His voice rang out, as she recalled from other times. 'I'll get you for this! I fucking *will*!' But by that time it was all over. Faith had been tentative at first, but as the abuse mounted, she increased the pressure, driving it into him with as much strength as she could muster.

Not that she needed strength, for Paul's anus had been well oiled and prepared; Jackson had seen to that. Faith could imagine him oiling Paul's backside on a daily basis until the anal ring was pliable, giving way even to her weak pressure. After an initial resistance the phallus made slow headway until the defences were overcome, when it slipped easily within the waiting sleeve. Paul gasped again, his head dropping in defeat, sighing contentedly as he felt the familiar sensation spread through him.

'Now, the whip.' Jackson held it out to her, handle first, willing her to take the short-handled, multi-stranded instrument, the ends loosely knotted.

Faith looked at it for a moment then, with a hesitant hand, took it from him. Paul was inert and he took a few deep breaths as though in preparation.

'Like this, my dear.' Martha Marryat was at Faith's elbow, positioning her arm for her. Under the woman's guidance, Faith swung the whip horizontally on to the pink, unprotected buttocks of the young man; lightly at first until Jackson told her to put some weight in it. Fewer strokes meant an easier time for Paul.

Gradually, Faith was coached in the application of the whip: how to judge the strength; how to place the strokes accurately; how to recognise when the weals left by the thongs were a hazard to further whipping. Yet, by the time she was finished, Faith felt shaken. Not that she disliked the action or found the lessons difficult to learn or execute. What was worse, she could sense the thrill within her; the exultant delight in using the fearsome instrument on another human.

Faith found to her dismay that she took a positive joy in administering the punishment, taking satisfaction at the sight of the naked, pink, quaking buttocks flaming before her and knowing there was nothing this young man could do to prevent her inflicting pain. Did Paul feel as she did? Did he thrill in anticipation? Did the pain mutate into passion as it had so often for her? The longer she went on, the more she enjoyed it, taking a pride in being able to strike the spot that either Jackson or Mrs Marryat specified. She was finding out more about herself at the Stables than she wanted; or had ever imagined.

Her breathing was quick when she finished, almost as though she had been exercising or making love. Jackson stopped her as she was about to swing again, catching her wrist to prevent the next blow landing, his serious expression bringing her down from the excited plane to which she had been lifted.

'Now,' Mrs Marryat said quietly, turning Faith away from where Jackson was releasing Paul, 'you have to "tease" him.'

'His ..?' Faith asked, her eyes widening at the thought of the upstanding erection.

The woman looked at her pupil for a moment, weighing up the different alternatives. It was always difficult teaching young women this skill. Either they were enthusiastic (in which case the subject suffered more than was necessary) or they were diffident, with the same result. She had to judge this finely, stepping in if necessary. But there was something about Faith which made her decide to continue.

It was true that Faith had begun to enjoy the whipping, but that was natural enough; many people in the same circumstances lost control of themselves and instead of a painful experience their passion had a negative effect. Yet Martha thought that Faith, if properly trained, might do quite well; she would have to lose some of her passion, of course.

Yet 'teasing' Paul would be entirely different because it was much more intimate. Faith would have to touch his erection; would have to squeeze it between her fingers and, in the intervals, take it in her mouth to massage some feeling back into it. That was the secret of 'teasing' – not letting the cock become so inured to pain that it became numb, for then the victim could ignore it.

'You'll take a strap to his erection, yes. You must strike hard – often and quickly – and in between, you must test it. I'll show you.'

Jackson had almost completed his rearrangement of the young man, who was lying back, groaning already in anticipation of what was the worst part of the punishment. Despite the times this had happened to him, he seemed to be unable to learn from the experience. Faith wondered whether he was, like herself, beginning to be attracted to the pain. Mrs Marryat brought Faith forward again and made her reach out to the purple end of the upstanding penis. Paul had been circumcised, so the foreskin had already slipped back to reveal the full, enlarged glans, naked to the world.

At Mrs Marryat's direction, Faith put her fingers on the hot, slippery end, her squeeze growing harder until a small quantity of hot fluid emerged on to her fingers.

'There!' Mrs Marryat said. 'Rub that between your fingers. Feel how oily it is? Clear? That's pre-semen; that tells you he has semen to release. When you've brought him to his climax, he'll still have an erection, but no pre-semen – not unless you rouse him again, which we won't do. So "tease" him, Miss Faith; tease him as hard and often as you can!'

Faith tried. She smacked the short, stiff leather strap up and down and side to side as she had seen Mrs Marryat do, ignoring Paul's pleas to stop and the threats and swearing he directed at her – something he never did when Mrs Marryat worked on him. From time to time Mrs Marryat had her stop, squeezing him again, and looking at the red, abused flesh. She showed her how to strike with the strap flat against the skin, so that the whole erection was struck at the same time. Yet despite the smacking, the erection remained stiff. If anything, it grew larger with the swelling of surface blood vessels.

An erection is a miracle of hydraulics, caused when desire drives a large quantity of blood into the penis. With ejaculation, desire dwindles to return the organ to normal size. With Faith providing outside stimulation, the blood flooded into the tissues, giving him an erection, but without releasing the desire which the manual stimulation of the prostate by the phallus had induced. Caught between the two fires, Paul could only groan.

When Mrs Marryat was ready, she stopped Faith again, feeling under the scrotum and putting Faith's hand there too, allowing her to extend her knowledge.

'Feel how tight he is now? That tells you he is beginning to be ready. Now, your mouth, Miss Faith; apply it to his erection. I know you know how to use it, so suck and lick him. Show him how nice a woman can be; show him that masturbation is a waste of an erection. Tease him again.'

Bending stiffly in front of him, her limbs trembling, Faith obeyed, taking the hot flesh into her mouth. Paul groaned quietly at the hot, soft, moist touch as she slowly allowed his erection in between her lips, running the inside of her lips closely over the glans and down the shaft.

She recognised the familiar taste from her previous experiences in this area – the salty, slippery, sweaty taste of Paul. The young man groaned again as Mrs Marryat brought Faith's hand round to hold his scrotum, the pulse within it gathering pace as she continued.

But Paul was not to obtain release so soon. Faith was ordered upright again for another five minutes of strapping his erect member. He no longer yelled, but begged her softly for release. The next time Faith felt it she was reminded of a drumskin stretched tightly across a frame.

For how long would this be prolonged? Faith wondered. Would Mrs Marryat insist on keeping this up much longer? She had doubts about her own ability.

'Now, Miss Faith. Sheath him as you sheath the standing man; squeeze him to his climax and yours.'

'What?' Faith's lips trembled as she looked at the shorter, older woman. 'Do it!' the woman snapped sharply.

Faith never knew quite how it happened. The woman had snapped at her and the next moment – or so it seemed – she was astride Paul, his huge, hot erection nested within her equally hot, aromatic passage. He, bent backwards over the bar and supporting her weight, groaned as she bestrode him, while Faith also groaned with the familiar contact. It was the first live penis she had experienced in some time and she meant to enjoy every second of it.

She was about to sigh in ecstasy when there was a familiar whistling noise as the strap cracked down on her buttocks with the familiar, stinging result. Almost automatically, Faith's muscles tensed up, squeezing Paul's erection in the process. Her vagina had been educated in control and even with the Burmese bells within her cervix, Paul was clearly too aroused to care.

He roared his gasping climax to the sky, while Faith jerked and shuddered in her own, aided by the judicious application of the strap to her tensed buttocks. With gasping breath, Faith allowed herself to fall forward on to the recumbent figure, shielding her flushed humiliation at taking her pleasure from the gallery of observers. They had been too far away to see more than Paul being efficiently flogged and 'teased'; too far to see the doubts and hesitations flit across Faith's expression. They only saw her outward appearance – the leather, the clamps and the shaven crotch.

After being plucked from atop the still-rampant erection and marvelling that it would not go down, Faith was hustled away to the saddle while Jackson removed Paul to his room where, chained to his bed, he could recuperate.

But for Faith it was more than just an incident. She knew that despite Susan's sweet, secret, lubricious attentions and despite the freedom it offered her from the seemingly eternal prospect of being bound, she still preferred a man within her hot body. Yet there was an aspect which worried her more than she cared to admit, even to herself, and the more she thought about it, the worse her dilemma.

For some time she was subdued as she thought about it, her face closed in thought while Susan massaged oil into her skin. Unlike previous massages, Faith made no protest or comment when the oil was worked into her anus, normally something about which she was sensitive. Susan's oily fingers were pushed deep into Faith's rectum without provoking anything more than an automatic grunt of acknowledgement.

'Are you ill, Miss Faith?' Susan's quiet, insidious voice was able to disturb even the most concentrated of Faith's thoughts.

'No,' Faith replied quickly. 'Just . . . just thinking.'

'No, Mistress,' Susan said quietly, reminding her that, despite outward appearances, the relationship between them remained the same. Though she was massaging Faith, she was still the mistress.

'No, Mistress,' Faith repeated, lowering her tone again and provoking a smile from the standing woman.

'Thinking?' she asked, amused by the idea for a brief moment. 'And what thoughts cause so much pain?'

'Pain, Mistress?' Faith started, trying to turn to look at the woman, but was pressed down again by the strong hands.

'Yes, pain,' Susan repeated. 'Something bothers you. I've seen you endure strappings with less emotion. What's bothering you?'

'Bothering? Yes, I –' Faith broke off, shaking her head at the leather beneath her, trying to formulate the words she knew she wanted but was unable to find.

'Was it, perhaps, the punishment? Paul *has* to learn, as do you.'

'I . . . I . . . I didn't . . . like doing that, Mistress,' Faith answered, keeping her face averted, hoping that the woman wouldn't recognise the half-truth.

'Didn't you?' Susan's tone told Faith that, unless she made some comment, she would be in danger of being punished for lying. But the masseuse was too quick for Faith. 'I watched you. Looking at you, as well as how you performed, and I didn't notice any revulsion, any disgust with what you were doing. You seemed to be rather enjoying it. Were you? Could it be that you're developing a taste for punishment?'

'That's . . . that's what I mean . . . actually, Mistress.' Faith felt her flush rise as her face burned. This woman was ahead of her at every stage.

Faith forgot that not only had Susan been trained in the self-same art, she had been a professional practitioner before she arrived at the Stables. Not only was she older than Faith, but she had trained several other young people. She was a shrewd observer of people who could be pretty accurate in her assessments. Not someone easily fooled by her feeble protestations.

'What's the matter, Miss Faith? Upset because you enjoyed strapping Paul?'

'Yes, Mistress,' Faith confessed quietly, hoping the woman would drop the subject.

'Why? Because you did a good job? Because you gave him the punishment he deserved?' She paused, waiting for an answer, then added, 'Or because you enjoyed doing it? He was helpless, fastened to the bar, unable to resist. Was that it? *Did* you enjoy it?'

'I . . . I think so, Mistress.' Faith's quiet groan made the woman smile.

'Do you think he'd have been so concerned had

your positions been reversed?' she asked. 'Do you think he wouldn't have enjoyed it?'

'I . . . I . . . I don't . . . know. It doesn't matter, does it, Mistress? It's what *I* feel that bothers me. Not *his* feelings.'

'Is it? You don't hold with doing to others what they would do to you, given half the chance. I see.'

Susan's fingers continued working into Faith's flesh automatically for a few moments until Faith asked, 'Is it . . . am I . . . wrong, in . . . in . . . liking . . . that, Mistress?' Faith was genuinely puzzled.

'Not wrong,' Susan replied quietly. 'And it's good that you realise it. You may have to administer discipline like that, one day, so you should know what to expect. But as for feeling remorse . . . Remorse is when you're sorry for what you've done, and you're not, are you? Your concern is the fact that you liked using the whip. But remember, up to now you've been on the receiving end, and you probably thought those using the whip were fiends; I know I did when I was being trained. I hated them all.

'I thought the people whipping me were perverted monsters; people with no feelings, no regard for human suffering. I found the reverse, in fact. They knew exactly what my feelings were, and judged precisely how much I could take. They showed me I had a very narrow, restricted view of my abilities, and also that pain in itself is nothing. It's a stage through which the body passes, provided the pain is carefully measured, of course. If I chose, I could inflict on you far greater pain than you have ever known, yet leave no marks a week later.

'You'd scream in agony behind a gag, plead silently for mercy, unable even to release the emotion. That would be *real* cruelty. We don't do that; though I believe some "schools" do. No. Pain has to be measured and very carefully applied. There has to be a relationship between the pain of punishment and the offence for which punishment is given, otherwise there's no point. Senseless brutality you can find anywhere, Miss Faith; on a street corner or in a stately home. More often in the latter, if my clients were anything to judge by. It's the intelligent application – the selective application of pain – which achieves the purpose.

'Paul masturbates. He knows he'll be punished for it, yet he persists. We could fasten his hands so he was unable to masturbate and you might say that's what we should do. It would prevent him being punished, but it wouldn't stop him masturbating when his hands were released. He has free will and it's his choice. He can stop masturbating any time, but he disobeys because of pride or defiance. He knows what will happen and, while he doesn't like being punished, in an odd way, I think he's trying to prove – if only to himself – that he can take whatever we dish out. There are times when I find myself admiring him. You've not seen him at his best.'

'I still feel . . . I don't know; ashamed, Mistress.'

'Ashamed of what?' The woman gave a sudden laugh.

'Of . . . of enjoying . . . that.'

'Think of it like this, Miss Faith. For a month we've been training you – bending you over that same bar, applying force, hurting you – though I know we've given you pleasure, too. Suddenly, with no warning, you're put in the position of being able to inflict some of the pain.' Susan paused for a moment, smiling at the tanned back presented to her. 'You enjoy it because you were able to displace your own fear and pain and pass it on to someone else – Paul. Had it not been you, someone else would have done it, so he'd still have been punished. With you watching, as before. For your disobedience, you'd have been next across the bar. You knew what had to happen . . . had to happen. Do you think he didn't want that phallus thrust into him? Or obtained no sexual arousal? We put it in a bucket of ice beforehand to make it cold so he won't *relish* it. His family had a choice; they either had him examined by a psychiatrist, which might mean anything from therapy to being restrained in an institution, or he came here.'

'I still don't like it, Mistress,' Faith grumbled.

'Turn over.' Susan tapped her side lightly in a familiar manner. Faith placed her shoulders on the leather top, looking directly up at the ceiling. 'I hope you don't, Miss Faith,' Susan said, startling Faith into looking directly at her as she leaned over, fingers already working on the muscles at her neck, a slight smile on her normally impassive face. 'You thought I'd encourage you? No. Using the strap or whip is not for you unless your duties as a pleasure slave require it. I dare say you could sexually rouse your master with it. If he wanted you to, you could probably rouse a woman too. You know by now how . . . delightful it can be. But no. Your role, your . . . vocation, is not discipline, but to give pleasure. If you remember that and nothing else we teach you, this training will have been worthwhile.'

Two nights later, as Susan was getting Faith into bed, Jackson entered the room, making her look at him in surprise. It was the first time he had been there since that first night when, with Mrs Marryat, he had examined her on arrival. After a moment, during which Faith was certain a look was exchanged between them, Jackson nodded, looking at her.

'Lie face-down on the bed, Miss Faith,' Jackson said quietly, gesturing towards the covers.

'Why?' she asked, flushing at the directness of the question. She knew that slaves were not supposed to question their masters or those set in authority over them, but her guilt was mitigated by the fact that, automatically, she was already moving in the direction he indicated.

'It's time to further your education. So I'm going to enter you.'

A cold sweat broke out on her face and she gulped, looking at him in alarm. She turned to find Susan was already seating herself on the bed where he had pointed, raising her white dress to expose her lack of underwear, the dark triangle of her pubic hair neatly trimmed. This had been previously arranged, Faith thought, for she remembered her removing her white briefs up on the hillside that afternoon. Jackson reached out, seized Faith's arm and threw her roughly on top of Susan, who pulled her into position.

Lying face down across the softness of Susan's thighs, her hands up by her head, Faith waited, feeling the warmth of the woman beneath her as she listened to the rustling clothes behind, aware of her own trembling. She could imagine the punishment he would inflict the following morning, or even that night, in the courtyard if she fought against what was about to happen.

'Part your legs,' Susan told her quietly, her left hand closing over Faith's soft, crushed, left breast.

The young woman was far too tense to obey as quickly as she should. Jackson parted her legs roughly with his strong hands while she had the sense to lie inert, making no resistance. He picked her up by her hips to settle her into a better position across Susan then, to her complete surprise, slipped his rather large erection into her lubricating passage, immediately thrusting deeply within and using his strength to

223

overcome the restrictions of the diminished size, ignoring the feel of the 'rin no tama' when the tip burst through to her cervix.

'There. Not so bad, is it, Miss Faith?' he asked cheerily as the easy movement of his hips moved her rhythmically on the covers.

Faith kept her beetroot-coloured face averted, not wishing to meet Susan's eye, but the woman turned her head back with the instruction, 'Look at me, Miss Faith. Look at me and when you feel pleasure, stick your tongue out as you were taught.'

With her eyes fastened on those of the woman, like a rabbit caught by a snake, Faith's nipples tingled at the touch of her hands on them. Her belly sent familiar sensations resounding within as the large, warm and gentle erection moved inside her. The three balls seemed to almost get out of his way when he drove himself upward and she tightened her muscles up on him. If this was what she was being trained for, then she would show them just what she was learning.

One hand moved from her hips to encompass her breasts, displacing Susan, who began to kiss Faith's pink tongue which was emerging from her full lips. Jackson's thumb and forefinger found her nipples, applying a pressure which delayed her orgasm while his other hand found her clitoris. The twin, contradictory pressures set up a conflict; one urging her on, one urging her back, both adding to her pleasure. Yet Jackson himself, even when Faith finally climaxed – her throaty cries unmistakable though muffled by Susan's mouth as she struggled within their grasp – refused to spill his seed.

Withdrawing slowly, letting her feel the full benefit of the slow, sinuous, liquid movement, he pressed the tip of his hot erection on her sphincter, making her catch her breath. She anticipated that at any moment

224

she would be painfully violated; that he would spear her vitals as she had Paul with the phallus. Tensing herself for the thrust, muscles tightening against him, she finally broke her silence.

'Please! No!' she begged in a quiet, hoarse voice once the woman released her mouth, her head shaking as the pressure increased slightly.

It would take hardly any pressure at all for him to penetrate her, but he hesitated, then asked in a surprisingly quiet tone, 'Why not, Miss Faith?' He waited, on the brink of penetration, for an answer.

Faith knew she could plead with him; knew too her pleas would be ignored. She had to have a reason, otherwise he would bugger her. He would quite calmly drive his erection into her rectum, despite everything she could do to stop him. Her bottom hole had been oiled and prepared daily by Susan; was it perhaps for this very assault? She could imagine his organ being thrust in and out of her anus, possibly damaging it.

'Because –' Faith stopped, swallowing harshly before she continued. 'Because . . . it's for my master.'

'Quite right, Miss Faith.' Jackson withdrew the pressure at once. 'Only your master should use you there, or allow you to be used there.' His gruff voice was almost tender. 'I have to admit, I'd like to take you there now. Best get to bed, though. Good night, Miss Faith.'

'Good . . . good night, Mr Clive,' Faith replied, unable to call him 'Master' the way she addressed Susan as 'Mistress', and speaking in a voice she hardly recognised as he turned away and left the room.

Susan's amused expression watched her for several minutes before she asked, 'Are you dribbling *very* much on the covers, Faith?'

'Yes, Mistress. I'm sorry,' Faith answered, her eyes dropping at once.

'What do you suppose I should do about it? After all, I've had to watch you take your pleasure, and had none myself.'

'Whatever you suggest, Mistress,' Faith answered at once, knowing that to hesitate would be to invite something far worse.

'No. What do *you* suggest, Faith?' Susan asked. If Faith only knew that *this* was the whole purpose of the exercise, she would have hesitated less. Jackson was an irrelevance. It was the willing yielding of herself – the surrender – that was important.

'I . . . I . . .' Faith buried her face in the covers to conceal her confusion and lust, for she knew that more than anything she wanted to be spanked.

'Ask me, Faith. Ask me for what you want,' Susan said quietly.

After a few trembling moments, Faith raised her face to look at the woman, surprise and horror in her eyes as she stammered out, 'Would . . . would you . . . please . . . s-s-sss . . . spank me, Mistress?' She buried her face again.

'Of course, Faith. I haven't a strap, so I'll have to use my hand. You'd like that, wouldn't you?'

'Yes, Mistress!' Faith howled, shocked by the realisation that without much prompting she was acknowledging that being spanked brought her pleasure; and after she'd had Jackson within her. After she had experienced an orgasm!

'One!' Susan began as she brought her hand down hard on the soft buttocks which Faith proffered so freely.

Lying alone in the darkness afterwards, Faith ran her fingers down her labial lips. The hair was growing back from where Susan had shaved it, even though it had only been done a few days previously. Yet feeling

226

the delicate tissue and opening herself up so that she could feel within herself, remembering what Jackson had felt like, Faith breathed comfortably. The skin of her buttocks glowed hot. The spanking had been intimate and Susan had made her spread her legs so wide that her fingers had often struck the tissue of those lips, which glowed from the contact. So much had happened to her, so many strange, new and wonderful experiences, yet she was still very excited by a man's cock squirming inside her. Thankful of that, and satisfied that she was still heterosexual, she fell asleep.

Chapter Thirteen

During the third week in June, another trial began for Faith, who had found herself gradually moving into an acceptance of the ways of the Stables, the restraints being only one of the many different conditions. At night, the chain at her throat and by day, having her wrists fastened behind her, became second nature. During other times she found herself even more secured, unable to move a muscle while Susan or Jackson plied the strap. To her surprise, neither restraint bothered her; she became accustomed to them, and even came to enjoy the feeling of security they brought.

Insecurity resulted from the gradual way in which they were dispensing with the tightness of the bonds during 'exercise', as the regular measures of instructional chastisement were called. If she was helpless, unable to resist should they wish to visit something on her, she could console herself with the thought that she had no choice.

But as the days progressed through hotter and hotter weather, Faith found herself being told to spread her unrestrained legs and to remain in those positions while the strap or paddle was applied. Her wrists would be unsecured at times so that she was, she found, merely standing still and allowing herself to be dealt with as they chose. The fact that not only did she go along with it but derived sexual satisfaction from it gave her food for thought. Not just that she took the easiest course of action – obedience – but that she found it perfectly right they should inflict pain on her. As always, with the pain came the sensations of arousal.

Faith also found the stinging of the strap or paddle on her buttocks was becoming less severe. Even when Susan deliberately brought the strap down hard across the inside of her thighs, attacking the soft flesh there, it failed to terrorise her. The delicate skin at the junction of her buttocks and thighs, perhaps the most sensitive of all, hardly attracted her notice when brought to a flaming hue by a length of leather.

Once, when spread out across the bar in the yard for some petty infraction, Gerald had been deputed to add some strength to Susan's arm (and shame to Faith's perception), bending her over the bar himself. He had leered at her knowingly and let his fingers tickle her gaping, moist sex before he began to work on her.

Gerald knew that for Faith to tense the muscles in her buttocks was to invite a greater discomfort, so he waited patiently until she relaxed, then deliberately brought some of the blows short, the end of the strap striking her lubricious labial lips, evoking a whimper of protest the first time, even as the pleasure shot through her.

Gerald had recognised the sound at once for what it was; the beginning of lust, and after that he ensured that more of his blows were short, building up her whimperings into gasping cries of pain and pleasure. He had stopped to allow Susan to rub Faith's own juices from her soaking sex over her perineum and buttocks before finishing – too soon in Faith's mind. She had fervently kissed the strap afterwards.

Within a day or two, this had almost faded from

her memory in the serenity she found in following the advice which was urged on her at every turn. She was beginning to submerge herself within the few remaining restraints and the pain, allowing herself to construct a mental carapace beneath which to shelter her emotions. Even when suspended by her wrists from a high pole in the yard, with two of them using their bare hands to spank her and laughing as she twisted and turned at first, frantic to escape their shaming slaps, Faith had found it possible to control herself. Later, when Gerald and Hilary took over with paddles, ensuring that from waist to knee her skin was a bright cherry colour, Faith never lost the ability to think of herself as standing outside her body, watching. Yet she found it difficult to control her arousal from that very same situation.

As the days passed and this punishment continued, she asserted sufficient control to remain quite still, her toes just touching the concrete while they slapped first her buttocks then her inner thighs. Even when Susan held her legs apart while Gerald spanked her open sex, reaching behind and below her to administer the most intimate spanking, Faith's control never faltered; though her sex dribbled uncontrollably.

She had little routine apart from waking, washing and meals. Each day she would be escorted first to the mirror room for the daily ritual of standing absolutely still, looking at her own reflection, while Susan (and occasionally Gerald or Hilary) watched over her with a paddle or strap, ready to use it if she moved. Some days, if they were honest in their work, Faith avoided being punished.

Afterwards, she went to the gymnasium to exercise, followed by the saddle to exercise her internal muscles, then usually in the afternoon she would walk in the woods with Susan, where in the privacy of the bushes she would be released to satisfy Susan's wants. Yet despite this constant attention, Faith barely responded to the Sapphic advances, and never initiated any.

There were occasions when Jackson or Mrs Marryat herself would escort her, always in her brace, corset and boots. Such walks, for all the different mental stimulation, would inevitably lead to her being bent over a tree-stump or a fallen log to have punishment administered, usually on the most flimsy of pretexts. This was done either by a series of hefty slaps or from a thin, whippy, newly cut switch. Afterwards, they would hold the backs of their hands to her hot sex, testing the temperature without touching her. One time she suggested that Jackson stick his fingers within, mostly to relieve her own need, though she could see his interest.

She never repeated the offer, for on arrival at the yard, she was punished on the bar with a strapping which took a thick application of Arnica cream to her buttocks and two days before the marks disappeared. Yet Jackson would occasionally visit her at night with Susan to use her vagina; always without discharging. It was as though the penetration, the working of her to her own climax, was justification enough. After which Susan would spank her and, relieved of the ache of lust which had grown again between her legs, she would sleep well content. She found it odd.

Coming back from their walk one afternoon, she found the whole pupil body in the yard, while Jackson and Mrs Marryat ranted at them. There had been too much slackness lately; people were becoming too blasé about what they were doing. The growing heat may have had something to do with it, but it was no excuse. Those who had not been sufficiently punished would receive it there and then, in the yard in front of everyone.

To her surprise, Faith found she was not included on the list of those who had not been sufficiently punished, but was shackled to the high posts with arms and legs spread wide where she could watch. For a few moments she was reminded of the strapping Mrs Marryat had first given her in that position, her full swelling breasts heaving with the thought of what one would be like now. She accepted that the woman had taught her a lesson rather than punish her.

A stool was placed directly in front of her, about two feet away, and before Faith's astonished gaze, Jackson bent Susan over it, lifting her skirt preparatory to entering her. Faith watched amazed, as the woman lay inert until Jackson actually entered her, pushing himself into one of her openings with something akin to a snarl. Then Susan seemed to come alive.

With a start, Faith found Susan reaching forward, gripping the crossbars of the stool with her hands to steady her while her tongue began to caress Faith's open sex, driving her to distraction within seconds. She knew she should stand still, ignoring the stimulation, and that she might be punished for it, but the feel of the soft, hot mouth on her was too much.

Her punishment, when it came, was to use the strap on the three newest arrivals, only one of whom had arrived subsequent to her admission. One after the other she went down the line, collected the young woman and, holding her by the arm, escorted her up to the bar, where she spread her out and began work. Unused to the strap, her handiwork was hardly of the same class as Mrs Marryat's or Susan's, but from the cries and groans, she knew they found it stimulating in the extreme.

* * *

Mrs Marryat went for Faith one morning rather than Susan and, as luck would have it, found Faith with her fingers between her thighs, the aroma of aroused young woman wafting under her nostrils. Faith made no attempt to explain or deny what she was doing, but knelt on her bed obediently, meekly awaiting whatever punishment might be decreed. For some time Martha stood still behind her.

'You were "diddling" yourself, Miss Faith,' the woman accused in a soft, silky voice.

'Yes, Madame.' Faith remained still.

'How should you be punished for that?'

'As it pleases you, Madame.' Faith had the right answer ready. If Martha wanted to trap Faith into requesting a light punishment, she was mistaken. She had seen what had happened when Roger did that with Gerald; taking note of the fact that the young man had been stiff for days afterwards.

'What is the most exquisite pain you know, Miss Faith?' the woman asked. 'What gave you the most severe pain?'

Faith remained silent for some seconds, thinking before she answered. 'When my Mistress made me stand in the yard with a thong between my legs, Madame.' She had wondered whether this would happen again. Her calves had trembled for days.

'Yes.' Martha nodded slowly, a slow smile unseen by Faith. 'I shall arrange that again. Up! Shower first and then to the mirror room. I'll paddle you dry.'

After being led by the chain on her collar to the mirror room (Faith was glad the woman failed to attach the clamps to her nipples), she stood before the mirror while Mrs Marryat paddled her behind. She made no attempt to justify it by her movements or posture, and such was the shame Faith felt that she was glad not to be taken out to the yard. The heat dried her off before she returned to her room for breakfast, after which, in boots, corset and clamps, the woman led her by the chain attached to her nipples to the gymnasium, where she was fastened to the wall bars.

Once standing with her back to them, Mrs Marryat tied the leather thong to the collar again before drawing it up between Faith's legs, lifting her on to her toes and making her grimace. Like Susan before her, she crouched to check that it was centrally placed before she tied it to one of the bars behind Faith, high enough to lift her on to her toes.

'Now, I intend to have you roused, Miss Faith. And the only way you get relief from that will be to drop from your toes, which will hurt. It will hurt the sweet little nut you love so much, won't it?'

'Yes, Madame,' Faith answered, already feeling the effects of the pressure and licking her lips.

'You're feeling that way already, I think. Still. We have to wait for Mr Clive.'

Jackson arrived when Faith was becoming desperate, for the aches in her calves were making it difficult to control her trembling limbs. He wasted little time and stripped Martha Marryat before Faith's surprised eyes, then fastened her facing the wallbars opposite. She made no protest as her wrists were secured at waist level and her feet moved wide apart, though she looked round to see whether Faith was watching, their eyes meeting in a blinding flash of understanding. It was clear to Faith that the woman was enjoying the preparations, just as it was equally clear what she was being prepared for.

When he began to strap her, Jackson used a thin, flexible belt which he brought down savagely across her buttocks for a good five minutes, during which time Faith saw the fair skin turn a deep red and heard her grunt a little every so often in a low, controlled tone. She could only admire the woman's self-control, for not a whimper or cry escaped her lips. It was not the first time Faith had thought about the immediate effects of a strapping, but Jackson was not finished. Martha had accepted this in silence, not even flinching, but then he changed his stance, and his aim.

He began to strike her with the belt at right angles to his previous direction, coating the insides of her buttocks at first, then lowering his aim to her sphincter, followed soon after by her vulva. Martha began to twitch under this abuse and stifled protests bubbled from her, running together until she was whimpering and the first wails began to emerge.

'Do you want me to continue?' Jackson asked, stopping for a moment and looking at the bound woman. Faith could see he was sweating, his chest heaving with the exertion, for he had been strapping her for almost quarter of an hour.

'Yes please, Clive.' Martha's quiet whisper just reached Faith's ears before the belt began again.

This time, as though the rest had undone her, the woman began to cry quietly, yet not just in pain. Faith listened with growing surprise and humiliation, becoming aware that Mrs Marryat was beginning to have an orgasm. Already, Faith could see the glistening moisture on her open, ruddy, sex lips; a moisture which increased as the strapping went on. Her cries began to catch in her throat, her breathing becoming shallow. Faith could almost feel her own orgasm releasing as she heard the familiar triumphant joy emanating from deep within Mrs Marryat, her head jerking up and back, her hips twisting and shaking as Jackson continued, driving her voice higher until it became a full-blooded cry, as loud as any Faith had emitted in the previous weeks.

The sound seemed to be sweet music to Jackson, for he stopped, looking at Faith, savouring the moment with a self-satisfied smile and listening to the jerking, twisting woman beside him whose thighs were now soaking with her own discharges. He made no move towards Martha but walked across to where Faith stood, and began to finger her sex, divided by the thong though it was. As she gasped and tried to move slightly, constrained by the securing thong and distinctly embarrassed to be witnessing such an intimate moment, he brought his erection from his trousers, laying it up along her lower belly. She knew that while he had been working on the woman, she had been quietly lowering herself on to the thong as a means of controlling her own arousal, but if he continued, she would have to be more severe with herself.

He was shorter than Faith so only the tip would have made entry had he tried to insert it. He rubbed that tip between her legs on the thong which split her, allowing her flesh to feel his erection. Faith's breathing became more laboured at the touch and she had to lower herself more on to the thong to prevent herself climaxing just at the thought. A month before she would have climaxed with the sensations which were coursing through her, but he nodded his acknowledgement of her control before returning to the bent-over woman.

Without ceremony, but careful that Faith could see every detail until the very last moment, he placed the tip of his erection at his housekeeper's sphincter, and pressed firmly. Faith was able to see the yielding pink ring swallowing the engorged erection before it was concealed by Jackson's body. Once again he waited until it was fully within her before he stood quite still, reaching forward to grasp her breasts while encouraging her to squeeze him, to move her behind, to deliver *his* orgasm. All of which she did, thanking him afterwards when he removed himself.

Faith could see the seminal fluid at her anus for some time, for Jackson walked out of the gymnasium, leaving his housekeeper fastened in that position. It was a cruel addition to the humiliation, Faith thought, being tethered like that with the evidence of the strapping on her rump and the evidence of his passion so clearly visible.

She thought she could see what they were trying to tell her; that a master could do what he chose and that it was a pleasure slave's business to accommodate him. That no matter how it came about, the master would also ensure that the slave was pleasured too, and that only total obedience would be tolerated. Masturbation was a means of circumventing this, and would therefore be ruthlessly stamped out.

Jackson was gone almost an hour, during which time Martha remained silent and unmoving while the semen trailed almost obscenely from her. When he returned to release her, she thanked him again and dressed while he released Faith. He then took Faith away for her morning ride on the saddle. She had several orgasms just thinking about what she had witnessed in the gymnasium.

One morning while Faith had breakfast, Susan left the room to return a few minutes later, placing a multi-stranded whip on the bed alongside Faith. The young woman's eyes were immediately drawn to it, her mouth opening in protest though no words came. Her breathing increased as she looked at the polished surface of the wooden handle and the long, lustrous strands of leather which would soon be kissing her behind. She knew then the panic which had gripped Paul in roughly similar circumstances, regretting having taken such pleasure in using the whip on him and later teasing him.

'I've been good, Mistress,' Faith said softly, lowering her eyes in case looking at Susan was taken as a measure of defiance. 'I *have* obeyed.'

'Yes, Miss Faith,' Susan answered quietly, her voice conveying sympathy and understanding. 'You have and are obeying very well, too.'

'Why must I be whipped, Mistress?' Faith sobbed into the cup before her.

'You know why, Miss Faith,' Susan replied quietly. 'You must be whipped to complete your training; otherwise, how can you go home? And you want to go home, don't you?'

'The whip'll hurt! I'm ... I'm frightened of it!' Faith sobbed, her face crumpling into a pitiful parody of anguish.

Susan did what she could to quiet Faith, dabbing her tears and clutching her head against her chest as if cradling a weeping child. When the tears were dried and the sobbing stilled, she tried to explain. 'Of course you're frightened; but you have been in one of the cages, which taught you to face your fears. Accepting the whip will do that too. You're afraid, but a sound whipping will show you that if you face your fears they become far less than you imagine.

'You used to think being strapped was terrible. I can remember – and I'm sure others do too – when you screamed when the strap even stroked your behind. Now you almost ignore it, don't you? The whip is only a little different; stronger in some ways, not in others. Why fear it? Why so afraid when you know we love you and would do anything not to hurt you?'

'Why must I be punished, Mistress?' Faith asked fearfully, looking not at the whip, but at the serious-faced young woman, whose expression could have been carved from granite.

'It's not a punishment,' the woman assured her at

once. 'It's a lesson; a lesson in obedience. When you've finished breakfast, you'll take the whip yourself, insert it as you've been taught, then bring it to me in the mirror room. No one will be with you. I'll wait. This must be *your* obedience; an indication you have absorbed the lessons we teach. Do you understand? We're not punishing you, Faith; you must believe that.'

Faith had settled down to making steady progress, accepting the restrictions without complaint, and any infraction of the rules she committed were petty. But if Faith had the idea that despite being obedient she was still punished, she would have little incentive to be obedient in future. What Susan was trying to do was to minimise any future difficulties.

'It's hard,' Susan agreed as she went on, her eyes finding Faith's. 'The whip's everything you hate and fear, but Mad Martha is right, Miss Faith. You have to learn. The first time is the worst. Like anything else, you fear the unknown. Come to me in the mirror room, Miss Faith, and bring the whip.'

Abruptly, she rose from where she had seated herself beside Faith on the bed, an arm spread encouragingly around her braced, naked shoulders, and left the room to leave the young woman to ponder alone. Faith was aware of Susan's internal tensions, not realising that it was differently based to her own. She thought Susan hesitated about using the whip on her, when she was actually tense about the fact that this was one of the final tests of obedience. If Faith were to join her in the mirror room and accept the whipping, then Martha would soon be able to inform the Chosen that their new recruit had completed her training; though telling her this would be wrong.

Once done, the Chosen would send someone for

her and one of their most difficult pupils would be off their hands. But there was no rush for Faith to make up her mind, for it was a stern test of character. For an organisation which demanded instant obedience to even the most mundane instruction, surmounting this obstacle was treated carefully. Fearing it, Faith would obviously take time to come to terms with the idea of the whip. Only if she had not appeared within a reasonable time would Susan go to find her, and then more to help than chastise.

In the event of total non-compliance, Susan would fall back on the methods used earlier: compulsion. She would make her splay her legs (secured if necessary) then insert the whip in the girl, who would be whipped far more severely as a result. This was a test for her but if she failed she would learn that compliance, instant obedience to orders, was preferable to having them enforced. It was a hard lesson to get across to someone like Faith, who feared the whole idea. But she had to be made to see that her compliance was something to be taken for granted. If she could not be trusted to comply, then the Chosen would wash their hands of her, and all that pain and suffering would be for nothing.

Forcing herself, Faith fearfully extended her hand nervously towards the whip on the covers beside her. The handle was towards her, feeling shiny and cold as she rubbed her fingers lightly down the shaft. It was like the one which she had used on Paul earlier. There were the same luxuriant strands on the far end; a profusion of thongs, their ends still knotted, which would release their pent-up energy against her skin in a burst of savagery. Gulping, Faith picked it up in one hand, running the fronds through the fingers of her other hand, feeling their firm flexibility.

She was more calm now, though still shaking at the

sight of it. It was a terrible thing, but it would pass, as all things *did* pass. What was it Susan had said? Pain is as transitory as pleasure? Yes, she believed that. She had to. She would be whipped as one of her lessons, as part of her training. But if she refused? The very thought made her catch her breath. If she tried to flee, or just refused to have anything to do with it, then she would be bent over the bar anyway, and she would be whipped; hard. Far harder than this whip would be swung at her buttocks this morning, if she took it to where Susan waited.

She knew all the reasons for going out there with a light heart and jaunty step; she knew all the submissions she had made of her pride and self; her complete self-degradation. Faith felt she had given enough and yet here was one more hurdle. There always seemed to be hurdles; tests of her humiliation, her will to survive and obey. Susan had been right about the way to accept what was happening to her – accept and subsume; welcome it, even. Could she do that? Could she offer up her body to the savage pain of this whip? Complicating the equation was the thrill she felt at the touch and smell of the leather; the anticipation of being aroused to a climax by such an instrument.

It came down to logic in the end; either a greater punishment or a less. The greater punishment would be excruciating and would be followed by others, probably just as painful. But if she surrendered yet again, abased herself *before* herself and cast out the last small fragment of her pride and independence, then the succeeding whippings would perhaps be less painful.

She might, of course, approach them with less terror. The terror of the whip she would vanquish within herself, not the pain of it. She would never be able to face a whipping with equanimity; even the delight of Mrs Marryat in the gymnasium, when she had been stripped and strapped, seemed far too advanced for Faith, yet unless she complied, she would always be in terror of this instrument.

Her breathing was emerging shakily from her chest as she rose; her mouth working silently as tears dripped relentlessly from her eyes. Frantically she blinked them away, wiping the backs of her wrists against first one and then the other to remove the occluding moisture. It was simple enough to place the whip upright on the bed, the fronds hanging down from the covers, then manoeuvre herself over it; unaware that she had a witness to the struggle.

Susan had waited ten minutes in the mirror room, feeling each minute like a day. Her hopes had been high that Faith would quickly follow her, for she had watched the improvement in the young woman with rising excitement. She had arrived with a reputation for being comfortable with bondage, which had subsequently been supported by the evidence. They had discovered in her a predisposition to accept the ministrations of discipline which, allied with her acceptance of being fastened, augured well for her master. Yet as the time had dragged on, her fears were becoming more pronounced until Mad Martha, who was waiting with her, said sourly, 'Doesn't look as though she's coming, does it?'

Susan looked at the door, praying she would see the girl opening it to join them.

'Give her time, Madame, please,' the younger woman protested quietly. If Faith failed, then it would be as much her failure – a failure of her judgement – and Martha and Clive would exact their payment for it in pain.

'She can't be ready, can she?' Mrs Marryat asked

sharply, eyeing the younger woman in the mirror. Susan looked pale and Martha could well understand why, too. She was in love with this one. It happened.

Every so often, one of the pupils would get beneath the carapace each erected to protect themselves from the thought of the consequences of what they were doing. Faith was beautiful and Susan was attracted; given her former profession it was little wonder she preferred women to men, but having to discipline her in the way of the Stables had been difficult. On balance, if she had to do it again, would she assign Hilary to the job, or Gerald? No, not Gerald; he was attracted to the girl and might have skimped.

'There's always one test, isn't there?' Susan asked wistfully, shaking her head. 'One test that gives more trouble. With some it's the standing man, with others it's the saddle. With Faith it's the whip. She has to learn to obey, that's all.'

'Go and fetch her,' Mrs Marryat said. 'She's had ample time now. If she isn't ready, Mr Clive will punish her with it in the yard.'

She knew she could trust Susan to play by the rules, for if she found the girl had made no progress, she would never insert the whip for her and lie afterwards to spare her. That would be counterproductive and love her though she may, it would do her more harm than good. The girl *had* to learn.

Chapter Fourteen

Susan had tears pricking her eyes when she saw Faith, splay-legged over the end of the bed, trying to insert the handle. Tears were still flowing copiously down Faith's crumpled face, yet there was a jutting edge to her jaw which spoke of determination. Trembling, she watched as Faith separated her labial lips to accept the tip of the handle, then taking hold of the black shaft, worked it gently up and down to lubricate herself. The poor thing must be as dry as a chip, she thought. I should have greased the handle first. Despite this it steadily vanished within Faith's body until all she could see were the fronds dependent from Faith like long, black pubic hair, her lips closing around them. Faith had obeyed at last!

Quickly Susan hurried to the mirror room to convey the exciting news, as Faith began to move, feeling the additional pressure within her. Faith had the three small '*rin no tama*' lodged in her cervix and this wooden intrusion felt enormous as it jostled with them for space, the eccentric movements setting off the usual lubricating feelings. Her breathing deepened as she realised that the physical conflicts being set up were actually helping her by changing the focus from impending pain to present lust. She began moving her legs, finding that her lessons with the boots had borne fruit, for it was easier to walk stiff-legged than to attempt to bend her knees.

The fronds tickled and caressed the back and sides of her legs as she emerged into the corridor, holding her wrists crossed behind her. She saw the pair of women standing by the mirror room door, apparently lost in conversation. She could not have taken too long, she thought, otherwise they would have got bored by now. Someone would have come seeking her. Gulping down her fears, Faith paced up the corridor until Martha Marryat turned to look at her, her expression letting Faith know she was aware of her struggles.

'Very good, Miss Faith,' she said quietly, then nodded. 'Over to the wall with you.'

A bar had been placed in the centre of the room, almost identical to those in the yard. Silently she stopped at it, automatically placing her feet beside the uprights. Susan secured her wrists behind her first, then her ankles to the uprights, before bending her forward with a hand on her back, stooping to gently ease the handle of the whip out. Faith blushed as she found that her muscles were so contracted that she was gripping the handle hard, making Susan put more effort into it than she had anticipated. She had ignored the familiar thrill in the feeling of terror at the prospect, but now that the moment had come, Faith was reminded of her own desires.

'You must hold that position while you're whipped, Miss Faith.'

'I'll obey, Mistress,' Faith replied in the otherwise silent room.

The whip whistled more than the strap, a hideous, insidious whistling which terrified Faith long before the blow reached her, so she was tense when it landed. The crack of the thongs against her buttocks, followed swiftly by the feeling of liquid fire in the tissue, made her jerk her head and shoulders up in a gesture of mingled pain and terror, blanking out her eyes as she looked in the mirror. She hardly saw her own strained expression – eyes bulging, the tendons in her neck sticking out like cords, the open mouth gasping – for the first stroke was followed almost immediately by another, delivered quickly and hard, almost in the same place, converting her soft flesh into a crazy modernistic design.

Her tears had not even started flowing when they were demanded even more urgently, but as her cry rang out, there was a different sensation. Soft fingers were pressing into her honey-pot, opening her liquid softness, stimulating her pearl to produce more, smothering her buttocks in her own juices, spreading them over each of the swollen weals which had been raised. And all the time, there was the soft crooning voice of Martha Marryat who crouched in front of her.

'My lovely darling, you were *so* good; so good. You took your whipping so beautifully, didn't you? And it hurt, didn't it? But it's over now; all over, all over for another day. No more whipping for Miss Faith until tomorrow, and you'll see; it won't be so bad tomorrow. Tomorrow, we'll wet your pretty behind so Susan won't hurt you so much, and you'll see. You won't hate the whip at all soon. It'll be no more than just a hard spanking or a strapping. You were *so* good! Such a brave girl!'

The curious thing was that Faith believed her.

Nothing could possibly match the terror she had felt as she had answered that she would obey, facing the unknown quantity of the whipping. She had suffered slaps, crops, wands, switches, straps, belts and all manner of lesser horrors. She had conquered them all, in time. Now she had experienced the whip and its terrors were known. She knew what it felt like to have it across her backside and she could judge her reaction to it.

As June ended, Faith was allowed to wear more of her clothes, although only in the afternoons when she walked in the woods. Her walks were different too, for here and there between the trees and on a long, bare slope of hillside, the country just beyond the confines of the privately-owned wood could be seen. Vehicles passing up and down the road that ran past the entrance to the Stables were visible. Even the drivers could be identified. Sometimes Faith wondered about life outside the Stables.

Paul seemed to be improving, though slowly. He was occasionally allowed to go with them, though always with his wrists cuffed behind him, a skimpy garment covering his thin, almost feminine hips.

In the mornings, in contrast, Faith was as naked as she had been at the beginning, although they no longer bothered to use the anklets unless there was a new lesson to learn.

After lunch, during the hour of rest, the chain was lengthened to enable Faith to sit at the dressing table to use her make-up and choose what clothes to wear for their walk. The boots had become almost mandatory, although occasionally Susan would insist she change into high-heeled shoes. On those occasions (usually as they walked across the yard and again on a very enclosed section) she would have Faith raise her skirt around her waist so she could see her legs and buttocks. Faith always complied, aware of Gerald's hot eyes on her every time. It was as though he found the concept of her legs encased in stockings and skirt more attractive than bare.

Faith would spend much of her time in the yard, watching the pupils being 'exercised', marvelling at the variety of painful lessons she had avoided.

'They're being trained differently to you, Miss Faith,' Susan answered when she asked about it. They were in the shrubbery, resting after one of Susan's carnal poundings.

'How differently, Mistress?' she asked.

'You're Chosen,' the young woman said, not looking directly at her. 'You have a sponsor who provided a basic set of requirements for your training. You're a pleasure slave; they're just slaves. They're not Chosen; they're not anything. Usually they're runaways or orphans; found on the streets by people. They're recruited in any of a dozen ways and brought here for training.'

'Training in what, Mistress?'

'Discipline, like you. But without a sponsor, Mad Martha doesn't have to answer to anyone for them, other than turning them out perfectly disciplined. Which is why they're all whipped far more than you were, and they don't get any of your pleasures, either. No standing man or saddle . . . or this.' Susan kissed the bare coral nipple closest to her. 'We've . . . I've rather spoiled you since I was put in charge of you.'

'Thank you, Mistress.' Faith was aware that her blood was turning cold; almost as cold as Susan's expression.

'Something wrong?' the young woman asked, her voice sharpening.

'It was only, Mistress . . .' Faith hesitated, shrugged and swallowed. 'That I wondered how you . . . you could do it? What you do to them.'

'Let's be honest; they're fodder,' Susan replied in a cold tone. 'Fodder for a dozen brothels and perverts. With no one to worry about them, compliance will be ingrained and they'll do well. It's as much as they can hope for; they don't have the drive, or the brains in many cases, to do better for themselves. Some come from wealthy or influential families, and they'll return more disciplined than they arrived. Who knows whether they'll remember the lessons?'

'That's . . . that's terrible, Mistress.'

'That's *life*!' Susan looked at her seriously, then smiled. 'You don't know much about life, Miss Faith. You've led a very sheltered existence, haven't you? But far worse things than this go on. At least someone is looking after them, giving them a trade, if you like. Most of them will probably live a lot longer than they would have done if they hadn't been brought here.'

On the first day of July, Faith was unfastened from her bed, and knelt with her hands behind her. Susan stood looking at her for a moment, then instead of unfastening the chain from behind the bed, quietly removed the collar from Faith's throat, standing back to look at her.

'How does that feel, Miss Faith?' she asked.

'Strange, Mistress,' Faith answered, unsure whether this was a test or not. She was a slave; she knew that. She was being trained in obedience, and she *was* obedient, but she was still a slave. People, having spent a lot of time and money on training a slave, didn't just suddenly free them.

'Too strange for you to shower by yourself this morning?' the woman asked, smiling at the prospect.

Faith frowned. 'There are other things, Mistress,' the young woman said, looking round at Susan with an uncertain expression, as though suspecting a trap.

'I'm sure you can remove the phallus yourself this morning, Miss Faith,' Susan returned.

'I can remove it, yes, Mistress,' Faith answered.

After a few weeks of using the suppositories, Susan had, for no apparent reason, gone back to inserting the dildo each evening, increasing the dosage to counter the effect of the increasing use of the whip. Sometimes, in the early hours of the morning, when she was awake before everyone else, Faith would ease it partly out of her bottom and, with the aid of a mirror, look at it. Each seemed thicker, or longer, than the last. As the dildo on the saddle decreased in size, these enlarged. She kept asking herself why. Unless her master was intending to make more use of the 'tradesman's entrance' than the normal one, why was this being done? Finding no answer, Faith kept her doubts to herself, privately thinking that it looked as though her master intended to sodomise her on a regular basis. After almost two months, she had accepted Mrs Marryat's premise that Alex was not her master as he had made no attempt to contact her; she belonged to the Chosen collectively.

'Good. Then do. There's tissue there in which to wrap it. I'll collect it later. When you're finished, I'll have your breakfast ready.'

'I shall not be secured, Mistress,' Faith said, as though it was just a fact, not the delighted question some of the others addressed to her in similar circumstances.

'No,' Susan answered. 'Does that bother you?'

'A slave should be secured, Mistress.' Faith gave the inevitable answer. 'I am a pleasure slave.' Faith's logic was as impeccable as her expression; carefully neutral yet enquiring at the same time.

'Do you *want* me to secure you?' Susan asked irritably.

'A slave should be secured, Mistress. A slave is valuable property,' Faith replied, not daring to allow her feelings of joy to intrude on her face.

She had endured the regime by locking up as many of her emotions as she could within the carapace of impassivity. Conversely, Susan, Jackson and his housekeeper had tried their best to have her pour her emotions out to them. Once out in the open they could judge her reactions and tailor their treatment of her accordingly, but the young woman was more intelligent than many of their pupils, and was outwitting them more often these days.

'After you have showered and had breakfast,' the older woman said in a chilling voice which accompanied the sharp, hard look on her face, 'I'll secure you properly!' Turning on her heel, Susan left the door open behind her.

Twenty minutes later when she returned, a freshly showered Faith was kneeling on the bed with her straight back towards her guide, wrists crossed behind her. Her hands rested just above the outswelling of her dull ruby-coloured buttocks, the last relic of the previous day's whipping. She could have been there ten seconds or ten minutes, such was her stillness and poise. After looking at her for a moment, the woman fastened her wrists and told her to rise and to follow her down to the mirror room.

Once there, Faith felt uncomfortable without the collar and chain around her throat. It had been such a feature of her life that she missed it. Susan waited until Faith looked doubtfully at her, then directed her to stand in the centre of the room facing one of·the walls. Before Susan could use the whip which she brought from the table, Mrs Marryat entered, looking surprised.

Susan allowed the silence to deepen for ten seconds before she announced in irritated tones, 'I tried to release Miss Faith this morning, Madame. It appears that she prefers to have her wrists fastened like a slave.'

'I see.' Mrs Marryat nodded her acceptance of the

report, looking towards the young woman. 'What do you mean by that?'

'I *am* a slave, Madame,' Faith answered, raising her head and meeting her eye. She had little fear of her these days, for apart from being abandoned for a lengthy period in one of the cages, she thought she had experienced all the horrors the Stables had to offer.

'Perhaps. You're under our directions while we teach you discipline, and we punished you for your mistakes. But I don't think you've been punished in a while, have you? Gradually, you've obtained more privileges and freedom. Your clothes, for example.'

'I'm naked, Madame,' Faith returned, and the woman smiled.

'Only until lunch,' Martha answered as though that was the clinching argument, nodding to Susan. 'Proceed. And release Miss Faith. She should not have her wrists fastened in future; she is disciplined enough to be "exercised" without restraint.'

'Of course, Madame,' Susan agreed at once. Faith felt that somehow she had been manoeuvred into a further, voluntary submission of some kind, but with the whip caressing her hot flesh, she had difficulty concentrating on anything.

Later, in the yard, watching Hilary gag the newest pupil (she had only been there three days and this was to be her first public strapping), Susan sighed.

'Why do they struggle and misbehave? It's useless.'

'How did I misbehave, Mistress?' Faith asked, interrupting her in the pause which followed.

'You . . ?' The woman stopped, looking at her, then sighed. 'You know that best yourself.'

'I did as I was told,' Faith answered. 'I did as requested by the person I knew as my master. I conformed.'

'Apparently not enough!' Susan gave her a frosty answer. 'But in any case, someone thought sufficiently of you to send you to us, to eradicate . . . whatever. You know yourself how much pride you had; pride you still have. Your sponsor, apparently, is pleased with your pride though.'

'Who, Mistress?' Faith asked hesitantly, 'Who is this . . . mysterious person you call my "sponsor"?'

'I don't know,' Susan answered without a pause. 'If I did, I couldn't tell you; it would be unprofessional. But I can't. I just don't know.'

'What will happen,' Faith asked, 'when I leave?'

'That's not our concern, Miss Faith. You could become a model – you have all the right qualities. The looks, the poise. You're Chosen, after all. There's nothing you couldn't do, if your master chooses to allow it.'

'When will I leave?' Faith asked.

'There is something that must be done first, Miss Faith. A final test,' Susan answered smoothly. 'Your sponsor will be contacted . . . probably through Mr Pellew, as he brought you here. Then someone will come for you. We don't know who or when – they'll call first. That's all the warning we'll get.' Susan hesitated, clearly concealing her own anguish. 'It makes for hectic packing.'

'Test? What test, Mistress?' Faith frowned at her.

'A test of your abilities, Miss Faith.'

Susan kept her features immobile. She had known that one day this would happen. That this lovely young woman would be taken from her, but it had not stopped her falling in love. Now the time of parting was drawing close and instead of it being easier to manage her grief, it was becoming more difficult. Mad Martha must suspect something too, for she popped up everywhere these days; even walked into the shrubbery when Susan had her tongue in Faith's channel.

That afternoon, walking through the woods with Martha Marryat, where the welcome shade of the trees broke up the close heat of the day, Faith asked, 'This morning in the yard, Madame, Susan said something about my future career. She said I could be a model or something like that, though I was in advertising. What was it she was trying to say, Madame?' Faith concentrated on trying to maintain a level expression and tone so that Mrs Marryat would not realise just how much importance Faith attached to her answers.

'What career in advertising are you talking about, Miss Faith?' the woman asked quietly. 'I understand you gave that up, or was it that you were sacked? It was something like that, I think.'

'I worked for –' Faith began but was interrupted.

'Yes. You worked; past tense,' the woman said as she looked off towards the A23, shaking her head. 'When you leave here, you'll go for further training in pleasure. Afterwards, you won't have time for a career in advertising or anything else. As Susan said, you could be a model. If that is your choice and your master agrees, then certainly. But your master will decide that.'

'My master,' Faith said quietly, almost content with the concept. 'Who *is* my master, Madame? All I know is that despite what both of you have said, I *am* a slave.'

'We are all slaves, Miss Faith. Each in our own way. A slave to our passions, to our employment, to our family and friends. Your training will make you more of a slave in some ways; free in others. Submerge yourself in the discipline as you have done; disengage your brain from the restraints as you have done. Do that and you will be happy.'

254

'A happy slave, Madame?' Faith laughed her question bitterly, no longer caring whether the woman knew her true feelings 'Was there ever such a creature?'

'Yes. I was a happy slave once,' Martha replied with a quiet confidence which surprised her listener. 'I was the happiest of slaves. I married my master and he was good to me. He whipped me when I needed to be, loved me all the time. Unfortunately, he died.' She fell silent, looking away again.

'You never thought of marrying again, Madame?' Faith asked, interested in spite of herself, heedless of the risk she was taking. At worst, it would only mean a whipping, and these were such daily occurrences that she could accept one more without fuss.

'Where would I find another master?' the woman asked, turning her grave eyes on the younger woman at her side. 'You may be passed from one master to another like a second-hand car, but one will *always* be yours, whether he's the first or the last.'

In Faith's mind, Lillian's comment about Alex giving her away to Max sprang immediately to mind. Though she knew Max well, and was his most successful pupil, the woman had been unhappy at the prospect.

'The unhappiest slave,' Martha continued, 'is the one in love with her master, or mistress, when that love is neither reciprocated nor appreciated. That *is* cruel; because in those circumstances, a slave has no other alternative but to continue to serve. I hope that fate never befalls you, Miss Faith.'

It was only later, in the quiet of the room before she dropped off to sleep, that Faith found the flaw in Martha Marryat's statement. If Clive Jackson was not her master, what was he doing usurping 'the master's right'? And if he was, why was Martha in charge? For it was obvious to Faith that she knew far more about the disciplining of young women (and men too, come to that) than her erstwhile employer.

After Martha's edict, Faith had been released from all restraints, trembling with uncertainty as Susan removed first the collar then the bracelets. She was told that she could more or less please herself about how she spent her time or dressed, though she was still to remain within the Stables, subject to the same strict discipline. For an hour the young woman sat silent, thinking about the problem in the isolation of her bedroom, her mind trying to come to terms with the new uncertainties of her situation. Not since she had first arrived in London had she felt so alone, and yet there was still a sense of belonging.

To Faith, there was little doubt that this was a test (perhaps the one they had mentioned) to see whether she was really disciplined. It would be typical of the convoluted approach adopted by Jackson and Mrs Marryat but if she obeyed then she would remain virtually a prisoner.

She noticed first the different attitude adopted by Susan, Hilary and Gerald; pointers to her new status. Susan was less in evidence, though she still woke her each morning, delivered her breakfast while she showered, and accompanied her to the mirror room. Yet in the stillness, while Faith looked steadily at the floor, ignoring her own reflection while the dark eyes watched for movement, there was a certain measure of deference. A feeling that bringing the strap or paddle across Faith's behind was a pleasure rather than a duty.

They still walked each afternoon through the woods to the hill where they sought the privacy of the shrubbery, though Susan no longer pressed her demands on Faith; rather, she was grateful when Faith removed her clothing. Hilary, from her lower height, looked up at Faith with a frank, open smile, regarding her more as an equal than a pupil, while Gerald stopped fondling her at every opportunity, even when Faith stretched herself naked between the poles, luxuriating in the discipline of the position. She was confident that, even were Mrs Marryat to come out to her with a strap or whip, she would maintain her poise.

Faith still insisted on sleeping with the collar on her throat; after it being a part of her life for so long, she found it difficult to be without. From finding it difficult to sleep with the collar on during her first night, it had become equally difficult to sleep without it. However, the key was placed beside her bed so she could release herself if she chose.

She managed to maintain her morning ritual, though; lying in bed until Susan arrived, when she would kneel as before, her wrists held behind her and her head bowed until Susan told her to rise and release herself. After her ablutions, performed once again in privacy, removing the phallus as usual, she breakfasted alone.

After the mirror room, Faith would go willingly to the standing man, squirming while she satisfied her need for release, then use the gymnasium and 'ride' for an hour, after which she showered. Susan, who helped with some of the other pupils, would then massage her. Faith appreciated the massage more with the increased workload. On alternate days, after her massage, Faith would be led out to the uprights to be disciplined, either with another strapping on her behind or on her more intimate flesh. On such occasions, all other activity in the yard stopped and she drew admiring looks from the other pupils afterwards as she was led out again.

She found a new serenity in the mental exercise, which ensured that she could maintain a calm, almost distant expression as this happened. Now and then Jackson would use the whip on her after breakfast, taking it to the mirror room. She never failed to insert it and take it to him in the yard where he waited, often following close behind him to go to the poles or the standing man.

Occasionally, she would kneel and press herself back on the sheepskin-covered block, her knees separating, after which Susan would take the small suede strap to her sex lips and anus, bringing both to a bright red flush while Faith whimpered, trying to control herself.

After walking in the woods – down to the iron-gated entrance, sometimes – she returned to the Stables for another hour in the gymnasium, then a shower and dinner, after which she invariably went to her room, chaining herself to her bed.

What had permanently changed was her relationship with Jackson and Mrs Marryat. Though she realised the lessons they were trying to get across to her, she still found she resented the way they had treated her.

Chapter Fifteen

Faith was in the gymnasium when Mrs Marryat, closely followed by Susan, came through the door, smiling. It was a reserved young woman who turned to face the older one and looked up from her squat thrusts, her expression of intent concentration falling into the usual neutral aspect as she waited.

Martha Marryat's face was flushed as she approached the younger woman, wringing her interlaced fingers as she crooned. 'We've just had a call, Miss Faith. You're to be collected within the hour. Imagine!'

'Do you know who's coming for me?' Faith asked, trying to conceal her very real relief at the news. With her return to freedom, she had stopped addressing Susan as 'Mistress' and Martha as 'Madame'.

'No,' Mrs Marryat answered. 'Except that it's your mistress. You must be pleased.'

'My ... my Mistress?' Faith felt a tremor rise through her legs. 'I thought you ... you said my sponsor was a man.'

'I *thought* your sponsor was a man, yes,' the woman agreed stiffly. 'Apparently I was wrong. At least, you may have a master, but your mistress is calling for you.'

'Is that ... usual? I mean ... both?' Faith disliked having such an uncertain arrangement made about her.

'It's not unheard of for a married man to . . . sponsor someone like yourself.'

'A pleasure slave?' she asked, bringing a flush to the woman's features before, for the first time, Martha dropped her eyes. 'Why did you keep it from me? Deny it when I asked?' Faith asked, trying to keep back the ripples of fear and uncertainty which threatened to engulf her in misery. She knew she was close to tears, and she had been so contented.

'We knew from the beginning,' Mrs Marryat said, looking up again. 'It wasn't something we could tell you, Miss Faith. The fact was that you were joining the Chosen as a pleasure slave. Apparently, it was your sponsor who realised how good you would be. I must say, you've shown . . . quite an aptitude for pleasure while you have been here.'

'I won't go,' Faith answered. 'I won't do it. They can't make me, can they?' Her jaw hardened into a scowl. The outburst made little difference to the woman.

'If your master wishes, Miss Faith, he *can* make you. It will be difficult, yes. You may be sent to another establishment; one where they specialise in enforcing even more strict discipline than is possible . . . or desirable, here. If you wish to show yourself such a disobedient pupil after all the love and care we've put into your training, then I can only suggest that it shows some defect in your own character.'

For almost a minute Faith faced the two women until Susan, no trace of her former indulgence on her face, said, 'I was going to ask Mrs Marryat to bend the rules for you, to enable you to meet your mistress with our assurance of your obedience. It seems, though, that we have to prove to her that you are obedient, so I won't even suggest you meet her prior to being tested. Outside in the yard, now!' Her voice snapped out, and she stood back to give Faith access to the gymnasium door. There was no trace of the pleased woman in that look, nor in the way she pointed stiffly towards the door. With almost contemptuous arrogance, Faith tucked up her legs and rolled quickly to her feet, luxuriating in her lithe ability. She was far more fit than at any other time of her life; stronger and more graceful too.

Faith walked proudly out into the sunshine, where the news had filtered through to the others. Gerald was helping Sophie up from the bar, his appraising look bouncing off the carapace Faith had erected around herself. She knew she had only a few more hours left at the Stables. At Susan's directions, Faith went to the familiar block where, without further instruction, she knelt while the plate secured her ankles.

'You can sit back until your mistress comes, Miss Faith,' her mentor said sourly. 'Then I shall blindfold you and you shall bend back when I give the word. I shall whip your sex and breasts before releasing you, because your mistress should see how obedient you are. Perhaps you'll disappoint her; who knows, eh? These tests can be *very* severe. But don't think that your test is over ... it has only just begun.

'Your wrists will be free the whole time and you'll maintain that position willingly, making as little noise as possible. Once that is done, you'll insert the whip and be guided to the bar where you'll spread yourself for a proper whipping. Your mistress will be asked to administer that herself, so you begin your relationship on the right footing for a slave. Do you understand me, Miss Faith?' Her voice was almost identical to the tone she used during the first few days of Faith's stay. It was as though the pleasant woman who had become something rather more than a dominatrix, though less than a friend, had vanished with the morning light. The conflict had been resolved in favour of severity.

'I understand, Mistress,' Faith answered with the faint trace of a smile, deliberately using the name she had abandoned some days before and bringing a flush to Susan's pallor.

This would be the last whipping she would endure in this terrible place. Surely her new mistress could hardly be worse than the twelve strokes she'd had from Jackson the week before. He had intended to give her more, but Susan had been quick to spot that he was near to drawing blood, which was, of course, completely outside the rules. Faith had been grateful at the time, but wondered whether Susan would do the same again.

As she waited, kneeling upright with her back to the sunshine, ignoring the activity going on around her, and facing the bar at which she would soon be bent for the final time, Faith allowed herself to consider the positive side of her predicament. In one way it was a wrench to be leaving the Stables, for she had gradually become used to the situation there, as well as the people and their little foibles.

She knew not to annoy Susan within the confines of the house or yard, but that she could take some liberties on their slow walks in the woodland. Jackson was less likely to retaliate with a sudden, savage punishment than his housekeeper, but when angered, his arm was very strong. He rarely came to her room at all now. It was over a week since he had last visited her, just after her whipping, in fact. Mrs Marryat seemed to have mellowed with the knowledge that so much of the training had been absorbed; perhaps she was just relieved at getting rid of her.

Faith had trimmed almost a stone from her comfortable weight of May (the product of too much dining out, she knew) and her tan was almost perfect. If asked, she could claim to have been working abroad. Her hair was far longer than she would have liked, but that could easily be remedied, providing her master and mistress approved. That was the only problem she could foresee; her new master and mistress. Trust the Chosen to have organised things like this. Keeping an eye on her right up to the last minute. In some ways, she was curious to see what they were like, and in others, wanted nothing to do with them.

Part of her mind told her that it was impossible in this day and age, late twentieth-century Britain, for anyone to be reduced to slavery, and yet she had seen the influence these people had. The Stables itself took money to run; and if there were other 'training centres' similar to this one, then it spoke loudly of organisation and wealth.

So the Chosen were probably amply protected from the usual hazards of modern life; policemen, journalists, the enquiries of family and friends. Her mother would hardly be worried about her; they had rarely corresponded during the time her parents had lived abroad. Normally they would meet once or twice a year to talk and catch up on each other's lives, but since her father's death her mother had cut herself off, living with her sister in Cumbria. There was probably no one to ask awkward questions, so who would know she was missing? She was almost the perfect victim, though Faith found she was relieved she was not like the others, with no one to care about whether they lived or died except the people training them.

They knew sufficient about her education and background, so they would have known all about her familial relationships. That would be the kind of research that would have to have been done as a matter of course while she lived with Alex. Alex was an excellent recruiter for the Chosen. He had asked questions about her previous life and her answers would have been sufficient to set them on the right track. It might be months or even a year before anyone realised that she was missing, by which time memories of her would have faded. Would anyone even bother to do more than enter her name and details in Missing Persons?

Contemplating this with the logical part of her brain (a brain which had been trained by some of the best tutors in the country), Faith took a deep breath as she considered her options. She could rebel when her new mistress came, but why? Letting her mistress take her out of the Stables was a sensible idea. Why not let her mistress take her where she was less securely held? Away from the restraints and whips at least and away from the well-oiled organisation. If she rebelled now, before her mistress arrived or during her visit, then she may be left for further training. Faith thought that was too awful to consider.

Once free of the place, she could reconsider the situation and plan ahead. It may take a day or so to devise a means of escape. They were likely to take pains to prevent her running away to start with. Yes; she would obey, but only for as long as it suited her. After all, there was the possibility that she might actually like it. Doubtful though she found that thought, it was an option she would be unwise to ignore.

'Pleasure slave' was an accurate enough term for her; perhaps someone had seen how roused Lillian Brampton had made her at that first party she had attended. Seen too how she had responded to the advances made. Yes; a master and mistress. If Lillian and Claire ... *and* Susan had reported on their advances, it looked as though she would be expected to serve both of them. Or was it 'service'? Susan had always stressed that it was 'service' not slavery, so she would be expected to provide for them both.

Even if they were old and ugly, it would be better there than in this place, though the thought of making the approaches to a woman sent a shudder through her. She had always been the recipient of those advances and none of the three women had ever made any attempt to take the passive role. Faith had not so much participated as acquiesced to what was happening; but would that change? A master and mistress suggested that it might.

Martha Marryat was surprised to see Faith's 'mistress' on opening the porch door to the speckled tarmac of the parking area. She stood about five feet nine in her flat white shoes, her blonde hair piled up, showing off her neck to advantage. The sun had bleached the hair gathered into a pony-tail on the top of her head, several shades lighter than when they had last met. Her pale eyes and colouring gave her the initial appearance of youth, though she was in her late twenties. As usual Lillian Brampton wore very little; just a loose, white, semi-transparent dress which showed her loose, swaying breasts, the darker nipples clearly visible, a tiny pair of white briefs and sensible white shoes as she was driving.

'Good morning, Madame.' The soft drawl that was typical of Lillian Brampton shook the pale-faced woman into silence but after recovering she led the way to where Susan waited by the windows overlooking the yard, where they could view Faith kneeling on the block without being seen.

'She looks delightful, doesn't she?' Lillian said, her indulgent interest sending grating feelings through Susan. This was where Susan lost her lover, and despite her willingness to see Faith settled, she resented the way this woman walked in and took her as though it were her right.

'We're very proud of her,' Susan answered, trying to keep her resentment concealed. 'She gave us a fright a few times, as you know; especially when she first arrived. But she's picked up since.'

'She'll take the whip now, which we despaired of at one time,' Mrs Marryat confirmed. 'Though she was terrified of it at first.'

'Damned things!' the newcomer snorted. 'I prefer the strap myself. Well –' Lillian sighed, raising and lowering her shoulders '– let's get this over with. I have an appointment in town this afternoon, as does Faith.'

'I'll blindfold her first,' Martha said quietly. 'You remember the procedure from before, of course?'

'Yes.' Lillian nodded, allowing her annoyance to show. It still rankled that she was a former 'pupil' of this woman, though hardly much younger. She could sense Susan's resentment, though she could find no reason for it other than the fact that she was obviously well-to-do and, in the opinion of many people, quite attractive. But that was this other woman's problem, not hers.

Lillian watched as Martha, in her oatmeal dress, walked slowly up the yard to stop in front of Faith, who knelt so upright – shoulders back, hands positioned perfectly behind her – all without restraint. They had done their work well by the look of it, and Faith should be eager to see the back of this place, but she should be kept in the dark about her identity until she was accepted. It would be terrible if Faith recognised her and then failed the test. If she was rejected then the only solution was for her to be retained for further training.

* * *

'Miss Faith?' Mrs Marryat said, clearly disconcerted by the slight superior smile the young woman wore. Faith's eyes were closed and her features composed. Mrs Marryat knew Faith's capacity for causing problems, and this was *so* important to them. That Alex Pellew had sent Lillian Brampton as Faith's mistress showed which way the wind was blowing. One day, Faith was going to *be* someone.

'Has she arrived, Madame?' Faith asked, her eyes remaining closed. She had knelt there, luxuriating in the silent peace of the yard since the others had all been quickly cleared out by Jackson. Listening to the sounds of footsteps coming towards her, she had felt the climax of her stay approaching; the doubt in her voice had been brought about by the effort of trying to identify the speaker.

'I've brought the blindfold.' Martha bent to the side, then moved so she could slide the elastic down the back of the young woman's head.

Blackness descended over Faith's vision as, with eyes still closed, she allowed the thick sleep-mask to be placed in position. It held no terrors for her now; she could have accepted the excuse that this was a lesson to be learned, had they the wit to use it.

'You won't shame us, will you? Please, Miss Faith; we *have* tried to be as kind as we could to you.'

'I'll obey.' Faith's smile hardly changed at the edge in the woman's voice. 'I am trained now.' There was no answer as the woman turned, beckoning to the window, and the new mistress began to make her way to the door to the yard.

Jackson emerged anxiously from the stable to stand watching as Faith heard the clack of heels on the concrete, taking a deep breath to steady herself. This was going to be her last ordeal and she knew she had to get through it in order to escape. But it was still going to be an ordeal, though perhaps not as severe as some of the encounters with Susan and Jackson had been.

As the clacking came to a halt in front of her, Susan said, 'Lean back on the block, Miss Faith. You are to be whipped.'

Obediently, Faith sank back until her shoulders touched the sheepskin, keeping her hands resting on the base of her spine. She was perfectly controlled.

'You see? Obedient.' Martha's voice held almost as much relief as pride. 'I'll –'

She stopped suddenly as Lillian placed her mouth close to her ear, asking in a whisper, 'Wouldn't it be better if *I* whipped her?' She looked directly into Martha's eyes.

Off to her right Susan stood silent, watching the final examination of her pupil, hoping she would be excused 'further training'. If Faith was rejected, then Susan herself would be at fault as much as the younger woman, and it would be Susan who would have to intensify the training with severities similar to those endured by the others.

For a moment there was a pause while the older woman considered, then, 'Of course.' Martha nodded. 'Miss Faith, your mistress intends giving you your first whipping. You will accept it without protest; and *no* noise.'

'I understand,' Faith answered, though the sun-darkened skin of her face lost some colour.

There was a hiatus while the visitor handed her handbag to Susan, taking the small suede whip from her. Slipping out of her shoes, Lillian silently approached the recumbent figure, then let the suede strap trail idly down the inside of the tense thigh of the younger woman, seeing the start in the muscles and hearing a sudden gasp. It was always better to let

268

the initial tension out before proceeding with the main business. Then she began, her hand hardly moving at all, flicking the whip at Faith's labia.

When the first strokes touched her pubic lips, Faith gasped at the stinging sensation, but closed her mouth again, pressing her lips into a firm line. There would be no cries from her; no pleas for mercy; no begging to be allowed release from the terrible sexual wanting this would engender. Her legs opened wider, allowing the whip to penetrate her more delicate flesh and yet, contrary to how Susan applied it, this whip was far more severe. This really stung when it struck her vaginal opening, and flicked against her perineum, perversely making her hips rise to meet the following blow. Once she saw the response, the visitor spent almost a minute flicking against the perineum, followed by a hard blow on Faith's clitoris.

This assault sent sharp spears of sexual suffering through her abdomen, for the blows to her love bud were accurate, hard and well timed. The pallor with which she had begun this ordeal fled as, trying to suppress her groaning with the rise of passion, Faith left no one in any doubt as to her state. Jackson bit his lip when at last Lillian stopped, bending close to Faith's face and allowing her mouth to lightly touch her parched lips.

'Delicious pleasure slave,' Lillian whispered, the sibilant hiss effectively disguising her voice, which Faith would have instantly recognised, 'I'm going to whip those lovely breasts of yours; those beautiful full teats. They are going to boil with lust and pain for me, and you are going to show when your pleasure comes, by poking out your tongue, aren't you? You are going to satisfy this, aren't you?' she asked in a voice hardly louder than deep breathing, giving no hint as to her accent.

'I-I-I'll obey.' Faith breathed hard, her chest heaving, concentrating on the concept of obedience as a means of diverting attention from the surges of lust which were running through her abdomen. If the woman did nothing to relieve her pleasure soon, she would climax. Which would bring shame and humiliation on herself, and in front of Susan too.

The stinging began on her breasts immediately, making Faith hiss at first, but banking down the fires in her loins. It was only temporary, Faith knew. If this cruel mistress did nothing for her, she would have to remember that pressure point on her thigh, which would probably enrage her new mistress but the need was too great to think of anything other than release. The whipping stopped as soft moisture was applied to her right nipple, making Faith catch her breath as the hot, moist tongue caressed the battered flesh. Faith was straining to arch her back to more than meet this mistress halfway. This woman, her mistress, obviously understood her needs.

After only a few seconds, the tongue was withdrawn and another strapping covered her teats, the flaring pain making Faith bite her lower lip for a few seconds before she became used to it. This woman knew what she was doing; balancing Faith between the pleasure, the pain and the release she so desperately sought. When the strapping stopped there was a few seconds' pause before the whisper was at her ear again, the voice so soft that for a moment she thought that she imagined it.

'Very good, my precious pleasure slave! Very good *indeed*, but are you ready? Are you truly roused? Shall we test you to the limit? Shall we . . . lick you, perhaps?' The hint of menace in the voice and the suggestion made Faith groan in a soft, shuddering gasp at the thought.

270

Then came the sweet, moist sensation of a tongue lapping the seepage from her vagina, running lightly up the edge of her lips until it flicked against her clitoris, to be followed almost immediately by the lash as Faith forced her hips towards her. The sudden stinging blow was not unexpected, nor was it excessively painful, but it increased the pressure of arousal just the same.

'That's enough,' Lillian whispered to Susan. 'Any more and the poor thing will explode.' She nodded to the silent figure of Jackson who appeared within her vision. The man's expression was grim at the sight of her, but Susan maintained a discreet smile as she turned towards her pupil. It had taken weeks to gain Faith's confidence to be able to receive the whip in this fashion, yet this newcomer had shown a complete mastery of the art.

'I'll give you the whip, Miss Faith,' Martha said. 'Insert it and rise.'

'No,' Lillian whispered in Martha's ear as Susan bit her lip. 'That will only bring on her pleasure and I want to keep her unsatisfied at the moment. Let her bend herself over the bar and I'll whip her. It would be as well if she became used to it.'

'Very well.' Martha could see her point. Faith's response to the whipping had been well beyond even her wildest hopes. She lay back with her back arched, knees spread wide, almost inviting being mounted or further abused in the same manner. None of them would have placed a bet on which Faith would prefer. 'You'll carry the whip in your hand, Miss Faith,' Martha said calmly. 'Your mistress knows you too well, it seems. Your pleasure will be denied you.'

Faith groaned with the knowledge that there would be another trial and no release. If she could be so cruel as to prevent her climax after that whipping, what would she do after –

'Rise and come to the bar. Your mistress will whip you, Miss Faith!' Martha's command broke in on her train of thought.

Faith's shock made her swallow, but she was already rising as she absorbed the information, her mouth opening as she reached the kneeling position again, pausing while the plate beneath her heels was removed. The whip was placed in her right hand, doubled over so that she could hold both the handle and thongs, making her aware of the instrument which would be used on her. But as she was helped down from the block by a hand on both arms, a soft, fragrant mouth was pressed against her own.

It was an expensive perfume, so it was neither Susan nor Martha. Her mistress? Already the woman's tongue was slipping insidiously across hers, to be withdrawn just as suddenly. Her journey (only three paces) was resumed until she stopped against the leather which fronted the centre of the bar. Spreading her legs automatically, Faith bent forward, the whip still in her hand until it was removed. She was not fastened, for this would test her obedience.

The soft voice returned to her ear, whispering, 'You are delicious, darling; better than I could ever have imagined, but place your hands on the bar, as wide as you can.'

Faith did as she was bid, finding that it steadied her body to be in this position, holding her body as level as she thought she could maintain. Already she could feel the trembling in her thighs, relics of the bent-back position she had just been made to adopt, and the fear of what was to come. Her first whipping by her new mistress. She tried to shut out the world, to ignore the whole thing, but someone (probably Susan) was . . . no. It was coming from her left so it must be her mistress. Her mistress was wetting her buttocks,

272

squeezing the sponge above her natal notch, allowing the water to trickle down over her anus and labia into her clitoris.

Already sensitive, this made those organs even more highly charged, ending all Faith's hopes of being able to keep her mind on something else during her ordeal. Her mistress must already know that trick, but then she had already shown that she was well versed in these arts. Then a soft hand took her left breast, fondling it gently and running the thumb lightly over the swollen nipple before, with a long, slow build-up, she heard the familiar hiss as the whip was plied.

The first blow made her jump, gasping as she jerked her body back and up, her back arching as she looked, sightlessly, at the hot roof opposite. The second dragged a groan from her which she knew was pure, unashamed pleasure. The third stroke brought another love-cry, almost incoherent. The woman seemed to understand Faith's body better than she did herself. Faith wondered whether this mistress was going to be something of a trial, knowing her so well. Was her master any more considerate?

'Three, my darling.' The voice was quiet as the woman's eyes met Martha's, nodding as she acknowledged Faith's feat. 'Three, and not a tear; not a whimper. You *have* been well trained. Shall we try four?' The whip descended across her behind with the same vigour.

This time Faith presented her buttocks to the whip, hollowing her back as her passion spread through from the soaking clitoris to her throat.

Susan looked in alarm as the visitor smiled then softly asked, 'Shall we see if five would make you cry? Five?'

She brought the whip down harder than before.

There were distinct marks on the skin now, for though she had less strength than Jackson, the woman knew how to use the whip. Faith's anguished cry was at the stimulation, not the pain, which she was using desperately to control her passion.

For a few seconds the woman paused, looking at Susan's anxious eyes while her thumb rolled the nipple gently. She had no intention of striking again for Faith had given every proof of the success of her training, but she hesitated.

'Very good, my beautiful pleasure slave,' Lillian whispered to her. She extended the whip towards the silent housekeeper, who took it as the woman's mouth neared the livid marks on Faith's buttocks. Her soft lips traced the line of some of them, making the younger woman shudder with repressed passion, waiting either for the next blow or –

'My!' The soft whisper sounded loud in Faith's ears. 'You *are* dripping, aren't you, you wanton trollop? No wonder they think you're ready. Would you like me to help?' Without waiting for an answer, Lillian slipped two fingers of her right hand within Faith's open cleft.

Immediately they touched her, Faith's body began to move, jerking slightly as she received them directly within her.

'Tense on that, my darling,' hissed Lillian. 'Release all that lovely, pent-up desire on my fingers. Show me what you learned on the saddle.'

Lillian's eyes were on Martha the whole time. The housekeeper's complexion paled as Faith's muscles sucked greedily at the fingers, drawing them slightly within, for she needed no second telling.

Faith tightened on them, grasping them with her muscles as desire to obtain relief from the agony of lust which her new mistress had induced took control

of her. Her hips were pumping up and down and pulling in and out on the fingers, building up to her
delayed climax. Faith's face burned with shame. This
woman had walked in and played her body like a fine
musical instrument. She had done things, ordinary
things which Susan had done a dozen times, and yet
she had built up such a desire within her that for a
few moments Faith forgot that she always addressed
her as 'my pleasure slave'.

Faith knew there were others watching but she
would have done the same had the whole Stables
been watching. Such was her lust that she would have
done the same in the middle of Trafalgar Square on
a busy Saturday afternoon in high summer, with
Japanese tourists taking photographs.

In that moment, Faith accepted the fact that she
would take more than a few days to plan her escape.
This woman knew her; knew her wants, her needs.
Even as her climax was making her cry out with the
release of desire, made more violent because of it being the last time she would be whipped at the Stables,
Faith was mentally ridding herself of the last of her
pride.

In her own mind, she was a slave, a pleasure slave,
either for the benefit of this mysterious group, the
Chosen, or as part of them. This woman was her mistress, who had delivered her of such pleasure that, at
that moment, she had no thought whether she ever
even saw a man again. This woman could take the
place of a man (which Susan never could) and could
give her the kind of pleasure and pain which she had
come to accept. In her own mind, Faith Small was a
pleasure slave, and would remain one.

When her orgasm had died, leaving Faith lying
helpless across the bar in the courtyard, there were
hands to lift her up. Someone tilted her to one side so

that her left leg was lifted, falling alongside the other. Tilted upright again, she found she could stand on her own feet; just. A soft mouth met her own in a brief kiss, a hand caressed her left breast and then a voice, at once alien and yet achingly familiar, said in a normal tone, 'I accept Faith. She has been well trained, thank you. Remove the blindfold, please.'

Faith's heart was in her mouth as she felt the hand behind her head and another holding the bottom edge of the mask, then light poured on to her eyes again. Deperately she blinked, narrowing her eyes, and was surprised to find that her hands had automatically returned to the small of her back.

Her buttocks were on fire and yet there was a sense that this was not a severe beating. The woman's voice had been too warm, too personal, too loving, to have administered a harsh punishment. There was something familiar about the shape in front of her, but the light was in her eyes. She had been turned around without her realising it.

Then the woman spoke again. 'Aren't you glad to see me, darling?'

Recognition followed the diminution of her pupils. 'Lillian!' Faith breathed, open mouthed.

'Your mistress, Miss Faith,' Martha said sourly. The open admiration Mrs Marryat had for the skills of her former pupil was too much for her severe soul to bear without some measure of reproof, especially as Lillian Brampton had been *such* a trial. In fact, Faith and Lillian deserved each other, for they had easily been two of the most difficult problems she had encountered.

'Come along, darling.' Lillian smiled and gently took Faith's arm, turning her towards the doorway. 'Time we went home.'

NEW BOOKS

Coming up from Nexus and Black Lace

Faith in The Stables by Elizabeth Bruce
March 1996   Price £4.99   ISBN: 0 352 33062 7
In this, the sequel to *The Teaching of Faith*, Alex sends Faith,
now ordained as one of the Chosen, to complete her education in
The Stables, a training centre in Sussex dedicated to the instilla-
tion of total discipline. Complete obedience is mandatory, no
matter how outrageous the command, and even Faith's liberated
imagination is stretched to its limits.

A Chalice Of Delights by Katrina Young
March 1996   Price £4.99   ISBN: 0 352 33061 9
Times are hard and fun-loving Gaelicia becomes the kept woman
of a lascivious nobleman, in return for a wide variety of sexual
favours. When she tires of this arrangement, she finds that the
earl is not prepared to let her off so easily; the terms of her contract are physically as well as legally binding.

Christina Wished by Gene Craven
April 1996   Price £4.99   ISBN: 0 352 33066 X
Three flatmates – unrestrained, raven-haired Christina, meek
Susan and Cathy, mysterious and immersed in a world of rubber
and leather – embark on a voyage of sexual discovery. Each must
face tests and undreamt-of pleasures, and push her sexuality to
its limits, before she can release the wanton inside her and revel
in the power of discipline.

Pleasing Them by William Doughty
April 1996   Price £4.99   ISBN: 0 352 33065 1
Into Dreadnought Manor, home to Robert Shawnecross and his
young and beautiful wife, come the puritanical Mr Blanking and
the wicked Sir Horace. They seek satisfaction through control
and cruelty and their hosts, along with the servants who have
been carefully selected and trained to cater to even the most bi-
zarre desires, must stretch their skills to find suitably extreme
pleasures.

Ace Of Hearts by Lisette Allen
March 1996   Price £4.99   ISBN: 0 352 33059 7
Marisa Brooke, a swordswoman and card-sharper with a taste for fleshly pleasures, lives by her wits amongst the wealthy, hedonistic elite of Regency England. Gambling dominates every gathering and, with love and fortune being lost more easily than they are won, Marisa has to use all her skill and cunning in order to hold on to her winnings and the young men she seduces.

Dreamers In Time by Sarah Copeland
March 1996   Price £4.99   ISBN: 0 352 33064 3
In a hostile world, four millennia from now, two thousand people remain suspended in endless slumber, while others toil for the means to wake them. Carnal desires have long been forgotten until Ehlana, a time-traveller and historian, finds the key to her own sexuality and, in so doing, unlocks the door to everyone's primal memories.

Gothic Blue by Portia Da Costa
April 1996   Price £4.99   ISBN: 0 352 33075 9
Set in a remote and mysterious priory in the present day, this dark, Gothic-erotic novel centres on Belinda, a sensual and restless heroine who is intrigued by the supernatural unknown. Written by one of Black Lace's most popular authors, it explores the themes of sexual alchemy and experimentation, the paranormal and obsession.

The House Of Gabriel by Rafaella
April 1996   Price £4.99   ISBN: 0 352 33063 5
Researching a feature on lost treasures of erotic art, journalist Jessica Martyn finds herself drawn into a world of strange, sexual power games and role-play, in the elegant, Jacobean mansion of the handsome, enigmatic Gabriel Martineaux. She also finds trouble, in the shape of her arch-rival, Araminta Harvey.

NEXUS BACKLIST

All books are priced £4.99 unless another price is given. If a date is supplied, the book in question will not be available until that month in 1995.

CONTEMPORARY EROTICA

THE ACADEMY	Arabella Knight	
CONDUCT UNBECOMING	Arabella Knight	Jul
CONTOURS OF DARKNESS	Marco Vassi	
THE DEVIL'S ADVOCATE	Anonymous	
DIFFERENT STROKES	Sarah Veitch	Aug
THE DOMINO TATTOO	Cyrian Amberlake	
THE DOMINO ENIGMA	Cyrian Amberlake	
THE DOMINO QUEEN	Cyrian Amberlake	
ELAINE	Stephen Ferris	
EMMA'S SECRET WORLD	Hilary James	
EMMA ENSLAVED	Hilary James	
EMMA'S SECRET DIARIES	Hilary James	
FALLEN ANGELS	Kendal Grahame	
THE FANTASIES OF JOSEPHINE SCOTT	Josephine Scott	
THE GENTLE DEGENERATES	Marco Vassi	
HEART OF DESIRE	Maria del Rey	
HELEN – A MODERN ODALISQUE	Larry Stern	
HIS MISTRESS'S VOICE	G. C. Scott	
HOUSE OF ANGELS	Yvonne Strickland	May
THE HOUSE OF MALDONA	Yolanda Celbridge	
THE IMAGE	Jean de Berg	Jul
THE INSTITUTE	Maria del Rey	
SISTERHOOD OF THE INSTITUTE	Maria del Rey	

Please send me the books I have ticked above.

Name ....

Address ....

....

....

..........................Post code ....

Send to: **Cash Sales, Nexus Books, 332 Ladbroke Grove, London W10 5AH.**

Please enclose a cheque or postal order, made payable to **Nexus Books**, to the value of the books you have ordered plus postage and packing costs as follows:

UK and BFPO – £1.00 for the first book, 50p for each subsequent book.

Overseas (including Republic of Ireland) – £2.00 for the first book, £1.00 for the second book, and 50p for each subsequent book.

If you would prefer to pay by VISA or ACCESS/MASTER-CARD, please write your card number and expiry date here:

....

Please allow up to 28 days for delivery.

Signature ....